mary-kateandashley
so little time
the love collection

Check out these other great

so little time

titles:

mary-kateandashley
so little time

the love collection

featuring

the love factor

dating game

boy crazy

HarperCollins*Entertainment*
An imprint of HarperCollins*Publishers*

A PARACHUTE PRESS BOOK

A PARACHUTE PRESS BOOK
Parachute Publishing, L.L.C.
156 Fifth Avenue, Suite 302
New York, NY 10010

HarperCollins*Publishers*

This edition published in 2004
by HarperCollins*Publishers* Pty Limited
ABN 36 009 913 517
A member of the HarperCollins*Publishers* (Australia) Pty Limited Group
25 Ryde Road, Pymble, Sydney, NSW 2073, Australia
31 View Road, Glenfield, Auckland 10, New Zealand
www.harpercollins.com.au

The Love Collection
ISBN 0732281563

Printed and bound in Australia by Griffin Press on 50gsm Bulky News

5 4 3 2 1   04 05 06 07

Contents

mary-kate and ashley
so little time
the love factor

by Rosalind Noonan

Based on the teleplay by Becky Southwell

HarperCollins*Entertainment*
An imprint of HarperCollins*Publishers*

A PARACHUTE PRESS BOOK

chapter one

"**C**hloe, are we here for a reason?" fourteen-year-old Riley Carlson asked her twin sister. "Or is this one of those unsolved mysteries?"

Chloe, Riley, and their friend Sierra Pomeroy were sitting at a table at a coffee bar called the Newsstand. Chloe only half heard her sister's question. She was busy watching Lennon Porter make coffee behind the counter. She was drawn to him – but why? Was it his crooked smile? Or the way his curly dark hair fell over his eyes…?

"Earth to Chloe?" Sierra pinged her shoulder. "Come back, girl!"

Chloe tore her eyes away from Lennon. She wasn't ready to admit that she came to the Newsstand just to stare at him. She didn't like him at all – she really didn't! He was such a know-it-all, but so cute…. So she tried to think of a non-Lennon reason for dragging Riley and Sierra to the café.

"Isn't this place cool?" she said lamely. "Look at all the magazines! They have lots of PCs and news-papers. And good scenery."

"Yeah, we're here for the scenery, all right," Riley said, turning towards the counter.

Lennon reached up and placed two glasses on a high shelf.

"Why don't you just admit it, Chloe?" Riley continued. "You like Lennon!"

"What are you talking about?" Chloe said. "I can't stand him." Chloe glanced over at him, then turned away. "Don't stare! You guys are so obvious!"

"Come on, Chloe. Come clean," Sierra said. "You're totally crushing on him."

"Crushing?" Chloe felt her cheeks heat up. "That is so not true. Lennon is an obnoxious jerk. He's so full of himself! How could you even think I like him?"

"Because it's true?" Riley asked with a grin.

Chloe rolled her eyes. She hated it when her sister was right. "Fine – he's cute, okay? Look at the guy! No – don't!"

Riley and Sierra had turned to glance at Lennon again. They jerked their heads back towards Chloe, giggling.

"You can't hide it, Chloe," Sierra teased. "You totally like him."

"That's impossible," Chloe protested. "He thinks he knows everything, and I hate people like that." The trouble was, Lennon really *did* seem to know every-thing. Or a lot, at least.

The waitress came by, and the three girls ordered coffee drinks.

Riley leaned towards Chloe, her shoulder-length blonde hair brushing the tabletop. "Maybe Lennon will clear our table when we're done. That'll give you a chance to talk to him."

Chloe sniffed. "I have nothing to say to the guy."

"That's a lie, and you know it," Sierra said. "You're *dying* to ask him out!"

"Talk to us, Chloe," Riley said. "We'll help you. I got Sierra and Larry together, and look how great that's turning out."

Sierra had started going out with Larry Slotnick, who was sweet but kind of goofy. Make that *way* goofy. But Sierra seemed to really like him. She thought he had a great sense of humour and that he wasn't afraid to be himself.

"Okay, you're right," Chloe admitted. "I've been trying to think of a way to ask out Lennon. But how? He's not like other guys. He's travelled all over the world and speaks twenty-five zillion languages."

"So?" Riley said. "There's nothing wrong with that."

"But he's so stuck up about it," Chloe went on. "He thinks he's perfect. And he can be so rude – and stubborn!"

She'd met Lennon when they both volunteered at a senior citizens' centre, and she had problems with him from the beginning. How could she even think of asking

3

him out?

"You know what?" Chloe said. "This was a bad idea. Let's get out of here." She grabbed her bag.

"We can't. Alex and Larry are meeting us here," Riley reminded her. Alex Zimmer was Riley's boyfriend.

"And we already ordered frappes," Sierra added. "Stay and face your fears!" she whispered in a spooky voice.

"I'm not afraid of him," Chloe insisted. "I'm just not sure how I feel about him. I'm all confused." She plopped back down and watched Lennon carry a bin of dirty dishes into the kitchen. His apron was slung low over his hips. His hair was a little longer than most guys' and curled over his collar. Lennon had a style of his own.

He came out of the kitchen and hurried over to a Japanese couple who were leaving. "*Domo arrigato*!" Lennon said, bowing.

The Japanese man and woman bowed, too. Smiling, they chatted with Lennon in Japanese. And he schmoozed right back.

"What a show-off," Chloe said. "Do you see? That is why I can't go out with him."

"I think it's sweet," Sierra said.

Riley rolled her eyes. "Chloe's right. The guy's totally showing off."

The Japanese couple left, and Lennon returned to the counter. Chloe looked around for something to distract her from him. She reached for a copy of her favourite magazine, *Teen Style*. "Hey, there's a quiz in this month's issue!" She flipped to the table of contents. "Let's take it right now."

"I already had a pop quiz in Spanish today," Riley complained. "Isn't one enough?"

"This is a really good one," Chloe promised. "It's called *The Love Factor: Is Your Boyfriend the Right Boy for You?*"

"I'll take it," Sierra offered. "Though it might not work for me. I mean, we're talking about Larry."

"It's true." Riley nodded. "Larry is definitely in a cat-egory of his own."

[Chloe: **Larry used to be crazy about Riley – before he fell for Sierra. But when I say crazy, I mean crazy! He bounced up to her bedroom win-dow on a trampoline. He collected all her used yogurt containers and built sand castles for her. I guess you have to give him points for creativity.**]

"'The Love Factor quiz is foolproof!'" Chloe read from the magazine.

Sierra shrugged. "Right, but is it Larry-proof?"

Chloe licked her lips. "We'll see about that. But I'll just have to keep score since I don't have a boyfriend. At least, not at the moment."

"Why don't you take it with Lennon in mind?" Riley asked.

"Please! Let's not even go there." Chloe clicked her pen and prepared to write. "Okay, question number one," she said. "'Your love gives you a gift wrapped with a big fat bow. You're thrilled... until you open it. It's all wrong for you! You... A. throw it in his face, B. tell him you'll cherish it forever because it's from him, C. admit it's not your style though you appreciate the thought, or D. take it home and sew it into a quilt.'"

"Who are they kidding?" Riley said. "All the choices are ridiculous."

"B," Sierra said firmly. When Riley and Chloe stared at her, she shrugged. "I guess I'm a lot more sentimental than people think."

"I'd say D," Chloe said. "If I had a boyfriend."

"You hate sewing!" Riley pointed out.

"But it's about cherishing a gift from your boyfriend," Chloe said.

"Unless he gives you a book... or his bowling trophy," Riley said. "They'd look pretty funny sewn up in a quilt."

Chloe was losing patience. "Would you answer the question?"

Riley sighed. "Okay, I'd pick C. I'd have to be honest with him."

"Okay," Chloe said, marking down their answers. She read off question number two. Then number three. The waitress brought their drinks, but Chloe put her iced mocha aside so that she could keep reading questions.

"Why don't we finish the Love Factor later?" Riley said, spooning some whipped cream from her drink.

"These quizzes are so lame."

"No, no! We're almost done," Chloe insisted. "Number nine. 'Your honey lamb asks for advice about a shirt. He thinks he's decked in slammin' duds, but he's a walking, talking fashion fright. You… A. hit him with your best shot – there's power in the truth, B. break it to him gently, C. tell him that you'd love him in anything, even burlap.'"

Chloe smiled as she logged in the final answers and tallied the scores. "That makes seventy-nine points for Sierra and Larry," she said, calculating on a scrap of paper. "And…" Chloe's heart sank when she saw the score for her sister. "Forty-two for Riley and Alex."

"That's it?" Riley asked. Then she shook her head. "Well, it's no big deal," she said.

"Really?" Doubtful, Chloe watched her sister sip her iced cappuccino. The quiz said Alex was not the right boy for Riley – it had to bother her. Or at least it would bother me if I got such a low score with my boyfriend! she thought.

"I'm not worried," Riley said. "I know what I have with Alex. And those quizzes are so silly."

The front door opened with a whoosh. In walked Larry, decked out from head to ankles in a red rubber wetsuit with black stripes on the sides. His nose was caked with white sun block.

"Larry, is that you?" Riley squinted at him. "You're all… red."

"You look like an alien," Chloe added.

"Check it out, Shred Betties!" Larry said, sidling over to their table. "I just got suited up at Zuma Jay's Surf Shop."

"I love it," Sierra said, squinting at the wetsuit's blinding brightness. "You'll never have to worry about drowning. A lifeguard could spot you a mile away!"

"But what is it for?" Chloe asked. "You're not actually going surfing – are you?" She shuddered at the thought of Larry let loose on the high seas with a surfboard.

"Why not? Zuma Jay's is sponsoring a free surfing clinic this afternoon," Larry said, stealing a sip of Sierra's drink. "Anyone want to hang ten with me?"

"I've always wanted to try surfing," Riley said. "But I can't go today. I'm hanging out with Alex."

"I've got to get home soon," Sierra said. Her parents were super-strict. "Besides, Mom and Dad would never let me try surfing. Anything that might cut into violin practise time is definitely out."

"I…" Chloe looked over at the coffee bar, then snatched a copy of *Le Monde* from the newspaper rack. Lennon was headed this way. She had to look smart. "I'm going to take up French," she said.

"He's coming over!" Sierra whispered.

"I know!" Chloe whispered back, trying to act casual.

"Are you going to ask him out?" Riley asked.

"Yes!" Chloe gasped. "No!" She lowered the newspaper. "I don't know. I'll play it by ear." She tossed her long blonde hair over one shoulder and leaned forward to sip her iced mocha.

Whoa! Sudden panic iced her brain. The frozen mocha was going right to her head. B*rain freeze*!

"Oh, no!" Riley gasped. "The frappe? You're frozen?" She knew Chloe's brain freeze symptoms. Whenever Chloe ate or drank something icy too quickly, her brain was paralysed with cold!

Chloe nodded, her hands fluttering under the table. This was terrible! She couldn't think. Her head was an ice cap. No way could she have an intelligent conversation with Lennon now!

"Hey," Lennon said, pausing at their table. "How's it going, Chloe?"

chapter two

Chloe lifted a hand in a flat wave, her eyes still frozen in panic. She pressed the other hand against her nose. "Owwwwww!"

Lennon folded his arms across his chest. "Chloe? Are you okay?"

Chloe nodded.

"She'll be fine," Riley explained quickly. "It's a brain freeze."

"Brain freeze?" Lennon laughed. "Yeah, I sometimes have that effect on people. I freak them out. They get intimidated by my incredible wealth of knowledge. I guess it's understandable."

Oh, put a cork in it! Chloe wanted to shout. But she could only work on thawing her head.

"Brain freeze. Ha!" Lennon said, moving away towards a group of guys.

Riley gave Chloe a sympathetic look. "Is that the

worst timing, or what? Your big chance with Lennon, and your whole head ices over!"

"My fault," Chloe said in a mousy voice. She shivered. "Why do I let myself go near anything with ice?" she added.

Chloe spotted Alex Zimmer across the room, sneaking up behind Riley.

He squeezed Riley's shoulders. "Guess what? I have great news," he announced.

Riley turned around and smiled at him.

Alex's dark eyes sparkled with excitement. "We have a gig for this weekend. Friday night at Mango's!"

"What? Are you kidding me?" Sierra cried. She and Alex played together in a band called The Wave. "This weekend? Awesome!"

Alex nodded proudly. "I just talked to the manager, and we're on for Friday night. It's a solid break for the band."

"That's fantastic," Riley said, nudging Alex's arm.

As they talked out the details, Chloe turned to the coffee bar looking for Lennon. Her embarrassment was melting with her brain freeze. Now she just felt a burning challenge.

She wanted to ask him out. She wanted to get an up-close and personal look at Mr. Know-it-all. And she wanted to prove that she wasn't afraid of him.

"I'd better tell Saul," Alex said, taking out his mobile phone to call the band's drummer. "He'll probably want to pull together a rehearsal this afternoon."

"There's no way I can rehearse today," Sierra said, disappointed. "I have to head home. My mom's expecting me."

"No problem," Alex told her. "I just want to try out a new song. If it works, you can learn it later in the week." Then he turned to Riley and flipped his phone closed. "Oh, Riley! I almost forgot. We were supposed to hang out this afternoon."

"No, it's okay," Riley insisted.

"We really need to rehearse," Alex said. "But I was looking forward to seeing you."

"No problem," Riley said. "I totally understand. Friday night is going to be great."

[Chloe: If I didn't know my sister so well, I'd buy that understanding bit, too. But I DO know my sister. And I can tell she's kind of disappointed.]

"Hey, Riley," Larry said. "Since you're not hanging with Alex this afternoon, that means you're free. You can come surfing with me!"

"Surfing?" Riley blinked.

Chloe smothered a laugh. Surfing with Larry was not Riley's idea of a great afternoon.

"You said you always wanted to try it, right?" Larry pointed out.

"Go for it!" Sierra said as she hitched up her backpack. "You like to try new things. And Malibu has some of the best surfing in the world."

Riley turned to Larry in his fire engine-red wetsuit.

Larry jumped on to a chair and struck a pose, arms out, as if riding a wave. "Let's ride the swells, Shred Betty!" he said.

Riley winced up at Larry's glowing red suit. "I guess…"

"Cool! Let's go!" Larry said, tugging Riley out of her chair. "We don't want to be late."

Suddenly Chloe felt a new panic. Everyone was leaving! Alex headed towards the door with his phone pressed to his ear. Larry dragged Riley. Sierra dragged her violin case.

"Hey, guys! Wait! You can't leave!" Chloe cried.

"Come with us!" Riley said.

Chloe hurried over to Riley and Sierra. "Don't leave me here alone," she whispered. "Lennon will think I'm a loser."

"But I thought you didn't like him," Riley said with a smile.

"I think I changed my mind," Chloe replied. "I'm going to make a move. Soon."

"Gotta go," Sierra said, ducking out.

"Sorry!" Riley called as Larry tugged her towards the door. "Good luck!"

That left Chloe to scurry back to the table alone. Grabbing her copy of *Teen Style*, she leaned back in the chair. Look relaxed, she said to herself. Totally cool. A girl glanced at her and Chloe smiled back as if to say: I've got it all together.

The page was still open at the Love Factor quiz. Chloe brightened. How perfect! She could take the quiz for Lennon and her.

She pulled out a purple pen and dug in. She answered question one and checked her score. The highest score possible. She answered questions two and three, then checked the answer key.

Another great score!

Her heart beat fast with excitement. She and Lennon were totally perfect for each other. She couldn't wait to finish the quiz!

With a secret smile, she looked around for Lennon. There he was, sliding his folded apron on to the coffee bar. He had his backpack on and…

Oh, no! He was leaving. His shift was ending. She had to grab him before it was too late!

Chloe dropped her pen and hurried over to the coffee bar. Forget about acting casual. This was her chance to get a date with the perfect boy for her.

Trying to pretend she wasn't nervous, she squeezed in next to Lennon at the counter. "Hey," she said.

Lennon turned away from the cappuccino machine and smiled at her. "Brain freeze over?"

"I'm totally thawed," Chloe said. Then she thought of an angle. "I didn't see you at the last party at the senior centre."

"I had to go to a wedding with my parents," Lennon said.

"Hey, Lennon," one of his friends called. "Over here."

"In a minute," Lennon called, turning back to Chloe.

She was close enough to see the tiny flecks of blue in his grey eyes.

"My friends are waiting," he said.

Chloe nodded. Enough small talk, she thought. Time to pop the big Q. "So I just found out my friend Sierra is playing at Mango's," she said.

"Really?" Lennon seemed interested.

"With her band, The Wave." Chloe's heart was beating hard in her chest. She wanted to do the safe thing and stop right now, but she plunged on. "They're performing this Friday night," Chloe said, bracing herself. "And I…"

Just then, someone turned on the cappuccino machine. W*hirrrrrrrrr*!

It drowned out Chloe's words: "*…I was wondering if you'd like to go with me*?"

Lennon squinted, his gaze on Chloe's lips as if he was trying to read them.

Did he hear me? she wondered as the machine stopped.

Lennon nodded slowly. "That's cool," he said.

"Hey, Lennon!" his friend called again.

"Look, I have to go," Lennon said. "But we'll talk later."

"Right," Chloe said. She smiled, trying to cover her

confusion as Lennon headed off. She replayed the scene in her head as she went back to her table.

Okay, she got bonus points for asking Lennon out.

The only problem was… she wasn't sure if he'd heard her.

Did she have a date for Friday night or not?

chapter
three

Riley breathed in the cool, salty mist that blew off the water. Today she was going to surf Malibu for the first time! She was going to try, anyway.

It was too bad that Alex had to cancel their afternoon together. But she'd always wanted to try surfing. And now that she was there on the beach, taking a lesson, she was glad. If only it wasn't with Larry.

Larry shuffled beside her in the sand, earphones on his head, dancing to some song playing on his Walkman. He had painted white sunblock squiggles on his cheeks. He was singing out of tune and kicking sand all over the instructor's surfboard.

Skeeter, the instructor from Zuma Jay's, waved a hand in front of Larry's face to get his attention. "Dude! Scale it down a notch."

Larry nodded, restricting his dance to a smaller area.

"Okay, surfers!" Skeeter shouted over the gentle pounding of the waves. "Place your boards flat on the sand and we'll go over the basics before you start surfing the 'Bu." The surf instructor walked along the line of students, his baggy shorts and yellow T-shirt flapping in the wind.

"We're ready to hang ten, oh mighty surf kahuna!" Larry called as he untangled his Walkman.

Skeeter lifted his shades to eye Larry.

"He's totally serious," Riley told Skeeter. "When Larry gets into something, he dives head-first."

Skeeter nodded, crossing his tanned arms in front of his chest. "Got it. Keep an eye on Larry."

Riley smiled. She felt a little like a seal in her black wetsuit with turquoise panels on the side. She slid her board onto the sand. She had rented them both at Zuma Jay's.

A guy in tropical-print swimming trunks and a sleek blue surf shirt dropped his board beside hers. "Hey, you're using a fun board?"

Riley looked down at the board she'd rented. The clerk in the surf shop had recommended a fun board, since they were shorter than most, and Riley wasn't very tall. "Yeah," Riley answered. "Do you think I made the right choice? I'm a total beginner."

"Should work for you," the guy in the flowered shorts said. "Not that I'm an expert or anything. But I surfed a few times in Hawaii."

"No way!" Riley cried. "If you're a hotshot, what are you doing here? This clinic is for beginners!"

The kid laughed. He had blue eyes and short-cut dark hair spiked just at the front. "I'm not that good. Actually, I stink. You'll see for yourself in a few minutes." He dropped down to the sand and stretched out on his board. "I'm Vance."

"Riley," she answered, sitting cross-legged on her own board.

"Okay, surfers," Skeeter said. He walked past the line-up of surfing students. "The main goal of this clinic is to give you the basics of surfing and to get you up on your board out there," he said, pointing towards the cresting waves.

"Cowabunga, dude!" Larry cried.

Skeeter eyed him. Riley couldn't tell if Skeeter thought Larry was funny or scary. "For starters, we're going to practise here, with your boards on the sand," Skeeter continued. "Let's have all of you stand up and take a stance on the board, one foot in front of the other."

Riley stood up on her shiny board and looked down. "Which foot goes first?" she asked.

"Good question," Skeeter replied. "It could go either way. Our stance is something that nature gives us. There's left foot in the front – that's regular. Or right foot in the front, which is called a goofy stance."

Riley looked over at Larry, who was leading with his right foot.

"Goofy stance!" Larry announced.

"Why am I not surprised?" Riley teased as she tried to find the footing that worked best for her. She stood on her board, arms out.

[Riley: Here I am... the wind gently blowing my hair back, the sun warming my skin. I'm a surf goddess, riding the crest of a wave and... Oof!]

Someone pushed her from behind!

She clambered forward, struggling for balance, and landed on the board with her left foot in front of her. She turned around to see Skeeter smiling behind her. "Hey! What was that about?" she asked.

"It's the best way to figure out your stance if you're not sure," Skeeter explained. "A sneaky push from behind always works. You're a regular."

Riley looked down at her feet. "All-righty, then. Thanks, I guess."

Next Skeeter showed them how to shift their weight to keep their balance. Riley bent her knees and gently shifted the board in the sand. It wasn't hard, but she knew it would be a different story out on the water.

Beside her, Larry toppled on to the sand. "Aw, man, I wiped out!"

"Larry, you're the first student I've ever seen wipe out before he hits the water," Skeeter said.

"Sometimes you have to learn the hard way." Larry brushed sand off his red wetsuit.

"I think you guys are about ready to get wet," Skeeter said, picking up his board. "Okay, surfers! Let's go in the water."

Riley lifted her board and ran into the foam alongside Larry and Vance. When the water was waist deep, she pushed the board under her and started paddling out.

Skeeter led the way. He paddled to a spot where half a dozen surfers lingered, waiting for a wave. Skeeter swung his board around so that he was facing the shore. "This is about far enough," he called to the group.

Riley swung her board around – and rammed right into Vance.

"Whoa! Got a licence to drive that thing?" Vance asked.

"Sorry," Riley said, trying to paddle backwards.

"It's okay," Vance said.

"That's one of the drawbacks of the 'Bu," Skeeter called. "Choice breaks are always going to be crowded. Now, let's get ready to take off."

Riley planted her feet on the board and looked back cautiously. A wave was rising behind her. She felt a surge of excitement as it moved closer. Still crouching, she faced the beach as her board was pulled forwards.

Knees bent. Arms out. Left foot in front.

Her muscles tensed as the board wobbled beneath her. But she was moving. She was up and riding, the wave whooshing around her.

It was great! She grinned. What a thrill!

As she swirled to a stop in the shallow water, Riley threw up her hands and let out a whoop of joy. "Yes!" she shouted. She grabbed her board and turned back to the others.

Larry and Vance stumbled in the surf, picking themselves up from their wipeouts. Their boards floated nearby.

"I totally ditched!" Vance exclaimed.

"Really." Larry put a finger in one ear. "I swallowed a ton of water."

"I love this!" Riley cried. She was eager to get back and try another wave.

She paddled out with Larry and Vance and hung out in the line-up. Skeeter gave them a few tips on how to spot the perfect swell. Then Riley was off again, rising to her feet unsteadily as water churned beneath her board.

She cruised in, loving the ride!

Larry came in on the next wave, howling in excitement. "That's it for me! I'm going to go hug the sand for a while."

"Thanks for bringing me here, Larry," Riley said. "It's so great! I'm going back in."

"Later!" Larry said, dragging his board towards the beach.

Riley paddled back in and joined the other surfers. They talked as they waited in the line-up. Then suddenly, everyone was moving to catch the next wave. Riley barely noticed as an hour flew by.

Surfing *rocks*! she thought as she reached the shore once again.

"Riley?" Skeeter darted over to her, his board under one arm. "You caught another wave? Nice!"

Riley swiped the water from her cheeks. "I got lucky."

"Looks like more than luck to me," Skeeter said. "You're a natural."

His words made her feel a swell of pride. "Thanks!"

"You're welcome." Skeeter nodded. "I'm sure I'll see you around. I'm here most afternoons. Or come find me at Zuma Jay's if you want some serious lessons." He ran back into the surf and paddled out.

Vance rode past him on a wave, kneeling on his board. He made a sharp turn into the wave and flew into the water.

Riley waited for Vance on the beach, smiling. "That was some stunt," she said.

"I'm practising for that show," he said. "The one that features Stupid Pet Tricks."

"But you're not an animal," she pointed out.

"Hey, don't blow my cover."

She nodded towards the beach. "I've got to go."

"I'll see you around," he said. "How about tomorrow? Now that you've got surf fever, you won't be able to stay away."

Riley glanced beyond him to the whitecaps and the blue horizon and the pink sunset. He was right. She couldn't wait to surf again. "See you tomorrow," she said. She plodded up the beach towards Zuma Jay's. It had turned out to be a spectacular day.

As she went to turn in her board, the clerk asked her if she'd had a good time.

Riley grinned. "It was great. In fact, how much more would it cost to keep the board for a week or so?"

The clerk smiled. "You're hooked."

Riley nodded. She couldn't wait to go surfing again. She was hooked, all right.

chapter
four

"So I started taking the Love Factor quiz for Lennon, and it was amazing! We're perfect together," Chloe told her sister that evening. She couldn't stop thinking about Lennon.

"Really?" Riley pulled back her hair, still wet from the shower. "So what did you do?" They were in the kitchen, trying to keep out of Mom's way.

"I didn't even have time to finish the quiz. Lennon was leaving! So I marched right over to him and asked him out."

"Go, Chloe!" Riley said. "And…?"

"And I'm not sure he heard me," Chloe admitted, wincing. "The cappuccino machine went on at exactly the wrong time."

"But you repeated the question, right?"

"There was no time!" Chloe said. "And he just said something like 'sounds cool'. So I don't know if that means yes or whatever!"

"Oh, no." Riley frowned. "What are you going to do?"

"I don't know," Chloe answered, wringing her hands. "The whole thing is kind of embarrassing."

"Ask him again," Riley said.

"I can't." Chloe paced across the kitchen. "But maybe I have to. Oh, I don't know!"

Riley peeked through the kitchen door. "Why are we stuck in here?"

"Mom's on the phone with Milan," Chloe explained. "That show in Italy? She's talking with a seamstress who's altering Tedi's gown." Tedi was one of the main models employed by Carlson Designs, the business run by Chloe and Riley's mom.

[<u>Chloe</u>: Our mom isn't a noise freak or anything. We don't usually whisper around the house. But she's under a lot of pressure lately, especially since she couldn't make it to her fashion show in Italy. Dad's in Santa Fe, and they don't like to be out of town at the same time. But let me back up. Our parents are separated. They used to be fashion designers together, but then Dad decided he needed a change of pace. So he gave up designing and stress and our big house on the beach. And Mom took on the whole enchilada – all of Carlson Designs.]

"I'm starving!" Riley said, lifting the lid on a steaming pot. "Surfing really makes you hungry."

"So you liked it?" Chloe asked.

"I loved it!" Riley told her all about the lesson and Skeeter and Vance. Chloe laughed when she heard about Larry's goofy stance.

"Maybe you can get Vance together with one of your friends," Chloe whispered as their mother's voice rose out in the living room.

"I don't think so," Riley whispered back. "I mean, Sierra is into Larry, and Vance is a little too outgoing for Joelle. And I'm not sure Carrie would *get* him." She stirred the pot on the stove and licked the spoon. "Mmm… Manuelo's stroganoff." Manuelo Del Valle was the housekeeper and cook who had lived with the Carlsons since the girls were babies. Over the years, he had become a part of the family. "When's dinner?"

Chloe peeked into the living room and saw their mom pacing nervously as she spoke on the phone. "I don't think Mom's going to be eating any time soon. There's a problem with some of the dresses."

"Oh, please, no! That could take forever! We'll be having stroganoff for breakfast." Riley stabbed a mush-room with a fork.

"Move over," Chloe said, hungry herself.

A breathless Manuelo suddenly appeared in the kitchen. "Ay! That wetsuit! It will have me up all night. I keep rushing to the patio to wet it again."

Riley shook her head. "Don't worry about it, Manuelo. As long as it's rinsed—"

"It's a wetsuit, don't you know?" he corrected Riley. "So I hose it down every half hour. I hear it's like a rhino's skin. If you let it dry, it cracks. Hopelessly ruined. Didn't you see the tag? No dry!"

Chloe held back a laugh. "I think that means don't put it in the dryer."

"I'm taking no chances," Manuelo insisted. Suddenly, he noticed the forks in the girls' hands.

Chloe shrugged. "The stroganoff is delicious."

"No touchy, touchy!" he told them. "Dinner is delayed. Your mother is on the phone. A crisis in Italy."

"Sounds like Mom's working on a diplomatic summit," Chloe said as the doorbell rang. "I'll get that."

"Would you please?" Manuelo asked. "I have gazpacho to prepare. And that suit. Oh, it's time for another wetting…" He disappeared towards the patio.

Chloe crossed the living room as quietly as possible. She opened the door and gulped.

It was Lennon!

[Chloe: Lennon is at my door! His eyes have little stars in them that shine only for me. He smiles that crooked smile and takes my hand. "Oh, Chloe," he says. "I just took the Love Factor quiz and I rushed right over to tell you that we belong together. We have to go out Friday night… and every weekend!" And this pink puffy cloud rises around us and lifts us into the sky and…]

"Lennon?" Chloe said in a dreamy voice.

He nodded, as if to let her know she got his name right.

Feeling like a total klutz, Chloe opened the door wider. "Come in," she said, turning to see her mom rake back her hair in distress.

"No, no, *prego*!" Macy Carlson shouted into the phone.

"Into the kitchen," Chloe whispered, ushering him past the living room. "My mom's on a call… business," she added.

Chloe stumbled and backed into the kitchen table. Lennon was here! She couldn't get over it. He was right here in her house, and she wasn't quite sure what to do with him.

Riley dropped the lid back on to the pot as she noticed them. "Hi there!" she said brightly.

"Hey." Lennon nodded at her. "Listen, Chloe, I just dropped by to give you this."

Chloe's heart began to hammer as he fumbled in his backpack. What had he brought her? A bracelet? Chocolate? Flowers?

He handed her a fat book.

"My algebra book?" she said. Her heartbeat slowed a little.

"You left it at the Newsstand," he said. "Thought you might need it."

"I do! I definitely do. Thank you," Chloe said, feeling like a babbling fool. Okay, it was only a book, but he'd brought it all the way over here. "I mean, I can't do my homework without it." It must have fallen out of my bag when I stashed away the Love Factor quiz, she thought.

"And her homework has to be done by *Friday*," Riley added, emphasising the day. "Big day, this *Friday*."

[Chloe: **Excuse me while I crawl under the kitchen table in total embarrassment. I know Riley's trying to help me. But does she have to hit Lennon over the head with the Friday thing?**]

"What about you, Lennon?" Riley asked as Manuelo rushed into the kitchen muttering something about being behind schedule. "Do you have any plans for *Friday*?"

Lennon nodded. "Actually, I—"

W*hi-r-r-r-r*! The blender shrieked as Lennon explained his plan.

Oh, no! Chloe darted a look at the blender, where Manuelo was mixing his gazpacho. Then she stared at Lennon, trying to read his lips. But it was impossible. Hopeless!

When the noise died down, Riley stepped forward. "What was that again?" she asked Lennon.

He smiled at Chloe. "Chloe knows," he said confidently. "We talked about it this afternoon."

No, no! No, we didn't talk about it! At least, I didn't hear you! Chloe wanted to shriek. But Lennon seemed so sure of her, she couldn't admit she'd been faking all along.

She followed him to the front door helplessly, Riley trailing behind them. Mom was pacing now, though the phone was hung up.

"We got cut off," Macy explained as they passed by. "Don't touch the phone, girls. I'm waiting for them to call back."

"Hold on a minute," Riley said, catching up to Lennon and Chloe at the door. "Let's just get this straight. Right?"

Chloe nodded. This time she was glad her sister was butting in. Yes, she wanted to know Lennon's answer, once and for all.

Riley took a deep breath. "The big question is…"

Just then the phone rang.

"Are you or are you not…" Riley tried to press on, but Mom was waving frantically at them.

"Quiet, please," Macy said. "Sorry, but I have to put Tedi and the seamstress on speaker phone, so I need absolute silence."

With a silently mouthed "Bye!" Lennon ducked out of the front door.

The girls leaned against the closed door and shared a look of disappointment.

Mom kneeled on the floor and leafed through an English-Italian dictionary. "How are the straps?" she asked.

"A little on the thin side," Tedi answered. "They're basically spaghetti straps."

Mom was shaking her head. "That's all wrong."

Poor Mom, Chloe thought, watching her mother fumble through the dictionary. Macy Carlson was a high-energy person, but the hectic pace of managing this show long distance was really pushing her to the limit.

"Tell her to make them thicker," she said, searching the book for a word. "Like… like…"

"Like fettuccine?" Chloe suggested.

"*Perfecto!*" Mom said, nodding at Chloe. "Did you hear that, Tedi?"

"Gotcha!" Tedi said. "And I'm worried about this rosebud. It's huge. Like a bird's nest."

"Tell her to make it small and delicate," Mom said. "Like a… a…"

"A tortellini!" Chloe called out.

"Right!" Mom said. "Did you get that?"

"It's a good thing you know pasta," Riley muttered.

Yeah, Chloe thought. Pasta was one thing she could handle. Setting up a date with Lennon was another story.

chapter
five

That night Riley was dying to tell Alex about her day surfing the 'Bu. She'd found something new and wonderful that she liked to do and she wanted to share it with him.

But when she called, Alex was tied up with band rehearsal. Then there was dinner with his family. Riley knew not to call Alex at dinner time. The Zimmers didn't like to be disturbed when they were eating. They were a little more conventional than Riley's family.

Then again, very few kids at school split their time between their mom's Malibu beach house and their dad's oceanfront trailer.

Riley's Love Factor score suddenly popped into her brain. According to the quiz, she and Alex were totally incompatible. She guessed it was true. They didn't have many of the same interests. Riley shrugged off the thought. The whole thing was stupid anyway. She didn't know why she was even thinking about it.

So we're different, Riley told herself as she sat at her computer, hoping Alex would come on-line. At least, our lives are never boring.

She was researching something for her European history homework when Alex's Instant Message flashed onto the screen.

AZIMMSTER: Wassup?

RILEY241: Surfing! I love it already!

AZIMMSTER: That's great. Did Larry survive?

RILEY241: He's still breathing. You should try it! Better than a roller coaster!

AZIMMSTER: Not into the water, remember? My sister says it's because I'm an Aries.

Riley sighed. She'd been secretly hoping that Alex would try surfing. It could be something fun they could do together.

Oh, well, she thought as a new message from Alex flashed on the screen.

AZIMMSTER: Band practice was great! We're going to really kick it up this weekend at Mango's.

No, Alex wasn't into outdoor stuff. But Riley loved to listen to him sing. And he was a great guy. So they didn't like exactly the same things. So what? He was still the boy for her.

• • •

On Tuesday morning Riley and Chloe left for school extra early. They didn't want to be around for Mom's next conference call to Italy.

Riley spotted Sierra and some other friends on the lawn outside the school building.

"Catch!" Sierra called, tossing a Frisbee at her.

Riley dropped her backpack on to a bench and ran to get the Frisbee. She tossed it back to Sierra, who was decked out in platform heels and black jeans that laced up at the sides. Her red hair was twisted into tiny knots held by cute little clips.

"Hey, surfer girl! I heard you aced the clinic yesterday," Sierra said.

"I loved it," Riley admitted. "How about Larry? Was he hooked, too?"

Sierra sighed. "Larry is hanging up his surfboard and moving on. He's already into a new thing. *Teen Jeopardy*. Didn't you see him handing out these flyers in the parking lot?" She pulled a piece of purple paper from her pocket and passed it to Riley.

Riley unfolded it. "*Teen Jeopardy* tryouts will be this Friday," Riley read. She and Chloe liked the show. "That sounds like fun," Riley added.

"But there's a bonus. Did you see who's giving the three-day crash course?" Sierra asked. "Ms. Cho!"

"No way!" Riley said. Ms. Cho was one of the most popular teachers at West Malibu High.

"And the course is supposed to be a great study aid,

even if you don't go on the show," Sierra said. "A great boost for scholastic exams."

"This is a must-do," Chloe said, reading over Riley's shoulder.

"Really," Riley agreed. "Where do we sign up?"

"Sign up for what?" asked a familiar voice.

Riley looked up to see Alex, his sandy blond hair catching the early-morning sun. Her heart did a little dance. "Alex, hi!" She showed him the flyer. "We were just checking out this crash course. Doesn't it look great?"

Alex nodded. "*Jeopardy*? Yeah, my parents are into that."

Sierra and Chloe headed off to play Frisbee. Riley sat on a bench. Alex dropped down beside her. "The crash course starts today after school," Riley told him. "Want to sign up with me?"

"Oh – I don't know...." Alex looked away.

"What's wrong?"

His brown eyes met Riley's. "I was hoping we could do something today."

"So then come to the course, Alex!" Riley tugged on his sleeve.

He shook his head. "It's not my thing. But I wanted to see you. I mean, I was sort of hoping... but if you're into this crash thing..."

"I want to see you, too." Riley admitted. "Really. How about if we get together after the study session?"

Alex winced. "My parents are cracking down on school nights. They're already a little bent out of shape with all the band practises."

"So when can we get together?" Riley asked. "Do I have to drag you out of rehearsal and take you to the beach?"

"And get my guitar all wet?" One corner of his mouth lifted. Almost a smile.

"You'd like surfing," Riley said.

"That made my night, thinking of you riding a wave," Alex said. "I want to come and watch you sometime. You wouldn't mind, would you?" he asked.

"No, but don't you want to try it?" Riley asked.

He shrugged. "Nah, but I'll come to the beach with you. Any time." He leaned closer, and for a minute Riley felt herself melting under his dark eyes. "After all, you're always coming out for me whenever I play with the band. And it gives me a boost, knowing you're there," he added.

"Hey, I really love watching you play guitar. How many girls can go see their boyfriends on stage? It is so cool." Riley smiled and leaned against him, wishing things were easier.

"So are you coming on Friday?" he asked.

"I wouldn't miss it!" Riley said. "But I do want to go to the crash course today."

Alex nodded. "Okay. How about tomorrow?"

"It's a three-day course. But it's only an hour tomorrow…"

37

"So I'll wait for you tomorrow, and we'll go over to my house together," Alex said.

"It's a deal," Riley said. She was still leaning against him, so she pushed a little harder until they both slid off the bench.

"Hey!" he laughed, pulling her back up.

Riley's hair fell into her eyes, and she smiled at him through the blonde strands. "Tomorrow," she said. "Be there or be square."

"He brought the book to your house?" Amanda Gray asked Chloe.

Chloe nodded as she went through her lunch bag. Manuelo had really hit it right today. He'd packed all the cute foods that Chloe could eat with dignity. Like easy-to-pop grapes. Mineral water. (It didn't make your tongue or lips turn odd colors!) And tiny peanut-butter crackers. No crumbs, no awkward crunches. Just neat, cute food.

Today would be the perfect day to "casually" run into Lennon in the lunchroom. She glanced over at Lennon's table. Was he watching? No, at the moment he was laughing with his friends. She didn't want to get caught staring, but it was hard to look away.

"It sounds to me like the guy is into you," Amanda went on. She flipped through a magazine as she ate. "I mean, he could have just left the book for you at the school office, if he didn't care."

"Do you really think so?" Chloe asked. She popped a cracker into her mouth, still feeling a little insecure about Lennon.

"I don't understand the problem," Amanda said. "If you're not sure whether he heard you, why don't you just ask him?"

Typical Amanda. She made way too much sense. "I've tried." Chloe bit into a grape and looked at Amanda's fashion magazine. "Hey, turn to the horoscopes, will you? Maybe we can find Lennon's. I wonder when his birthday is…"

Amanda turned to the horoscopes and nodded. "That's it! Here's the reason you're having trouble. Mercury is in retrograde. So, like, every sign in the zodiac is in for some problems this week." She read: "'Messages will be mixed up. Minor snafus. Nothing to worry about. Take a bubble bath!'"

"Really?" Chloe read over her shoulder. "So I just need to keep trying?" She sank back with relief. This was going to work.

"I have been so worried about this. I was beginning to think Lennon and I weren't meant to be together. But after I took the Love Factor quiz and…"

It hit her. She never finished the quiz!

"Oh, wow! I have to finish it!" She turned to the cover of Amanda's magazine, but she was reading *Giggle Girl*. Chloe would have to wait until she got home to find out her final score with Lennon.

"I've heard of that quiz." Amanda brightened. "You've got to show it to me. I've been dying to take it."

"No problem," Chloe said. "I'll bring you a copy tomorrow. I can't believe I didn't finish. When I scored the first few questions, Lennon and I got a perfect score."

"Really?" Amanda blinked. "That's pretty amazing. The Love Factor is supposed to be foolproof."

Chloe nodded, watching Lennon. "I know."

Amanda followed Chloe's gaze. "You're staring at him. Why waste time? Just go right over to his table. Now's your chance if you really want to ask him."

Chloe took a sip of water. Amanda was right. What was she waiting for? She dabbed her napkin at her mouth and stood up. "I'll be right back," she told Amanda.

Feeling energised, Chloe pushed herself to *casually* walk by Lennon's table. As she listened in, Chloe realized Lennon and his friends were quizzing each other. Someone had a book of sample questions from *Teen Jeopardy*.

"The category is kings," one of Lennon's friends said. "He had six wives."

"Who is Henry the Eighth?" Lennon said without looking up from his pizza.

"Okay," someone else said. "This one is under Space Facts. It's the only man-made structure visible from outer space."

"What is the Great Wall of China?" Lennon answered.

Lennon rattled off one answer after another. Chloe had to admit she was impressed. "Hey, Lennon," she said, acting as if she were just passing by. "Are you going to Ms. Cho's seminars?"

"No way," Lennon said. "Those things bore me. Why sit through that stuff when I already know the answers?"

Chloe cringed. This was the side of Lennon that drove her nuts. Mr. Know-it-all. "You don't seem to mind the boring questions now," she pointed out.

Lennon's friends laughed, pointing at him.

"Busted!" one kid said. "She's got you nailed."

"We're just hanging out, having lunch," Lennon said. He bit into his pizza, flashing a challenging look at Chloe.

Was he mad at her? Chloe wondered. He was the one who was showing off.

"Toss a few more at me," Lennon told his friends.

The boys fired off a few more questions. As Lennon answered he watched Chloe and smiled. It was as if he was teasing her.

She wished he would miss just one answer, but he got them all right. The boy knew everything. If he weren't so cute, he'd be a nerd.

Chloe felt a pang as he gave her a crooked smile. How could she ever have fallen for him? Lennon was obnoxious with a capital O!

"Well," Chloe said, "I'm going to the crash course. I don't know everything. At least, not yet."

"Ooh!" Lennon's friends said, turning to him. "She burned you again!"

"Gee, that went well," Chloe muttered to herself as she turned away.

"Hey!" Lennon called after her. "Maybe I'll go to the crash course after all! There's got to be at least one fact I don't know!"

I doubt that, Chloe thought. She walked steadily back to the table and faced Amanda. "He's smart!" she gasped. "Really smart – and he knows it."

"So are you," Amanda said flatly. "So what's the big deal?"

Right, Chloe thought. She did well in school. Always on the honour roll.

"I get good grades," Chloe admitted, "but I don't act like I know everything. He can be so full of himself!"

"He'll get over that," Amanda said. "You'll help him get over that. Maybe Lennon just needs a girl like you to keep his ego under control."

Hmm. Chloe liked the sound of that.

"Maybe that's why you two are a perfect match," Amanda said. "You're both smart. You can teach him not to show off about it. You belong together."

Chloe popped a grape into her mouth. Maybe Amanda was right. Maybe she and Lennon *did* belong together.

"So… are you going out with him on Friday night?" Amanda asked.

"Yes," Chloe said. "Lennon might not know it yet. But we *will* go out Friday night."

chapter
six

"I can't believe it," Riley whispered to Sierra as they entered the auditorium for the *Teen Jeopardy* crash course. "Vance is here. I told you about him. He's my surfing buddy from yesterday."

"Really?" Sierra looked around. "Where?"

Riley nodded towards him. "He's by the flag. Short black hair. Nice tan. Blue eyes."

"You didn't mention that he was totally hot," Sierra whispered.

"I didn't—" Riley stopped herself as she got her first real look at Vance. She liked his easy smile and the way he wore his short brown-black hair spiked over his forehead. Okay, she had noticed his pale blue eyes before. But somehow the whole package didn't register with her until now.

Vance was gorgeous.

"Wow, he really is cute," she murmured.

"Told you," Sierra said. "And you're just noticing? Where've you been?"

Riley shrugged. "Since I already have a boyfriend, I guess it didn't cross my mind."

Sierra's eyebrows shot up as she gave Riley a curious look. "I'm crazy about Larry, but I can still appreciate a hottie when I see one."

Riley turned away from Vance and tried to focus. She hadn't expected to see him here. She didn't even know he went to West Malibu High. "How weird is that? I never noticed the guy before, and now, twice in two days, I run into him."

"Life is full of random weirdness," Sierra said. "Speaking of weirdness, there's my cutie." She pointed across the room.

Larry bounced up and down, waving them over to seats he'd saved.

The girls went to sit with Larry as Ms. Cho called for the meeting to start. "Let's jump right in," Ms. Cho said. "Today we're going to do drills. That means we need to break into smaller teams. I will assign them so that we don't all end up with our best friends. Okay?"

As the teacher went down the rows giving out numbers, Riley hoped she could be on Sierra's team. But what were the chances?

"Okay, let's have all the ones here, all the twos here," Ms. Cho said, assigning areas to the different teams.

When Riley went to find her teammates, there was Vance. It gave her a funny feeling in the pit of her stomach. Sort of giddy. Nervous. Excited.

Riley bit her lower lip. What was that about? It wasn't as if she liked Vance or anything – was it?

"I'll race you up the hill!" Riley called, pedalling her bike hard.

"You'll never beat me!" Vance challenged, switching gears. "If you pull ahead, I'll just crack you up again."

Riley could barely pedal, she was laughing so hard. Vance had just told her a funny story about how he'd once ditched his bike in a puddle of melted ice cream.

After the crash course ended, Sierra and Larry left together, and Riley found herself walking to the bike rack with Vance. He'd biked to school that day, just as she had. He talked her into taking a detour, since it was such a beautiful day. They rode up the paved path that wound along Malibu beach.

As they pedalled over the rise of the hill, the ocean came into view. The sun was low, hiding behind pink clouds that hung over the sparkling blue water of the Pacific. She wished that Alex were here to share it, but then, he wasn't really into riding bikes.

"You can stop pedalling, Riley," Vance called. "I give up. Victory is yours."

She cruised to a stop and stepped off the seat. "Check out that sky."

Vance circled, then braked beside her. "Yeah, every-thing looks awesome from up here. Too bad we don't have time to hit the beach."

"I want to go surfing tomorrow," Riley said. "But not today — it'll be dark soon. Besides, I have too much homework."

"Me, too," Vance said. "I've got algebra assignments coming out of my ears. Maybe we should get started on it. There's a pizza place up ahead with outdoor tables. We could crack open the books and knock off our home-work. And I wouldn't mind grabbing a slice."

It sounded like a good idea to Riley. "Let's go," she said, swinging on to her bike again.

They cruised along until they came to a stretch of beach with a café, a bookstore, and a pizza parlour. Vance ordered two slices and sodas. Then they cracked open their books and got to work.

"I do okay with this stuff," Vance said as he scratched out an equation. "But I don't see how I'm ever going to need it. Not with what I want to do."

"And that is…?"

"Professional snowboarding." His blue eyes lit up. "Have you ever tried it? It's my ultimate favourite sport. Especially the stunts. Flips and spirals."

"I've skied in Tahoe a few times," Riley said. "But I've never flipped down the slope. At least, not on purpose," she added.

"You have to try it!" Vance said. "My dad got me into

it. He works in an office, so he loves tearing out of there on long weekends. And I've got this wild uncle who loves camping and stuff. We go kayaking and hiking. Surfing and skiing. Depending on the weather."

"Sounds great," Riley said, chewing her pencil. She had a lot of fun with Vance, biking and surfing… and even at the crash course today. Vance had managed to psych up everyone on their team. He taught them some tricks to help them remember the presidents, the planets in the solar system, the periodic table of elements.

Their bubbling hot pizza arrived. Riley took a bite and thought about all the active, outdoorsy things she enjoyed doing, like hiking and swimming and surfing. It had been ages since she went camping or hiking. Why had she been hanging back lately?

> [Riley: I almost choked on my pizza when it hit me. Alex! Not that he stops me from biking or swimming… but Alex isn't into those things. So we usually hang out at his house or walk along the beach. It's nice. We have a great time together. Really. But sometimes I miss doing all those other things, too.]

Vance talked about canoe trips he'd taken with his dad. Riley listened as she ate her pizza. She laughed at Vance's stories and watched as the sun set over the ocean, all pink and purple and gold.

It was sort of the perfect date. Sort of.

Because it wasn't really a date at all. And Riley was still crazy about Alex.

Really, Riley thought as Vance leaned close to help her with an algebra equation. Vance is just a friend!

"I can't believe I skipped the crash course to chase a guy," Chloe said as the waitress delivered three coffee frappes to their table.

[Chloe: Correction: two frappes and one hot latte. I made one important promise to myself yesterday. No more cold drinks in front of Lennon. At least, not until our third date!]

Chloe enlisted the advice of her other good friends Tara Jordan and Quinn Reyes. And they convinced her that if she wanted to zero in on Lennon, she had to report to the Newsstand immediately. As Tara pointed out, it was already Tuesday. If Chloe was to finalise her plans for Friday, she had to get an answer from Lennon.

"Believe it," Tara said.

"Come on, Chloe," Quinn pointed out. "Do you want to go out with Lennon or not?"

"I do, I do – I think," Chloe said, taking a sip of her warm latte. "You should have seen him in the lunchroom, spouting off answers to those quiz questions. The guy is a brain wrapped in a hottie package." Chloe shook her head. "He's way too perfect. Except for the fact that *he knows* he knows everything."

"Well, you'd better figure out how you feel about Mr. Perfect pretty fast," Quinn whispered. "Because he just came out of the kitchen."

Chloe swallowed hard as she turned towards him. She didn't want to like the boy genius – she just couldn't help it!

"Oh, Chloe," Tara said, shaking her head. "You've got it bad, girl."

"I must be crazy," Chloe said.

"Okay, you're crazy," Quinn said as Lennon went to talk with some of his friends. They had taken a table near the newspaper rack, and they were joking about headlines. "Now go talk to him. Find out exactly what he's doing on Friday night."

Chloe stood up and straightened her ruffled shirt. "Right. I can do this. It's a simple question, right?"

"Right!" her friends answered.

Marching over to Lennon's table, Chloe felt a sudden stab of panic. What was she going to say?

[Chloe: At times like this, I can count on my brain to come up with mush. Just take a look at my conversation starters: 1. Did anyone ever tell you that you look hot in an apron? 2. Did anyone ever tell you that you're incredibly obnoxious? 3. Did anyone ever tell you that you're the guy for me?]

Okay, maybe those were all the wrong things to say. She should focus on Friday night. But that seemed so blunt.

Suddenly hesitant, she squeezed her toes around her flip-flops as she reached Lennon and his friends.

"Hey, Chloe," Lennon said, looking up from a news-paper.

"Hi!" Chloe said. The word flew out of her mouth like a lone moth, and that was it. Empty. Nothing else to say.

"What does that one say?" one of his friends asked Lennon, who was holding a copy of a French newspaper called *Le Monde*.

"The headline is about a demonstration in Marseilles," Lennon answered. "And this is a story about how little snow they've had in the French Alps."

"Cool," another boy said. He shoved a different paper at Lennon. "What's this?"

"It's German, from Stuttgart," Lennon answered. "The lead story is about… how they're opening a new factory to make Porsches."

"Wow, is there any language you don't speak?" someone asked.

Lennon rolled his eyes. "Plenty! I just picked up a lot when my family moved around Europe. But I'd be lost in China or the Middle East."

Was that a flash of modesty from the brilliant Lennon? Chloe wondered. Maybe he wasn't a totally stuck-up snob.

"Pretty impressive," she admitted, thinking of how she'd struggled with Spanish until Manuelo had started coaching her.

As the guys shoved other newspapers at Lennon, Chloe's gaze landed on a photograph of Tedi.

"Whoa!" She pulled the paper towards her.

"You know her?" Lennon asked.

"That's Tedi, the main model for my mom's label. Mom's a designer," Chloe said. "And this Italian show has been really hard for her."

Chloe thought of the crunch Mom had been under with this latest show. Talk about stress! Mom had been up most of the night, worrying over design changes.

She studied the headline. Since it was an Italian newspaper, the only thing she could decipher was Tedi's name in the caption. "I wonder what this is about."

Lennon leaned closer. "Good press for Carlson Designs," he said. "It says that Tedi is one of the beautiful models in Milan for the fall show. Actually, it says she *is* the most beautiful."

An idea buzzed in Chloe's mind. "You speak Italian?"

Lennon nodded. "Sì."

If Lennon spoke Italian, he could help Mom! There wasn't a moment to lose. Mom needed him to translate. She was probably struggling through an overseas phone call right now.

Without another thought, Chloe grabbed his arm and gave a tug. "Why didn't you say so! My mom has been going nuts trying to talk to Italian seamstresses!

She needs you desperately!"

"I'd like to help," Lennon said. "But I'm not totally fluent. I just know a few words."

"That's more than Mom knows," Chloe said, tugging on his arm. "You've got to come with me. Now!"

chapter
seven

"Let's move on to the evening gown," Macy Carlson said with authority.

Lennon translated for the seamstresses on the other end of the speakerphone.

Macy turned to Chloe, who put down the sketch of the suit she'd been holding and grabbed the sketch Mom needed.

This is going great! Chloe thought.

With Lennon translating, Mom was free to think about the design. Even Chloe was able to help, finding the right sketches and measurements so that Mom could focus on the most important thing – perfecting the details. Working as a team, the three of them had made it through alterations on most of the Carlson collection.

Chloe grinned. She liked being on Lennon's team. When he wasn't trying to impress his friends, Lennon was a great guy.

"Is the bodice snug enough?" Mom asked.

"It fits like a glove," Tedi answered. "I'm just not sure about this hemline. It goes up in front."

Chloe sifted through the sketches to find the dimensions of the gown. She handed them to her mom.

"It should rise a little," Macy answered. She looked down at the notes Chloe had found. "Just enough to reveal some toe cleavage."

Lennon translated for Mom, and the seamstress shot back another question in Italian.

Chloe listened carefully, trying to anticipate Mom's next move. This was fun! Not that she was totally obsessed with high fashion or anything, but the air was crackling with excitement.

"I've decided to make it pasta night, in honour of your show," Manuelo announced from the kitchen door. "Four different types. Spaghetti, radiatori, percatelli…"

"Shh!" everyone hushed him.

"Oh! Sorry!" Manuelo's hand flew to his mouth. "I thought you were finished."

"Now… where were we?" Mom asked.

"The hemline," Chloe said, pointing to the sketch. Now she was the one keeping Mom on track. That was a switch!

"Right. Is the hemline falling properly in the front?" Mom asked. "It shouldn't buckle around the seam."

As Lennon translated, the door opened and Riley breezed in. "Hey, everybody!" she said cheerfully.

"Shh!" Manuelo said. "Can't you see they're in conference?"

"But we're almost finished," Chloe said quietly.

Manuelo threw up his hands and returned to the kitchen.

As Lennon and Mom talked, Riley edged over to Chloe. "What's going on?" she asked.

"Lennon is translating," Chloe whispered. "He knows Italian. Can you believe it?"

"How great is that?" Riley said.

"It's totally great!" Chloe tried to keep from bubbling over with excitement.

"I think that covers everything," Tedi said over the phone. "And it's a good thing. I'm walking down the runway tomorrow."

"That's it," Mom said, raising a fist in victory. "We did it! Call me if you need me, Tedi."

"Will do," Tedi said. "*Ciao, bella*."

Mom swept the design board out of Chloe's hands and danced her around the room. "*Finito!* I am so relieved! Now I can collapse and watch that Daffy Duck marathon on the Cartoon Network."

"I didn't know there was a Daffy marathon today," Lennon said. "I love Daffy Duck! He and Elmer Fudd are my favorites."

"Elmer is good, too," Mom said. "But nothing beats twelve straight hours of Daffy."

Chloe stared from Lennon to Mom and back again.

Was this really happening? Was the boy she liked bonding with her mom in one easy step? She wanted to rush forward and throw her arms around both of them.

No… that would be a little pushy. First she should get a date with Lennon. T*hen* she would throw her arms around him.

"And Lennon," Mom went on, "thank you so much! My show would never have been ready in time without you."

"Yes, thanks, Lennon," Chloe said. "You were awesome. Especially when that seamstress shot back questions in rapid-fire Italian."

Lennon gestured around the room. "We make a great team. By the way, what in the world is toe cleavage?"

Chloe and Riley looked down at their own flip-flops and started laughing. "You don't want to know," Chloe teased Lennon. "It's definitely not a guy thing."

Lennon laughed.

He's so nice! Chloe thought. How could I ever have thought he was a snob?

Mom gathered up the sketches. "Manuelo, I'll be parked in front of my cartoons."

"Dinner in ten minutes, Mrs. Macy," Manuelo called from the kitchen. "That gives you time for one episode of Daffy."

"I guess I'd better get going," Lennon said.

As Chloe walked him to the door, she thought of

how much had changed in the past hour. She'd seen a deeper side of Lennon, and his talent with languages had made Mom's day. She followed him out of the door to put the perfect ending on the afternoon.

Chloe pulled the door closed behind her. Suddenly they were face-to-face. Chloe felt the electricity between them. She couldn't help staring at the little flecks of blue in his pale grey eyes. A warm feeling swept over her as he reached out and touched her arm.

"I'm glad you brought me home with you, Chloe," he said. "I had a good time."

Chloe felt herself melt. "Me, too. Thanks."

"Any time," Lennon said. Then he turned to head up the beach road. "See you tomorrow."

"Bye!" Chloe waved after him, deciding to wait until he was gone to break into her happy dance. She had dragged Lennon to her house. He had said they made a great team. How hard could it be to coordinate a date for Friday?

Friday! She almost forgot.

"Oh, wait. Lennon?" she called.

Just then a jet plane passed overhead with a loud rumble.

"Lennon! Are we…?" But Chloe's voice was totally drowned out by the noise. "You've got to be kidding me," she muttered as Lennon disappeared around a corner.

Frustrated, she headed back into the house. For two

people who are supposed to be a perfect match this was getting pretty weird. Why was it so difficult to find out if they had a date?

Then Chloe remembered something even more urgent. The Love Factor quiz! She had to finish it!

chapter
eight

Riley stretched out on her rosebud quilt to do her homework. She opened her algebra book. Duh! How could she forget? She'd already finished her algebra with Vance at the pizza place.

She closed the book and laughed, remembering how Vance had talked his way through the algebra problems. He pretended the variables were spies. "I'm going to neutralize you, Agent X," he'd said. "I'll find out your equal, Agent Y."

It was goofy, but she liked it.

Just then the bedroom door burst open. "You're never going to believe this!" Chloe announced, beaming. "Not in a million years!"

Riley lifted her head. "What?"

"Lennon and I aced the quiz!" Chloe bounced onto the bed beside Riley.

Riley tried to focus on the copy of *Teen Style* that

Chloe shoved in front of her face, but the whole bed was jiggling from Chloe's bouncing.

"You're making me seasick!" Riley said, gripping the magazine. "You took the Love Factor quiz?"

Chloe nodded. "And we totally maxed out on every question!"

"I had a feeling," Riley said. "He seemed pretty comfortable helping Mom this afternoon, too."

"Didn't he?" Chloe hugged the magazine to her chest, then tossed it on to the bed. "This is so great! I'm not going to let anything else get in the way. I'm calling him right now!"

Just then the phone rang, and Riley laughed. "Well, if the Love Factor is right, that's probably Lennon calling *you* right now!"

Hopeful, Chloe grabbed the phone, and said hello. "Oh, hi, Alex," she said. "Sure, she's here. Hold on." She handed the phone to Riley, saying, "I'll use the business line downstairs."

Chloe left, and Riley pressed the phone to her ear. "Hi! How's it going?" she asked, looking down at her maths notebook. She noticed a little doodle Vance had scribbled on a page. A silly face with a moustache. Feeling a pang of guilt, Riley quickly closed the notebook and turned round.

"I'm great," Alex said. "What did you do this afternoon?"

"I…" She choked on the words. Why was he asking

that? Had he heard something? "I... nothing special. I went for a bike ride. Homework. Things like that."

As Alex told her about a history project he was working on, Riley wondered why she didn't tell him about Vance. It was an innocent thing. But it would sound as if she was making a big deal out of it. Wouldn't it? And it would only underline the fact that Alex didn't like to go biking or surfing...

"What did you end up doing after school?" she asked him, hoping to change the subject.

"The usual. I played guitar a while. Came up with half a song. Played it for Saul over the phone."

"Did he like it?" Riley asked.

"He's cool with it," Alex answered. "It still needs work, though."

"Uh-huh." Riley bit her lower lip. She didn't know what to say next. Sometimes phone conversations with Alex were like that.

"So how was that whole *Teen Jeopardy* thing?" Alex asked her.

"Really fun," Riley told him. "We learned a cool trick to memorise the presidents and the planets and constellations. I know it sounds boring, but Ms. Cho makes it interesting."

"Yeah," Alex said. He had Ms. Cho for social studies. "She's great."

Riley took a deep breath, trying to get past the tight feeling in her chest. "Well..." She tried to think of something else to talk about, but suddenly her afternoon with Vance weighed on her mind. His face loomed there, reminding her of the good time they'd had together after school.

She just couldn't tell Alex about it.

"I guess I'd better go," she said. "I've got a pile of presidents to memorise."

Riley clicked off the phone and let her head drop on to the bed. She felt so awful! She hated hiding anything from Alex.

Chloe burst in again with an update. "Okay, I called Lennon, and he was home! But someone beeped in, and it was a call his dad had to take. So he's calling me back."

"Great!" Riley said. She really was happy things were working out for Chloe, but she couldn't shake her bad feeling.

"What's the matter?" Chloe asked.

"It's nothing," Riley said.

"What?" Chloe pounced on to Riley's bed. "What happened between you and Alex? I can tell something is wrong. Tell me!"

"Nothing happened with Alex," Riley admitted. "It's Vance."

"The surfer boy?" Chloe asked.

Riley nodded. "He turned up at the *Teen Jeopardy* crash course today. He landed on my team. And when the course was over, we walked out together. We ended up going on a bike ride. Then we stopped at this pizza place to do our homework."

"So?" Chloe shrugged. "Sounds innocent enough. What are you so worried about?"

Riley sighed. Chloe was right. It was no big deal. Vance was a cool guy, and Riley liked to hang out with him. So what? Why should she feel guilty?

"Alex is your boyfriend," Chloe said. "But you're still allowed to talk to other guys."

"I know," Riley said. "That's why I don't understand why I'm afraid to tell Alex about Vance. Does it mean something?"

"Let's see what *Teen Style* has to say about this," Chloe said, leafing through the magazine. "According to the Love Factor, you don't need to feel guilty if—"

"Chloe?" Riley interrupted. "Can we just forget the quiz? I can't get into it right now."

"Okay," Chloe agreed. "You need to do what's right for you. I mean, just because the Love Factor worked for Lennon and me..." She put the magazine aside and jumped up. "I've got to go call Tara and Quinn. They're going to freak when they hear about my incredible score!"

Chloe left, and Riley flopped down on the bed.

That dumb quiz! At least Chloe was happy about it.

But if Riley believed the Love Factor's scores, she and Alex were in trouble. Which was ridiculous, since everyone knew they got along just fine.

The magazine sat on her nightstand, practically

calling at her to open it and take the quiz again. I shouldn't, she thought. It will only confuse me more.

She could hear Chloe's voice in her head. "The Love Factor is foolproof!"

With a deep breath, Riley sat up and grabbed the magazine. She didn't believe in the quiz. Not really. But it was tempting.

She could take it again… this time for Vance. Just to see how they did together.

No, that was silly.

She glanced at the first question. "'Your love gives you a gift wrapped with a big fat bow!'" she read aloud.

Oh, why not?

"Tara thinks I should call Lennon back," Chloe said as she burst into the bedroom a few minutes later.

Riley dropped her pencil and shoved her score sheets under the magazine. Caught! Even though she wasn't doing anything wrong. But she didn't want Chloe to know she was taking the quiz *twice*.

"But Quinn has a different theory," Chloe went on, leaning into the mirror to unhook her shell necklace. "She thinks that forces may be keeping us apart. Supernatural forces."

"I don't know about that." Riley frowned. "A noisy jet and a whirring blender wouldn't really make it on *The X- Files*."

"But you've got to admit it's weird." Chloe turned away from the mirror and sat across from Riley. Her gaze fell on the open magazine.

Riley squirmed.

"What's this?" Chloe reached over and slid out the two pages of answers in Riley's handwriting. "Riley? Two sets of answers? You took the Love Factor quiz over again?"

Riley winced. "I was just goofing around with it. I didn't finish," she admitted, hoping Chloe would just forget about it. "No big deal."

"So go on and finish it!" Chloe insisted, looking at the papers. "This one is done, and this one..." She blinked. "You took the test with Vance as a boyfriend?"

Riley winced again. "I told you, I was just goofing around."

"So finish!" Chloe repeated. "We've got to see how this works out."

Biting her lower lip, Riley finished the last three questions and handed Chloe the answer sheet.

Chloe nodded as she scored Riley's answers. "Nice score! This is great. It says you are a great match for... Vance!"

Riley blinked. "Vance? But what about Alex?"

"Not so great with him," Chloe admitted. "But you knew that already."

Uh-oh, Riley thought.

"I think you know what this means," Chloe said.

Riley hugged her knees. "I was kind of afraid of this," she admitted. "But I guess… maybe… I like Vance. As more than a friend. At least a little."

"What are you going to do?" Chloe asked.

"I don't want to do anything to hurt Alex," Riley said. "So I guess, starting tomorrow, I'll just have to stay away from Vance."

chapter
nine

"Chloe, the gig at Mango's is the day after tomorrow," Quinn said on Wednesday morning at school. "And you still don't know for sure if Lennon is going there with you."

"You have to act," Tara ordered. "Now."

"I know," Chloe moaned. "He never called me back last night! No matter how hard I try to pin him down, something always gets in the way."

"Well, you can't let *him* get away." Quinn sat on the step beside Chloe. "Lennon is major boyfriend material."

She reached into Chloe's backpack and flipped open Chloe's mobile phone.

"What are you doing?" Chloe asked.

Tara held out a slip of paper with a number on it. "Lennon's mobile phone," she said.

"He has a mobile phone?" Chloe snatched the

paper. "How did you get this number?"

"Never mind that," Tara said. "He's only supposed to use the phone for emergencies. But this definitely qualifies. Now dial. He's probably on his way to school."

Quinn handed her the mobile phone. "Call him. Ask him. Do it now."

"Okay, okay!" Chloe tapped in the mobile number and waited as it rang. She bit her lower lip. "He's not answering," she said. "And I'm not getting voice mail."

"Maybe he's on the other line," Tara said.

Quinn frowned. "Still ringing?"

Chloe held out the phone so Quinn could hear. "No go." An image flashed through her mind – Lennon the show-off, shooting off answers to quiz-show questions in the cafeteria. She felt annoyed. "He's probably on the other line with some girlfriend in Sweden. Some girl he can actually connect with. Because that's Lennon, the big, important world traveller. Mr. Know-it-all."

"Chloe?" There was a voice on the line. Lennon's voice.

Chloe gasped. When had the ringing stopped? How much had he heard?

She pressed the phone to her ear.

"Is that you?" he asked.

Panicked, Chloe pressed the button to hang up. "I blew it!" she moaned.

"What happened?" Tara shrieked.

"Did he answer?" Quinn asked.

Chloe nodded.

"Did he hear you?" Tara asked. "*What* did he hear?"

"I don't know!" Chloe moaned. "It took him such a long time to answer the phone. I figured he was never going to pick up."

"It's okay," Tara said. "You are totally covered. He has no way of knowing it was you."

"Right," Chloe said, nodding. "Except that I think he recognized my voice. He said my name." She pressed her chin against her fist. "I am so busted."

I have total willpower, Riley thought. I'm in complete control.

She looked up from her history book and glanced around the library. She'd made it all the way to study period without running into Vance once.

I can do this, she told herself. She chewed her pencil. If she stayed away from Vance, she would have no problem. Soon she'd forget how much fun she had with him and stop liking him.

Yes, that was the plan. Now if only she could stop thinking about him and focus on her work.

Okay… back to the Battle of 1812.

"Riley! Hey!" Vance waved to her and walked across the library, straight for her table. He grabbed a chair and sat down.

Riley grinned. So much for willpower.

"How's it going?" Vance said. "I just got a mondo

paper assigned in social studies. I like to get that stuff out of the way during study period. I mean, who needs to be doing homework after school when you can get out and bike and surf and stuff?"

"Totally." Riley nodded.

"So, do you mind if I study with you until next period?" Vance asked.

"Um – no, I don't mind," Riley replied. What could she say? No, you can't study with me? No, this library is for my personal use only?

This is ridiculous, she thought. How can I avoid someone who goes to the same school as I do? And why should I? Vance is a fun guy and I like to hang out with him. So what?

"So what are you doing after school?" Vance asked.

"I've got the *Jeopardy* course," Riley said. They were on the same team. There was no way she could avoid him there. But that wasn't her fault, was it?

"Oh, right! So do I." Vance nodded. "How about after that? Do you want to hang out?"

Yes! Yes, I do, Riley thought. But… "I can't," she said. She had plans with Alex.

"Oh." Vance was scribbling something in his note-book. "How come?"

She hesitated. Should she mention Alex?

"Too much homework," she said. *Chicken*, she scolded herself.

"Tell me about it," he said. "Sometimes I think the

teachers just want to torture us. Maybe all this home-work is a plot to keep us busy while the teachers secretly try to take over the world."

Riley laughed. "Somehow I can't see Mr. Vargas running the world." Mr. Vargas was a science teacher. He had very thick glasses and tiny little teeth like yellow Chiclets.

"No, see, he's got a great cover," Vance said. "You'd never suspect somebody with glasses that thick. But underneath he's a villain right out of a spy movie. He definitely gives the most homework, anyway."

Riley laughed again. Before she knew it, study period was over – and she hadn't got much studying done.

chapter
ten

I haven't seen Alex all day, Riley thought as she settled at her desk in Mr. Bender's English class. That's strange. She usually had lunch with him on Wednesdays. But Riley had just finished lunch, with no sign of Alex.

Rrrrrrriiiiiinnnnnggg! The fire alarm blared through the school. Fire drill!

"Leave your books where they are," Mr. Bender said. "Proceed out of the door to the left. Single file!"

Riley hurried out of the classroom. Another line of students marched down the hall. She walked alongside them, keeping an eye out for Alex.

"This is all part of the plot," a familiar voice said in her ear. "Fire drills, I mean."

Riley turned around. Vance!

"While we're all outside learning about fire safety, Mr. Vargas is in the chemistry lab, cooking up some kind of secret potion," Vance said.

"Yeah, a mind-control potion," Riley said, going along with the joke. "He'll take over the school. First West Malibu High, then the world!"

They laughed as they headed down the outdoor stairs of the annexe. Riley stared at the sea of students assembling on the school lawn.

Where was Alex? Why didn't *he* run into her during the fire drill?

Riley liked hanging with Vance, but this was getting crazy. How could she avoid him when he seemed to pop up everywhere?

At last! Chloe thought when she spotted Lennon in the hallway. She was late for science class, but she didn't care. Now was her chance to clear the air once and for all. Did she have a date with Lennon on Friday night or not? And did he hear what she said about him over the mobile phone? Was he mad at her?

"Lennon!" she called. He stopped and turned around. "I've got to ask you something—"

Rrrrriiiiiiinnnnnggg! The fire alarm clanged. Chloe couldn't believe it. How could this be happening *again*?

"We'd better get out of here," Lennon said as the classroom doors popped open around them.

Chloe sighed and followed him down the hall. Major humiliation! Maybe it was fate. Maybe it was her destiny *not* to be with Lennon.

At least he didn't mention the phone call.

"Sorry I didn't get back to you last night," Lennon said. "My dad's business call took forever."

"That's okay," Chloe said. She wondered if she should apologise about the mobile phone hang up. No, don't go there, a little voice warned her. Instead, she changed the subject. "Tedi called back last night to ask about our mysterious translator. All the seamstresses in Milan want to meet you."

Lennon laughed. "How did your mother's show go?" he asked.

"Actually, it should be starting any minute," she said, "and without any problems, thanks to you."

The bell rang. That was the signal to return to class.

"I'm going to stop by my locker," Lennon said. "Catch you in bio."

I hope so, Chloe thought as she turned towards the lab. I hope you catch every word I say to you! Because biology was the only class they had together. It was time to make her move. She passed a notice board covered with flyers and notices.

The power of the written word. Maybe that was the way to go. That's it! she thought. I'll put my question in writing. What could be more definite than that?

She would write him a note. Then, at least, she would know whether the answer was yes… or no.

There was no time to lose. Definitely no time to run the note by Tara and Quinn. Chloe would have to make the pass during science class. That was the only time she was guaranteed to see Lennon. She opened her notebook and thought about what to write. Something short and sweet. To the point. A no-frills note. She took out her purple pen and wrote:

> *Are we on for Friday night?*
> *—Chloe*

She thought about a border. Maybe some stars and hearts?

No, she decided. Keep it simple. She folded up the paper and tucked it into the pocket of her Capri pants. She was ready....

She walked into the biology classroom. Half the class was already there, sitting on stools at the high counters in the lab area, adjusting their goggles. Oh, no! It was a lab day!

Oh, great! She was going to have to confront Lennon wearing steamed-up goggles and smelly latex gloves. Way to look cute.

"Let's settle in as quickly as possible," Mr. Levine, the teacher, said. "We're going to dissect sea anemones today, and it will take the entire period."

"Gross!" Chloe took her seat next to Amanda, her lab partner. Mr. Levine came around with a huge jar of the spiny creatures. "They smell terrible!"

"That's the formaldehyde," Amanda said. "It's, like, a preservative."

"Couldn't they add a little perfume to that stuff?" Chloe said, pressing the goggles against her nose.

The class settled in as Mr. Levine began his instructions.

"I need a favour," Chloe whispered to Amanda. She reached into her pocket, trying to play it cool. Like most teachers, Mr. Levine was not a fan of note-passing. "Pass this on for me. To Lennon."

Amanda nodded. She took the note and slid it along the black countertop. It zipped past Matthew Kazorowski and stopped right in front of Lennon. Perfect! Amanda was a pro.

"Thank you!" Chloe whispered.

But Lennon was focused on Mr. Levine and didn't see the note. Matthew spotted it, though. He reached over and flicked it with his forefinger.

The folded note skittered across the counter, back towards Chloe. A perfect table-hockey puck.

"No!" Chloe muffled the word as she reached out to snatch it. The note bounced off her arm and glided over to Mike Malone.

Mike grinned and shot it back across the shiny black counter.

"Stop it!" Chloe hissed in a panic.

But the guys were too amused to listen. The note went to Preston Phillips. Then back to Matthew. Then Mike. Then over to Preston, who shot it off the counter.

"That's it," Chloe muttered, slipping off her stool to

go and recover the note. She snatched it off the floor and returned to her seat, feeling discouraged. She would have to abandon her mission. When it came to communicating with Lennon, she couldn't seem to do anything right!

She set the note on the counter in front of her. Maybe she could catch Lennon at the end of class when he was on his way out of the door.

She sighed and turned her attention to Mr. Levine and the sea anemones. But then, out of the corner of her eye, she sensed movement nearby. She glanced down at the note. A hand covered it and plucked it off the counter.

Chloe's gaze moved past the hand, up the arm, and rested on the pimply face of Dylan Greenley. He was sitting across the counter from her, clutching the note.

What was he doing? She didn't know him well, only that he was shy and sort of nerdy. Totally into video games. He carefully unfolded the note and read it.

Oh, no, Chloe thought. She began to panic. Dylan thought the note was for him!

"Friday night?" Dylan smiled, and Chloe squinted in the major solar flash from his braces. "Sure!" he said.

Chloe swallowed hard. This couldn't be! But there was Dylan, refolding her note.

"Okay," Chloe said, nearly choking on the word.

Across the table, Lennon was watching. What could she do?

She could barely get the words out. "Then we're on for Friday, Dylan."

Chloe picked up her scalpel with a sigh. Somehow, cutting up a smelly sea creature didn't seem so gross now. It was a lot more appealing than her current social life.

chapter
eleven

"How's the *Jeopardy* thing going?" Alex asked as he set a plate of cheese and crackers on the table.

"Great!" Riley settled into a corner of the basement sofa. She was glad to see Alex at last, glad to be at his house, glad that the day was over. "I'm learning a lot and Ms. Cho makes it fun." She didn't add that Ms. Cho had tried a different format that day, with different teams. That left Vance on the opposite side of the room, far, far away. When the course ended, Riley had ducked out of the side door and dashed off to meet Alex in the school library.

And now here she was, settling in with Alex. He popped a cube of cheese into his mouth, swung his guitar on to his lap, and started picking out a melody.

"Well, I'm glad we could get together today," Alex said. "Between my band practice and your *Teen Jeopardy*, things were looking kind of dismal there."

She smiled. He'd missed her.

"Hey," Alex said, "let me play you the new song I've been working on."

Munching a cracker, Riley watched him intently as he sang.

"*Through a window, see her there. Through a doorway, lost somewhere. Listen closely for the sound. Feel the silence. Look around.*" His fingers moved over the neck of the guitar, picking out a riff.

Riley nodded, waiting for more.

"That's all there is right now," he said. "I'm still working on a bridge."

"It's great," Riley said. "How do you come up with such creative lyrics?"

"They usually just pop into my mind," he admitted. "But sometimes I have to keep working them. Over and over." He picked up a cracker. "You must get bored, hanging out in a basement, listening to me practise."

"No! I love it," Riley said as he started playing a familiar song. It was the one he wrote for her.

"*Pass her in the hall… Try to catch her smile*," he sang, his eyes on her. "*Don't you know you're all I need for a while?*"

She leaned back into the worn sofa and watched Alex, her heart swelling. Sure, she liked Vance, but she liked Alex, too. They were like two different sides of her, the quiet and the adventurous.

Everything seemed so complicated – more complicated than anything a teen magazine quiz could handle.

• • •

Riley walked home from Alex's house along the ocean path, feeling good. It was a beautiful afternoon, and the sun still had a few hours to go before it set. As she approached the Malibu beach near her home, she spotted a few kids out surfing.

What a great idea!

She decided to rent a board at Zuma Jay's, then jogged home to change into her wetsuit. Soon she was hiking through the sand into the salty foam. She tried to remember everything Skeeter had taught her, but as soon as the first wave swept past her it all came naturally. Paddle out. Turn. Watch for a wave. Feet on the board, left foot first and…

Whoosh!

She took off.

Riley felt a zing of pride as she rode her first wave in. She paddled out again, this time talking a bit with the other kids there. They'd had a good afternoon, though the surf was a little too calm for some of the guys.

It was fine for Riley. As a beginner, she found mellow waves just her speed. As she mounted her board for another wave, Riley thought about Alex and Vance. Vance was cool and fun to hang out with. But she cared about Alex, too. She didn't want to hurt his feelings. And she wanted to be fair to him.

She stood halfway up, then flopped off her board into

the water. Oh, well. Maybe I should focus on the waves instead of thinking about guys all the time, she thought.

She paddled out and waited for another wave.

"Riley!" someone shouted. "Riley…"

She gazed towards the beach. Someone splashed into the surf and paddled towards her on a surfboard. Vance.

She sat up on her board.

[Riley: Okay, I know I promised to avoid him. And it's a big, big ocean. But there's really no escape when you're floating on a board and someone is headed right towards you. I mean, what am I supposed to do? Paddle off to Hawaii?]

"Hi," Riley told him. "The surf is great. Not too rough."

"And the water looks so blue today," he said. "I just grabbed my board and booked out here."

A wave rose up behind Riley. "Here comes one!" she called. She was glad Vance was there – surfing was even more fun when he was around.

She mounted her board and threw her arms out for balance…

And she was riding another wave!

She and Vance surfed until they were exhausted, although Vance had done more stunt falls than anything.

Riley dragged her board up on to the hot sand of the beach.

Vance dropped his board beside hers and sat on it. "Another great day!"

"Really!" Riley sat on her board. "I totally love surfing. It's so much fun!"

"But it really zaps the energy," Vance said, stretching out on his board. "Wake me up when it's time for school."

"Oh, come on, Mr. Rock-Climbing, Triathalon Snowboarder!" Riley teased. "*You're* tired?"

"Hey, even pro athletes need naps," Vance said.

Riley stretched out beside him, loving the smell of the salt water and the feel of the late-afternoon sun on her skin. She knew it was about time to head home for dinner, but she couldn't leave yet. When she was out on the beach, her troubles seemed so small.

"The ocean is amazing," she said. "When my parents first split up, I used to hit the beach a lot. There's a lifeguard stand by my house, and I would sit there after hours. Try to work things out. Argue sides in my head."

"Really?" Vance asked. "And who won?"

"That's the great part about arguing with yourself. You always win."

Vance laughed. "I sort of do the same thing. When I've got something on my mind, I jump on my bike or take off running. Sometimes when things slam you, you just have to kick it and let loose."

Riley sighed. What was she supposed to be worrying about?

Oh, right… Alex and Vance. Somehow it didn't seem so important when she was in the water, floating, waiting for the next wave. Or lying on her board, relaxing in the sand.

She felt a light tug on her hair then looked up.

"I thought I saw a strand of seaweed," Vance said. "Or was that your hair? Salt water is a killer."

Riley laughed. "Oh, right. You'd better rush home and give your hair a moisturising masque."

"Hey, I do it every night," Vance joked, shaking out his spiky hair.

Riley sighed. She didn't want the day or the afternoon or this moment on the beach to end. She wished she could stay right there forever.

chapter
twelve

"**S**o you had a great time surfing with Vance?" Chloe asked Riley in the kitchen that evening.

"Well, yeah," Riley admitted. "Though I totally failed at avoiding him."

"It's no wonder," Chloe said. "You can't run from your soul mate!"

"Vance is not my soul mate," Riley said.

"He is, too!" Chloe didn't understand why her sister kept denying the truth. "The Love Factor doesn't lie, and today was proof."

Riley shook her head. "It's just a quiz, Chloe. I'm not going to believe it."

Frustrated, Chloe looked around the kitchen. "Okay, I'll prove it to you. Manuelo? Can you come here a second? I want to ask you a few questions…"

Five minutes later Chloe wanted to shriek as her purple pen ran down the page of Manuelo's answers. She had asked Manuelo to think of one of his true loves and fill out the quiz. But she had never expected such fabulous results!

"How did I do?" Manuelo asked.

"This is the most perfect score you could possibly get!" Chloe said, looking up from the Love Factor quiz spread out on the kitchen table. This would prove, once and for all, that the quiz worked.

"You're kidding," Riley said, pushing her algebra book aside to take a look. "Manuelo, how did you do this?"

Chloe gaped at him. "The real question is, who is your secret love? I mean, according to this you should run to the nearest courthouse and seal the deal with your soul mate forever."

"Aha," Manuelo said, nodding. He pursed his lips, trying to restrain himself. "That could be a problem."

"What?" Chloe asked. "What's so funny?"

Manuelo dissolved into giggles. "Last time I checked, you could not wed a crustacean. My 'secret love' is not marriage material. When I filled out the quiz, I had but one thing in mind. The love of my palate. Lobster!"

"What?" Chloe sank down in her chair. "A lobster? You can't have a love affair with a lobster!"

"Right. How does that work, Manuelo?" Riley asked.

"It's so simple," Manuelo said, gesturing with a spatula. "Don't you see? To have a relationship with a lobster, there is so little conflict. It never gives me silly gifts. I never get sick of it. And, yes, I did learn my love was not perfect. All that cholesterol! But these small things I can forgive. For that smooth, succulent flesh. The buttery afterglow—"

"Okay!" Riley interrupted him. "I think I've heard enough!"

"Me, too," Chloe said as Manuelo returned to the stove to stir a pot. She was disappointed that the quiz wasn't all it was cracked up to be.

Chloe looked across the table at her sister. "You were right all along. This quiz isn't foolproof. At least, it's not as accurate as I thought."

Riley nodded. "There's no wisdom in the Love Factor," she said.

"I'm sorry I sort of forced it on you," Chloe said.

"That's okay," Riley said. "It made me realise something. I don't really want a boyfriend right now. I just kind of want to go with the flow. Do what I want and not worry about it."

"But that means—" Chloe began.

"I know," Riley finished. "I've got to do something about Alex."

I've got to get out of this date with Dylan, Chloe thought the next morning. But how? She leaned against a brick wall outside the school, wondering how *Teen Style* would handle this.

> [Chloe: A. Tell him you're not feeling well. (But then I can't show up at Mango's. And I can't bear to miss the fun, especially if Lennon shows up!)

B. Spill the truth. The note was intended for someone else. He's a great guy, just not your crush. (Ouch! That would be hard to do. I'm not used to being so blunt.) C. Find a friend for him and tell him it was all about a blind date! (Like that's going to happen. I'm having enough trouble getting my own date for Friday night!)]

There's got to be a better way, Chloe thought as Lennon came up the path towards school.

"Hey," he said. "Did you hear about bio class?"

Chloe shook her head.

"We're meeting in the library today," Lennon told her. "Some loser stuck a sea anemone in the air vent, and the lab totally reeks. They've got to air it out before we can go back."

"Gross!" Chloe winced. "Who would do something so stupid?"

Lennon shrugged. "No clue. I don't know everything. Though I can be a know-it-all sometimes."

Chloe felt a wave of embarrassment as she sank against the wall. "So you heard that?"

He nodded. One corner of his mouth lifted, almost in a grin.

"I'm sorry, Lennon. But you do act like the authority on everything."

"And that bothers you?" he asked. "Or does it kill

you because I'm usually right?"

Chloe couldn't help but laugh. "You know, Mr. Know-it-all, now that you're here, let's put this to rest. About tomorrow. Are—"

The morning bell rang, right in their ears.

Chloe stared up at it, furious. This was just too much! She wasn't going to fight it anymore.

Lennon made a show of rubbing his ears. "What? What were you saying?" he asked as the bell finally stopped.

"Oh, never mind!" Chloe said, heading for the stairs. It was not meant to be. Fate was keeping her from dating Lennon. And the sooner she accepted that, the better off she would be.

She trudged up the outdoor stairs to the annexe. The corridor that lined the second storey of the building was already crowded with students on their way to class. Weaving through a group, Chloe spotted Riley walking slowly just ahead of her.

"Riley!" she called, catching up with her. "It just happened again," she said. "I asked Lennon about Friday night, and the bell rang right in our ears."

"Oh, no!" Riley touched her sister's arm. "This is getting bizarre."

"I'm giving up," Chloe said.

"You can't!" Riley insisted. "You really like Lennon."

"But things don't always work out just because you like a guy," Chloe said.

"That's for sure." Riley looked down at her feet.

"Riley!" someone called. It was Alex, hanging with Sierra and Saul at the end of the corridor. "Over here!"

Chloe glanced at him, then back at her sister. "Alex is calling you." Just then, Chloe saw Vance pop up from the stairs at the opposite end of the outdoor platform.

"Hey, Riley!" he shouted.

Riley spun round.

"Got a minute?" Vance asked.

Riley was stuck in the middle, glancing from one boy to the other. "Come on!" she said, grabbing Chloe by the arm. "Time for the artful dodge." She pulled Chloe through the nearest bathroom door.

"Oh, Riley," Chloe said sympathetically. "You have to face them sometime—"

Just then a boy pushed past them. Chloe turned round and saw the backs of a few other boys lined up to…

"Ohmigosh!" she exclaimed, pushing Riley back out of the door. "Wrong room!"

"The *boys'* room!" Riley clapped her hands to her face. "I've been thinking so hard, I must be suffering from brain drain!"

Chloe found the door to the girls' room next door. "Girls," she said, double-checking the sign before she and Riley ducked inside. They squeezed past a line of girls and went over to the row of gleaming white sinks.

"Phew!" Riley said. "That was close."

"I think you'd better make a decision here," Chloe

said. "Before we run out of doors!"

Riley grabbed a paper towel and ran some cold water on it. What should she do? she wondered, pressing it against her neck. "I wish there was an easy way," she told Chloe.

Chloe gave her a look of sympathy. "It's not as simple as the Love Factor quiz makes it sound," she admitted. "But you've got to do something. You're on a collision course with two guys out there."

Riley nodded. Chloe was right. All this worrying was taking up too much space in her brain. And it wasn't fair to Vance or Alex.

She had to set things straight. Right now.

"Wish me luck," she said, heading towards the door. "I have a feeling I'm going to need it."

chapter
thirteen

"**D**o you want a snack?" Alex asked after school that day. "I can get some crisps or iced tea or something."

"No, thanks," Riley said, sinking into the worn sofa in his basement. There was a knot of tension in her throat. She knew what she had to say, but it was hard.

His fingers moved over the guitar strings, picking out a familiar melody. It was the song he'd written for Riley.

"*Make me want to change… Make me want to speak… Tell you how I feel… You're the one I seek.*"

Tears stung her eyes, and she lifted a hand to swipe them away.

But Alex noticed. He stopped singing. "Wow. I didn't think I was that far off key."

"No," Riley said. "It's not the song. It's me."

He watched her, waiting to hear what she had to say to him.

She couldn't say it. She liked him so much. She didn't want to hurt him.

But she had to be honest.

Just say it, Riley. Say it! she told herself.

She swallowed hard and pressed her hands into tight fists. "I can't be your girlfriend any more," Riley blurted out.

"Wow." Alex stopped strumming and rested his hand atop the guitar. "Why not?"

"Alex, I really, really like you," Riley said. "But I like hanging out with other guys, too. And there's so many different things I want to try, like surfing and *Teen Jeopardy*, and a million other things. I don't want to hurt you—"

"Is this about that Love Factor quiz?" Alex interrupted.

Riley stared at him. "What?"

"My sister has been talking about it all week. This dumb love quiz. She made me take it."

Riley tried not to laugh. "*You* took the quiz? About me?"

Alex nodded. "Yeah, and my sister said we didn't get a very good score. But I don't believe in those things. Do you?"

Riley shook her head. "No. And this isn't about the quiz. I just think we need to be free to hang out with other people. Both of us."

Alex took a deep breath. "Yeah, you have a point. You know, I was thinking the same thing myself."

"Really?" Riley tried to look into his eyes, but Alex was leaning over his guitar now, head down.

Suddenly Alex strummed his guitar. "*I know a girl, her name is Riley,*" he sang. "*To make her stop crying, I'd walk a mile-y…*"

Riley laughed through her tears. Leave it to Alex to make *her* feel better when *she* was breaking up with *him*. Well… sort of.

"Are we okay?" she asked him. "You don't hate me?"

He shook his head. "I'm going to miss being your boyfriend."

"We'll still be friends," Riley said.

He nodded. "And who knows? Down the road, we could hook up again, right? If we feel like it. I mean, we're only in ninth grade. Anything can happen."

"Anything can happen," Riley said, liking the sound of that. She squeezed his hand. She was so relieved! Everything was turning out okay.

Anything can happen, she thought. And that was how she needed to take things right now – with an open mind and a wide-open date book.

chapter
fourteen

On Friday afternoon Riley floated in the line-up with a half-dozen other surfers. She had met Vance on the beach after school, and together they tried to catch some waves.

She'd been surfing for more than an hour, and this was going to be her last wave. She had places to go.

"Heads up," someone called as a wave swelled behind them.

"See if you can ride this one all the way in," Vance said. "I dare you."

"Oh, right!" Riley teased. "You're the one who was just eating sand."

"I meant to do that," Vance said with a huge grin. "I was trying to do a handstand on the board!" His last words were drowned out as the surfers rose on to their boards.

Riley heard the familiar whoosh of water as the

wave kicked up around her, pressing her forwards. She held her hands out, working to balance herself. This would have to be her last wave of the day. She wanted to make it count!

She managed to ride it in until it turned to foam.

"Nice one," Vance said from where he'd landed a few feet away. He turned his board and took a wave sideways. "Let's grab another one!"

"I can't," Riley said. "I have to go."

"No way!" Vance insisted.

"I've got plans," Riley said. She had to get showered and dressed for The Wave's show at Mango's. Maybe she wasn't Alex's girlfriend anymore, but she wanted to see Alex and Sierra perform. She had promised to be there to cheer them on.

"Okay," Vance said. "Well, maybe we'll hook up this weekend."

"Maybe," Riley called back to him. "I'll definitely be spending some time here on the beach."

"Later!" Vance shouted as he headed back into the water.

She wrung the water from her hair and carried her board across the sand. So far things were totally casual between her and Vance. Chance meetings. Easy-going jokes. And she liked it that way.

They'd never even kissed.

Something to look forward to, she thought as she trudged up the beach.

• • •

"Where's Riley?" Quinn asked. She sat across the table from Chloe at Mango's.

"Don't worry. She'll be here," Chloe said, scooping some whipped cream off her decaf coffee drink. Beside her, Dylan stirred his fifth packet of sugar into his iced tea. He had insisted on buying drinks for all the girls — Chloe, Quinn, Tara, and Amanda. It was very sweet of him, but Chloe didn't want him to be quite so nice. After all, this was probably going to be their one and only date.

"I can't wait to see The Wave perform," Amanda said. "This is so exciting."

"I'll bet Riley is thrilled," Tara added. "I mean, her boyfriend is the lead guitarist in a rock band!"

Chloe didn't reply. Alex wasn't Riley's boyfriend anymore. But Riley had asked Chloe not to say anything to anyone, at least until the gig was over. Riley didn't want the gossip to overshadow the band.

"I think Alex is a little hurt," Riley had told Chloe when she came home that day. "But he's not mad. It was hard, but now that it's over I feel so much better."

Chloe knew it was for the best. Now she sat at Mango's with her friends, biting her tongue, struggling not to tell them the news. She loved to be the first to break a juicy bit of gossip. But she'd never let Riley down that way.

"Is Sierra nervous?" Quinn asked. "I don't know how

she does it. I would be so freaked getting on stage in front of all my friends."

"I don't think it fazes her," Chloe said. "I guess her parents started her early with those violin recitals."

"Do you know what this place used to be?" Dylan asked. When the girls shook their heads, he answered, "A video parlour! I used to come here all the time. Then California cuisine hit, and the owner turned it into this fruity, organic teen club."

"Really?" Chloe said politely. "I didn't know that. Are you into video games, Dylan?"

He smiled, a silver flash of braces. "I'm pretty much an expert. I know most of the tricks to get to the top level. Now I mostly do computer games."

Chloe smiled back, trying to appear impressed. Dylan wasn't a bad guy... just not her kind of guy. There was definitely no Love Factor with him.

"They've got some decent games here," Dylan said. He looked longingly at one of the PCs where his friends were gathered. "Do you want to see?"

Chloe could tell he was dying to get away. What? He'd rather be playing games with his friends than on this *sensational* date with her?

Chloe laughed to herself. I guess the Love Factor thing works both ways, she thought. I don't have "the factor" for him any more than he has it for me.

"I can show you a few short-cuts in the games," Dylan said.

"Maybe later," Chloe said. "But why don't you go check it out, Dylan? We'll be right here, saving the table for when the band starts."

Dylan took a swig of tea, then swiped at his mouth. "Okay. I'll catch you later."

"He's sweet," Tara said.

Chloe nodded sadly. "But he's not Lennon. I guess I really messed up."

"It's not your fault," Quinn insisted. "Besides, your friends are here to save the night. We're going to have a blast – no matter what boys show up."

"Thanks, guys," Chloe said. She was glad Tara and Quinn had agreed to stick with her. If you've got your friends, nothing else matters.

Riley breezed in, the back of her hair still wet. She scanned the crowd, searching for her sister.

Chloe waved to her. "Over here!"

Riley plunked herself down in an empty chair. "I didn't miss anything, did I?"

"They're just about to start," Chloe said. "Alex and Saul have been testing the sound system."

A few minutes later the band members took their places. Alex leaned into the mike. "Hey, everybody," he said. "We're The Wave. Now let's rock!"

Saul counted off on the drums – "One, two, three, four!" – and the group launched into a song.

As Alex sang, Chloe saw the look he shot at Riley. Wow! He still liked her! At least, it seemed that way to Chloe.

But Riley had made her choice.

Someone tapped her shoulder. Chloe turned, and her heart started beating like crazy. "Lennon?"

[Chloe: He's here! He showed. Happy dance in my heart! I would do it on the dance floor, but that would look stupid with the song the band is playing.]

He stood behind her, grinning. "Hey. Mind if a know-it-all sits at your table?"

Chloe let out a breath. "I'm glad you came." She couldn't take her eyes off him as he sat down beside her. Was he here by coincidence, or did he really get the message about their date?

"Hey, I wouldn't miss our date," he said. He glanced over at Dylan, who was heavy into a game at a computer. "Even if you are double-booked."

"That note was meant for you," Chloe said. "But you knew? You knew what I was trying to ask you all along?"

"Only because one of my friends heard about it from your friend Tara," he said. "What, were you afraid to ask me? Why couldn't you spit it out?"

Chloe sighed. "If only you knew!" she cried. "I guess I'm not the best communicator in the world."

Lennon moved closer. "You—"

Just then the band launched into a loud rock song, overpowering his voice.

"What?" Chloe yelled above the music, dying to

know what he had to say. But she couldn't hear a thing.

Lennon smiled and leaned very close, until his lips were touching hers in a soft kiss.

Breathless, Chloe closed her eyes and kissed him back. Now *that* message was perfectly clear!

Chloe
and Riley's

SCRAPBOOK

mary-kateandashley
so little time
dating game

by Kylie Adams

Based on the teleplay by Becky Southwell

HarperCollins*Entertainment*
An imprint of HarperCollins*Publishers*

A PARACHUTE PRESS BOOK

chapter
one

"**S**top! That is so gross!" Riley Carlson cried.

Fourteen-year-old Chloe Carlson hushed her twin sister. "No, wait," she insisted. "You have to hear this part, too." Trying hard not to laugh, she read aloud from the school newspaper: "'There is so much grease on the pizza served in West Malibu High's cafeteria that it hovers over each slice like smog.'" Chloe closed the paper and shook her head. "I would love to trade places with this kid. The biggest problem he can come up with for the 'Sound Off' column is greasy pizza. Hello? There are other issues in the world. Doesn't he watch *Entertainment Tonight*?"

Riley groaned. "You know, I might write a 'Sound Off' myself."

Chloe checked her watch and relaxed. There were still a few minutes to spare before homeroom started. "Really? About what?"

"For starters, the boring assignments I get stuck with for that paper," Riley said.

"Well, you *did* sign up in the middle of the semester. Instead of a staff writer, you're a floater. I guess that's kind of like being an intern at a big company. You know, boring, no glory, no perks…"

Riley raised her hand. "Enough—I get the point."

Chloe smiled. "But there was that story you did on the new coffee machine in the teachers' lounge. You know, that was really exciting. It should've been a two-parter." She laughed.

Riley pursed her lips.

Uh-oh, Chloe thought. Maybe I took the teasing a step too far. "You know I'm kidding, right?" she asked, giving her sister a friendly shove.

"Well, you shouldn't really talk about my skills as a journalist," Riley said. "What have *you* written lately?"

"Do I have to remind you how many e-mails I get in a week? I'm *constantly* writing," Chloe replied with a grin.

"E-mails don't count," Riley protested. "I'm talking about real writing, like an article. Maybe *you* should do a 'Sound Off.'"

"On what—the mysterious meat loaf?" Chloe laughed at her own joke.

Riley cracked up, too. "I think we can move beyond the cafeteria. I'm sure there's a cause out there that you feel strongly about."

Something clicked in Chloe's brain. How could she

have forgotten? "Actually, now that you mention it, the plight of endangered sea mammals is something I'm *very* passionate about."

"Since when?" Riley asked.

"Since Mom told me that we could take boys to this year's Save the Seals benefit," Chloe replied. Save the Seals was a fancy charity dance that was tons of fun. The Carlson family attended it every year.

Riley grabbed Chloe's jacket sleeve. "Are you serious?" she asked.

Chloe nodded. "Yes, and it's this Saturday, so we have to work fast."

"*Saturday*?" A look of panic swept across Riley's face. "But it's Monday!" She paused. "Wait a minute. This would make a great first date with Vance."

Chloe had known that was coming. Vance Kohan was the cute boy Riley had met at a surf clinic. They weren't exactly dating, but as far as Chloe was concerned, they should have been.

"Vance surfs in the ocean," Riley went on. "Seals *swim* in the ocean. What could be more perfect?"

"If Freddie Prinze were single—that would be more perfect," Tara Jordan said, joining them.

Chloe laughed at Tara's one-liner. The girl was hysterical. And she was looking very state of the trend in her low-rise jeans and vintage rock tee.

Right beside her was Quinn Reyes. They were two of Chloe's closest friends.

"By the way, what are we talking about?" Quinn asked just as Ms. Raffin passed by.

Ms. Raffin was an English teacher and the faculty sponsor for the student newspaper. "Let's not dawdle, girls," she said. "You'll be late for homeroom."

Riley managed a quick wave and made a speedy departure.

As Chloe, Tara, and Quinn started off in the direction of the science wing, Chloe filled them in on Save the Seals.

"Cool," Tara chirped. "So who are you going to ask? Hold on. Let me guess. Lennon, right?"

Just hearing his name caused Chloe's heart to skip a beat. Lennon Porter was smart and funny and supercute. But Chloe didn't want to let Tara know just how much she liked him yet. Tara was a true friend but also a big talker. One false word and everybody at school would think Chloe was madly in love with Lennon. Including Lennon.

"Maybe," she said casually. "We went out on a date two weeks ago. It was fun. I think he likes me."

"Then you should definitely ask him," Quinn said.

[Chloe: So here's where you think: Okay, Chloe's going to ask him, right? I don't think so. Granted, this is the twenty-first century, the era of female power and such. But I'm tired of always making the first move. I mean, what's wrong with a little romance? Boy asks girl. Girl says yes. Boy

shows up with candy and flowers. Girl locks herself in her room and changes her outfit at least
twenty times. Yes, that's what I want—an old-
fashioned date!]

Chloe felt a flutter in her stomach. "You know what?"

"Lennon's got a cute brother who's a junior but doesn't mind dating freshman girls?" Tara asked hopefully.

Chloe laughed. "Sorry. Anyway, you're the one with the cute older brother, Tara."

"I know," Quinn said, practically swooning. "Kyle is amazing."

Tara shook her head. "I don't know why all the girls go crazy over my brother. He's a six-foot-one goofball."

"You didn't let me finish!" Chloe cried. "I'm *not* asking Lennon to the dance."

"Why not?" Tara asked.

"Because I want a little romance, thank you. Why do I always have to ask out the boy? If Lennon likes me, then *he* should be the one to ask *me*. I mean, let's face it. Boys are getting lazy. Somebody has to take a stand."

"Yeah," Quinn agreed. "Way to go, sister!"

Tara glanced at Quinn and wrinkled her nose. "Whatever...*sister*."

"All I have to do is plant the seed and let him know that I want to go to the dance," Chloe announced, smiling. "But Lennon will have to do the asking."

115

"Well, I hope you have a green thumb, because he's heading this way," Tara said.

Chloe glanced up and saw Lennon striding down the corridor, looking exceptionally cute in way casual baggy jeans and a T-shirt.

He made a beeline toward her. "Hey," he said. "What's up?"

"Funny you should ask that," Quinn said.

Chloe silenced Quinn with a look. "Actually, something *is* up," she told Lennon. "My mom said I could take a date to the Save the Seals benefit this weekend."

Lennon nodded. "That's cool. Well, I'll talk to you later. I'd better get to class." And off he went.

Chloe just stood there for a moment. 'That's cool?' Didn't he realize that telling him about the dance was his cue to ask her out?

"That was a perfect setup, and he totally missed it," Tara said as Chloe watched Lennon disappear down the hall. "Are you sure he's in the honors program?"

Riley could not get the old song "Surfin' USA" out of her head—probably because she and Vance had met while learning to surf.

I wonder if the band at Save the Seals will play it, she thought. Then Vance and I could dance to it. And we could make it our song!

But first she had to ask him to the benefit.

More excited than ever about her first real date with

Vance, Riley scouted the crowded halls with a determined gaze. She hadn't run into him even once today, and this was a situation that definitely couldn't wait until tomorrow.

"Dude! You are so busted!"

At the sound of his voice, Riley craned her neck to see Vance goofing around with some of his buddies.

"Vance!" she called out—a little too eagerly.

Vance and his friends turned in her direction. Vance grinned right away. One of his buddies whispered something to the other, and they proceeded to crack up.

Riley went hot with embarrassment.

Vance stepped over, waving the guys off. "Don't pay any attention to them," he assured her. "They always act like morons."

Riley took a deep breath. "There's something I really wanted to—"

"Hey," Vance cut in. "Guess what? My cousin scored me a VIP ticket for the Tribal Council concert Saturday night. Isn't that cool?"

Riley knew the band. She loved their new song, "Bad Versus Beautiful," and she'd already heard about their upcoming concert at Visible Lines, a new teen club in Beverly Hills. But right now the fact that it was happening *this* Saturday night didn't seem so cool. Her spirits sank.

"What's wrong?" Vance asked. "You look like your goldfish just croaked."

Riley attempted a smile but managed only to curl her lips into a weak grin. "There's a big Save the Seals benefit this weekend. I thought we could go together."

Vance winced. "Do you have any idea how lucky I am to be holding a VIP ticket to Tribal Council? They're, like, huge."

"Oh, I know," Riley quickly agreed. "That's too amazing to pass up." She tried to snap out of her funk. No reason to make Vance think that her world had come to a crashing halt, even though it had, at least temporarily. "I'll figure out something."

"You will have no trouble finding a date," Vance said. "Trust me on that." He shot a look back to his buddies. "Listen, I'll talk to you later. We're meeting some other guys to play basketball."

Riley watched Vance go, feeling a minor sense of panic. No doubt Chloe had made plans with Lennon. Would she be the only one without a date for Save the Seals?

Chloe spotted Lennon at his locker, loading up his backpack with textbooks. She made a quick move in his direction. Obviously he hadn't picked up on her hint earlier. She had stewed over the situation throughout the day and decided that Lennon simply wasn't a morning person and that it was better to catch him in the afternoon. Swooping in, Chloe leaned against the locker next to his.

Lennon shut his door to lock it and saw her. He smiled.

Chloe smiled back. "How was your day?"

"Better than my night will be." He pretended his backpack weighed at least one hundred pounds. "The homework they pile on is no joke."

Chloe saw her opening and went for it. "Tell me about it." She sighed. "But sometimes it doesn't seem so bad when you have something fun to look forward to on the weekend."

Lennon laughed. "It's only Monday. You're living for the weekend already?"

Chloe halted. Was this a trick question? If she said yes, she might appear desperate. "Not exactly. It's just that there's a big event on Saturday for Save the Seals, and my mom said I could take a date, so that's the kind of thing I have to plan. You know, finding something to wear, figuring out who might want to be my date…"

Lennon said nothing and went to work on his locker combination. "I knew I'd forgotten something." He glanced at Chloe. "My Greek mythology book."

Chloe shut her mouth tight to stop herself from screaming. For a boy so responsible about homework, Lennon certainly was clueless! Would she have to hire a skywriter to fly by West Malibu High and spell it out: ATTENTION LENNON: ASK CHLOE TO THE DANCE!

She left in a minor huff. Tara, Quinn, and a few other girls were waiting by their lockers around the corner.

"So did he ask you?" Tara demanded, following her down the hall.

"No!" Chloe said hotly. She spotted Riley heading their way.

"Chloe, you'll never believe this," Riley said, joining them. "Vance can't go Saturday night. He——"

"Oh, I can believe it," Chloe cut in. She picked up her step, Riley right beside her, Tara, Quinn, and the girls directly behind them. "The boys at this school are in serious need of a talking-to."

"What good will that do?" Tara asked. "The damage was done a long time ago. Maybe their mothers didn't hug them enough when they were little or something."

Chloe marched on. She shot Riley a glance. "You know what? I think I *am* going to do one of those 'Sound Off' articles. Why waste the space on complaints about pizza when there are serious issues to put on the table?"

[Chloe: I know, I know. It's not exactly a world crisis along the lines of global warming or a peace summit. But here we are. Chloe and Riley: two girls in need of dates and two girls without them. Yikes!]

chapter two

When Riley walked into the house with Chloe, she sensed trouble right away. The look on Manuelo's face told her something was wrong. "Are you okay?" she asked him.

Manuelo released a heavy sigh. "You know the old saying 'Don't shoot the messenger'?"

Riley nodded.

"Well," Manuelo continued, "in this case, it's don't shoot the postman. But at the very least he deserves a kick in the—"

"Manuelo!" Chloe exclaimed, cutting him off before he had a chance to say it.

"I was going to say *caboose*," he said, gesturing wildly toward the kitchen. "Ever since he delivered today's mail, those two have been…"

Riley marched directly into the kitchen to see what all the fuss was about.

Chloe followed her.

"Then how do you explain this, Macy?" their father, Jake, was asking as he waved an envelope in their mother's face. "The Save the Seals invitation is addressed to Mr. *and* Mrs. Carlson."

Riley could tell by the vague sense of victory in her mother's eyes that she was hardly stumped for an answer.

"*Obviously*," their mother began, "the mailing list has not been updated to reflect our status as a *separated* couple."

Riley felt kind of weird. Her parents hadn't really argued since before they were separated. And what was it about? A silly invitation?

[Riley: Well, I guess it makes sense that they wouldn't always see eye-to-eye on things. Mom and Dad are what you might call TOTAL and COMPLETE opposites. Mom is into power lunches, power workouts, and power bars. And Dad's... well, Dad's not. He's into meditation and yoga and the power of relaxation. Now he's living in a trailer park near the beach. He says the simple life is helping him find his true self. Meanwhile, Mom has happily taken over their fashion design business.]

Suddenly Riley experienced a feeling of dread. If Mom and Dad decided not to go, then she and Chloe would not be attending either. And Save the Seals would be so much fun. Plus, it was tradition for Mom and Dad to burn up the dance floor at the event during the disco songs.

Jake grabbed a protein bar from the pantry and shrugged his shoulders. "Let's just go together. We'll chaperone the girls. What's the big deal?"

"It *is* a big deal," Mom argued.

Chloe turned to Riley with a worried look.

"Well, if we're separated," Macy went on, "don't you think it's in the best interest of all concerned that we remain…*separate*?"

Riley leaned in to whisper to Chloe. "I've got an idea," she said. "We should help them find dates for the dance."

"Before or after *we* find dates?" Chloe whispered back. "So far nobody is picking *us* up on Saturday night."

Riley nodded in miserable agreement.

"But you may have a point," Chloe murmured under her breath. "Because if we don't find *them* dates, there will be no reason to find ourselves dates."

"I know," Riley said. "So, how should we—"

"We have the perfect solution," Chloe said out loud. Her voice rang with a great air of confidence.

Mom and Dad looked at them with interest.

"We'll find you dates for Saturday night," Chloe said.

"Uh…yeah," Riley stammered even though she wasn't quite ready for Chloe to blurt out this idea. They didn't have a plan yet.

Dad beamed at Mom, then nodded thankfully to them. "I think I'll take you up on that. Make sure she's smart and beautiful." He laughed a little.

But Mom didn't look so thrilled about the idea. She cleared her throat. "I don't need my children to help me get a date. I'll find my own escort, thank you."

Riley breathed a sigh of relief. She knew that Chloe felt it, too. Their chance to go to the dance was safe— for the moment.

Dad chomped down on the protein bar, grinning as if he didn't have a care in the world. "This is great, girls. I'd better try on my suit and make sure it still fits. See you later!" He headed out of the house.

Mom sighed and started for her office. "Girls, you might want to make a snack. I've got a conference call scheduled with a buyer overseas, so we'll be having dinner a bit later than usual."

Almost instantly Chloe opened the fridge and pulled out yogurt, strawberries, pineapple, and skim milk, then reached into the cabinet for the wheat germ and raisins.

"What are you doing?" Riley asked.

"Making a smoothie," Chloe said. "Want one?"

Not feeling very hungry, Riley shook her head. "Where are we going to find a smart and beautiful woman for Dad in five days?"

Chloe shrugged. "I don't know, but wouldn't it be great if she came with two smart and cute boys for us?"

Riley giggled, in part because the idea sounded ridiculous, but also because she had to admit, at the same time, it sounded great!

Chloe was channel surfing, listening to the radio, sipping her smoothie, and talking on the phone with Tara—all at the same time.

"I can't believe that Lennon didn't ask you to Save the Whales," Tara was saying.

"Save the Seals," Chloe corrected her.

"Whatever," Tara chirped. "Whales, seals, baby dolphins—the point is, he *didn't* ask you. And you dropped some serious hints. I mean, you were looking pretty desperate there for a minute."

Desperate? Chloe thought. Was it really that bad?

[<u>Chloe</u>: Here's the best part about moments like this: One day they will be over. Right now it seems so tragic. I mean, it's practically Shakespeare, or, at the very least, a really dramatic episode of *7th Heaven*. But in some not too distant future, it will barely register as a memorable event. Of course, right now I'm totally freaking out and thinking I might have to move to Iowa to escape the humiliation.]

"Are you there?" Tara asked.

"Yes, I'm here," Chloe grumbled. "I'm trying to factor the social damage. Did everyone see me throw myself at Lennon and be completely ignored? Did it look really bad?"

"No," Tara said. "It was all pretty low-key."

Call-waiting sounded in Chloe's ear. "Hold on, someone's beeping in." She hit the flash button on her phone. "Hello?"

"Is this Chloe Carlson?" a female voice asked.

The woman sounded very familiar, but Chloe couldn't quite place her. "Yes, who's this?" she asked.

"It's Ms. Raffin, dear. Listen, I'm so glad that I caught you. The school paper's in a terrible bind, and we need your help."

"But Riley's the one who writes for the paper," Chloe said.

"Oh, I realize that, dear. But I couldn't help over-hearing you in the hall today discussing your interest in writing a 'Sound Off.'"

On that note Chloe reached for her smoothie and took a generous sip. Ms. Raffin didn't exactly overhear as much as she eavesdropped. Sometimes she knew more about who was starting up, breaking up, and making up at West Malibu High than the students themselves!

"Could you work up something by tomorrow morning?" Ms. Raffin asked.

Chloe paused to allow the smoothie to go down. It was true, she *had* said she wanted to write a "Sound Off" this afternoon, but she wasn't really serious about it. "Well, I—"

"I'm staring at empty column space where the original 'Sound Off' column should have gone," Ms. Raffin continued. "But no matter how bad the pizza is, I can't dedicate two columns in a row to the subject. I'm so glad you're helping me out, Chloe. You're the best! Bye, dear." Then she hung up.

That was the other thing about Ms. Raffin. She had a way of not letting you say no.

Chloe sucked in a breath. Now what was she supposed to do?

Riley walked into the room. "Dinner's almost ready," she said.

Chloe couldn't imagine sitting down to eat just then. Her mind was racing a million miles a minute.

Riley's gaze zeroed in on the phone in Chloe's hand. "Who are you talking to?"

Suddenly Chloe remembered Tara on the other line and pressed the Flash button. "Tara, I'll have to call you later."

"Was that Lennon?" Tara asked.

"I wish." Chloe groaned. "I have to go. Bye." She hung up and buried her face in a pillow.

"What's wrong?" Riley asked.

Chloe removed the pillow and brought Riley up to speed on the entire Ms. Raffin incident.

Riley perched herself on the edge of the bed. "This is no big deal. The 'Sound Off' columns are short, like maybe one page."

This news did nothing to calm Chloe. "But I have no idea what to write about, and she expects it tomorrow morning!"

Riley considered this for a moment. "I remember seeing a famous author on television, and her advice for all new writers was to write what you know."

Chloe felt the urge to push Riley off the bed. "That still doesn't tell me what to write!"

Riley gave her sister a shrewd look. "Think about what you know."

Chloe tried to concentrate, then gave up in frustration. "Ugh! I can't even think straight. This whole Lennon thing is driving me nuts. Can you believe him? I mean, when a girl tells a boy that a dance is coming up, he should take that as a hint to ask her out!"

Riley smiled. "My point exactly. Write about that."

Chloe was stunned. "Seriously?"

"Why not? It's an issue that you feel passionately about. That's what the 'Sound Off' column is there for. You know, to vent."

Chloe warmed to the idea. "You're right!" She stomped over to the desk and snatched her laptop, booting it up as soon as she returned to the bed.

"Don't get started now," Riley said. "We're about to have dinner."

Chloe was already turning on the word processing program. "Tell Mom I'm not hungry. I'll put something in the microwave later."

"Okay," Riley said.

Chloe barely noticed her sister leave the room. She was too wrapped up in her first "Sound Off." And once Lennon read it, he would know exactly what to do.

Hopefully.

chapter three

"Riley!"

She spun around to see Ms. Raffin rushing toward her.

Secretly Riley wished that she hadn't been spotted. The last thing in the world she had time for was another lame newspaper assignment along the lines of new furniture for the principal's office.

"Turns out the Carlson girls are my most valuable players this week," Ms. Raffin gushed. "Chloe saved the paper last night, and now I need you—"

"Ms. Raffin," Riley began, hoping to beg off another lame assignment, "I'm completely swamped—"

"Oh, dear, please don't tell me that!" Ms. Raffin's face crashed in disappointment. "Peter Brenner is out with strep throat—"

"Wait a minute," Riley blurted out, suddenly entertaining a change of heart. "Peter Brenner? He's the sports editor."

Ms. Raffin's nod was serious. "I know, and there's a very important story on the varsity football team that has to be covered right away."

Riley's mind went into hyperdrive. The football team was full of cute boys. Granted, a jock wasn't her first choice for a date, but one would do in a pinch.

Seemingly deep in thought, Ms. Raffin bit down on her lower lip. "But since you're so busy, I suppose I could ask—"

"I'm busy, yes," Riley interrupted, "but I'm never too busy for the school paper. At heart I'm a journalist. I realize how important it is to get the story."

Ms. Raffin beamed. "So young and already so professional. You are going to go very far, dear."

Riley was already at work thinking up an angle for the article. Maybe a profile on the cutest players without steady girlfriends. Yes! That would definitely interest West Malibu High readers. After all, a true journalist always thinks of her audience.

[Riley: I admit it. I don't really care about the West Malibu High audience. You and I both know that I have a personal interest in this story. Somewhere underneath all those helmets and protective gear is a cute boy who would love to take me to the dance!]

"Coach Lee is expecting to talk to you during your lunch period," Ms. Raffin informed her. "Bring back a hard-hitting piece about the team's new offensive line."

"Yes, hard-hitting," Riley assured her, lowering the pitch of her voice to what she hoped was a serious and capable tone.

All the excitement burned away Riley's appetite, but she realized that she had to eat something and gobbled up an energy bar on her way to see Coach Lee.

His office was located just off the weight center in the gym. The door was ajar. Riley peered inside to see Coach Lee sitting at his desk, reviewing video footage from a previous game on a small television.

She observed him for a moment, then rapped on the door. "Coach Lee?"

He peered up and smiled instantly. "Are you that nosy sports reporter I've been expecting?" His tone was teasing, and his eyes crinkled with amusement.

Riley smiled and stepped inside. "Is this a bad time?"

Coach Lee reached for the remote, zapped off the TV, and spun around to face her. "You have my undivided attention." He gestured to the empty chair in front of his desk. "Have a seat."

"Thanks," Riley said, settling in and fishing through her backpack to retrieve a small notebook and pen. Coach Lee seemed approachable enough, and Ms. Raffin probably wouldn't mind her unconventional angle on the story. In fact, she just might admire Riley for going with her instincts.

Coach Lee's chair squeaked as he leaned back and folded his arms. "Fire away."

Riley was struck by Coach Lee's surroundings. A large aquarium filled with exotic fish dominated the credenza, and an assortment of enormous seashells served as paperweights on his cluttered desk. Tacked on the wall was a giant picture calendar, also ocean-related. This month featured seals.

What an amazing coincidence! Riley thought. Mom has no date for Save the Seals, and sitting before me is a very nice and cool man who obviously appreciates seals. Riley casually let her gaze fall on Coach Lee's hands. No wedding ring. Hmmm. Very interesting.

[Riley: Sure, Mom says that she can find her own date, but chances are she'll get caught up in work and forget all about it. I'm sitting in front of a handsome, apparently single man who obviously has a thing for the sea. It's not such a stretch to think that he would enjoy attending Save the Seals with a beautiful and successful woman. Don't you agree? Me, too.]

Riley pointed to a large seal pictured on his calendar. "Isn't it a shame about the plight of the seal? I wish everyone understood how endangered some of our sea mammals are."

Coach Lee returned a grave nod. "Some of the research is downright frightening. My grandfather was an oceanographer, so I was taught an appreciation for sea creatures early on."

"You know, there's a Save the Seals benefit this weekend," Riley said.

"I didn't know that."

"Are you a good dancer?" Riley asked.

"I can hold my own." Coach Lee gave her a quizzical look. "Do you plan on asking me any questions about the football team?"

Riley waved off the suggestion. "Oh, we'll get to that in a minute." She scooted her chair closer to Coach Lee's desk, as if letting him in on a conspiracy. "I have it on good authority that a very attractive woman about your age is holding an extra ticket to the Save the Seals benefit on Saturday night."

Coach Lee grinned. "Is that so?"

"Yes," Riley said, glancing around to make certain there were no prying eyes or ears. "Of course, this is all very confidential."

"Oh, of course," Coach Lee said.

"But if I were in your shoes, I would keep my date book open for Saturday night."

"As it happens, I'm free."

Riley couldn't believe this stroke of luck. Chloe would be thrilled.

"So, can you give me a hint? Who is this mystery woman?"

"My mom," Riley said.

Coach Lee did a double take.

"But it's a secret. She doesn't like the idea of someone helping her find a date, so when you meet her, don't let on that we've had this conversation."

"My lips are sealed," he said. "I do have one question though."

"What's that?" Riley asked.

"How are the two of us supposed to meet?" Coach Lee replied.

Riley leaned back. "Leave that to me."

"So you have a plan?" Coach Lee asked.

"Yes…well, not exactly…uh…all the particulars are still being worked out." Riley could feel her left eye twitching, which always happened when she lied. Luckily Coach Lee was not hip to this fact. He seemed to be buying her story. But Riley would definitely need Chloe's help to finish the job!

Coach Lee checked his watch. "We'd better get on with the story, Riley. Time is getting away from us."

"Oh, yes," Riley agreed. "You're absolutely right." She cleared her throat and sat up straight. "Speaking of the story, I was thinking of mixing things up and coming at this from a whole new angle."

Coach Lee gave her a strange look. "I thought this was just a simple announcement of the new offensive line."

"Well, that's probably how Peter would have approached it. But he's a boy." She paused to emphasize her point. "And I'm a girl. So instead of printing another laundry list of players and positions, why not offer our readers something different?"

Coach Lee grinned. "Such as?"

"Pictures of all the guys and their current dating status," Riley said.

Coach Lee was laughing now. "Well, that's certainly a different approach."

"I'm serious," Riley insisted. "Can you think of a better way to get girls to read the sports page? Or buy advance tickets to the games?"

Coach Lee shook a finger at her. "You just may have a point there, Riley." He stood up. "Okay, you've convinced me. Let's do it." From the top drawer of the filing cabinet he grabbed a thick brown envelope. "You're in luck. Our official team photos just came in. Every player in the starting lineup posed for an individual shot, too."

Riley dug right in and began sorting through the pictures as if they were playing cards. Wow. There was definitely something to be said for boys who played football. Drop-dead-gorgeous guy. Big-muscles guy. Supercute guy. Going-to-Princeton-on-an-athletic-scholarship guy.

Her head began to spin. "I don't know where to start!"

Coach Lee squinted at her. "You wouldn't be going into this story with a personal agenda, would you?"

"No, of course not," Riley said quickly. "That would be unprofessional." She glanced down at the image of the drop-dead-gorgeous guy. "Let's get started. What's the lowdown on him?"

"That's Brad Collins," Coach Lee said. "He's our star quarterback. A sure bet to go pro one day."

Feeling anxious, Riley glanced at her watch. How could she politely tell Coach Lee that she didn't have time for a whole biography on every player? Basically she just needed to know the name, current dating situation, and whether or not this Saturday was open.

[<u>Riley</u>: I know, you're probably saying, "Where is the romance? Is this girl looking for a date or ordering a sandwich from the deli?" But the clock is ticking! At times like these, a girl can't be choosy. If he's cute and unattached, I'll take him. At this point he doesn't even have to dance that well.]

She suggested to Coach Lee that he just go down the starting lineup with the information she needed. "Otherwise I'll be late for my French class, and Mrs. Lerman always gives a pop quiz during the first five minutes."

Riley shifted uneasily in her chair as Coach Lee ticked off each name and delivered the bad news. Each and every one of these boys seemed to have a girlfriend, and they weren't just regular girls like Riley. They were cheerleaders or so beautiful, they were probably members of the Future Supermodels of America Club or something. A handful of the guys were unattached, but all of them were stuck with community service on the weekends for pulling a prank on a rival school.

Except for one. A huge boy Coach Lee called T-Rex. Named after the dinosaur, apparently. He weighed over two hundred and fifty pounds and could block three players at a time during a game. And he liked to roar when doing so.

Riley decided to pass.

chapter
four

"**I**'m dying to read it," Tara was telling Chloe over the phone.

"Yeah, me, too," Amanda Gray said. She was Chloe's very shy friend, and Chloe couldn't believe she had agreed to a three-way call with Tara. Maybe the girl was beginning to come out of her shell.

Chloe giggled. "Everything will be revealed tomorrow morning," she said, enjoying the fact that she had them in suspense. "I will tell you this much—the title of my 'Sound Off' is 'Saturday Sounds Perfect.'"

Chloe was kicking back in her room, switching channels and fending off Tara and Amanda while waiting for Riley to get home. An anxious feeling settled in the pit of her stomach. The clock was ticking. They needed to get started on finding Mom and Dad dates.

"Come on. Give us a sneak preview!" Tara begged.

"Yeah," Amanda agreed. "Don't make us wait until the school paper comes out. We're your friends."

Just then Riley stepped into the room and announced, "I've got *major* news."

Chloe signed off with the girls and crossed her legs on the bed. "Okay, spill it."

"I found a date for Mom," Riley said proudly.

Chloe could hardly believe it. "Who?"

"Coach Lee," Riley replied.

Chloe *didn't* believe it. "No!"

Riley smiled. "Yes!"

Chloe got off the bed and practically jumped up and down. "This is crazy!" But then she paused to think about it. Coach Lee was about Mom's age, kind of cute, and single. Why not? But there seemed to be one little problem. Chloe's excitement came to a sudden halt. "But don't we have to get them together without letting Mom know that we're getting them together?"

Riley plopped down onto the bed. "I know," she said. "That's the hard part." Then she took in an excited breath. "I've got it!"

Chloe's heart picked up speed. "What?"

But just as quickly, Riley's enthusiasm faded. "Never mind. That would never work."

Frustrated, Chloe stood up and began pacing. "Let's put Mom aside for a minute. At least we're halfway there. An idea will come to us. We're just thinking too hard right now. The real problem is Dad! We are *nowhere* on finding him a date."

Riley fell back on the bed as if exhausted. "I walked into this room in a great mood. What happened?"

"Reality set in," Chloe informed her. "Okay, if I were a single woman and met Dad—"

"Yuck. I cannot even think like that," Riley said, scrunching up her face.

Chloe shuddered. "You're right. Too weird." She paced another moment or two. "Let's take a different tack. What are Dad's hobbies? We'll try to find someone with his interests."

"Yeah! Like pen pals or something," Riley said, nodding.

"Exactly," Chloe said. "Okay, we know that he never misses his yoga class."

"And he prides himself on knowing who makes the best granola in Malibu," Riley put in. "Oh! And don't forget his discipline for soulful meditation."

"Or his routine of reading his daily Buddhist wisdom e-mails."

Riley tilted her head. "I forgot about that one." She shut her eyes tight. "Think, Riley, think," she chanted to herself, then let out a heavy sigh before opening her eyes. "I've got nothing."

Chloe had to admit that she was coming up empty, too. She looked down at Pepper, their black-and-white cocker spaniel, who was looking up in expectation of attention. "Pepper, do you have any ideas?"

Pepper's tiny tail wagged back and forth.

Chloe scanned her bedroom, trying to get an idea. Her gaze fell upon the laptop sitting on her desk. Impulsively she booted up and logged on to the Internet. "Maybe we'll find an idea on-line," she said.

"Good thinking," Riley agreed.

Before Chloe could click on to a search engine, one of those annoying pop-up advertisements filled the screen. She huffed. "I get so sick of these..." Her voice trailed off as she realized that the pop-up ad in question was boasting a Southern-California-based on-line dating service. Chloe tossed a look to Riley. "I know what we can do for Dad!" she exclaimed.

"What?" Riley asked, rushing to the computer.

"The answer just popped onto the screen!" Chloe exclaimed. "Everybody is finding dates on-line. Why shouldn't Dad?"

By the time the fourth-period bell rang on Wednesday, Chloe's first "Sound Off" column had found its way into the hands of every student at West Malibu High. It was a crazy feeling.

Amanda had already read the article three times. "This is a modern classic for our generation! Whenever my parents argue, my mom makes my dad read *Men Are from Mars, Women Are from Venus* all over again." She paused. "Did I get the planets right?"

Chloe laughed. "I think so."

Amanda glanced upward, brushing back her shiny brown hair. "I wonder which planet *boys* are from," she said.

"Probably one of the unidentified ones in another galaxy," Chloe replied.

"Excuse me, aren't you Chloe Carlson?" a girl said.

Chloe spun around to face the voice. It belonged to a pretty junior whom she recognized but had never met. Clutched in the girl's hand was the school newspaper, folded back to reveal the "Sound Off" page. Chloe smiled and nodded.

"I'm Krista, and I just read your article. You go, girl!" she said, pumping her fist in the air.

Another girl moving down the hall in the opposite direction reached out to high-five Chloe. "I couldn't have said it better myself!" she said.

Chloe, stunned by the response, just stood there.

"You have a gift," Amanda said. "Wouldn't it be great if you had your own talk show? You could be the teenage Oprah. Maybe you should look into getting an agent!"

"Uh, no thanks," Chloe said. "This is insane. But it's also kind of a relief. Now I know that it's not just me who thinks boys are lazy when it comes to dating. Obviously other girls feel the same way that I do."

"Exactly," Amanda agreed. "You've definitely struck a chord with the female population." She glanced at a group of boys who were playfully shoving each other and barking like junkyard dogs. "I'm not sure about the other half though. You might have to put it in a rap song to reach them."

"Let's hope not," Chloe said. "I'm no rap artist, that's for sure."

They were just heading into the cafeteria as the first lunch shift was filing out. For a moment it was total body crush. Somewhere in the crowd Chloe spotted Lennon coming toward them. She felt a familiar storm of nervous energy.

Had he read her "Sound Off"? Did he get the picture now? Would he ask her to the Save the Seals benefit?

As the questions piled up in her mind, the mob inched her and Lennon closer and closer together. Finally, just as they reached each other, the crowd opened up. She sighed her relief. At last! Room to breathe.

Amanda announced that she would secure seats at their table and left Chloe to deal with Lennon one-on-one.

Lennon touched Chloe's arm and gently led her to the side, out of the path of comers and goers.

Chloe practically swooned. It was so sweet the way he'd just looked out for her safety and everything.

[Chloe: Don't laugh. I'm serious about this. What Lennon just did was a heroic act. If you've ever been around a bunch of hungry teenagers, you'd know what I'm talking about. Obviously he wants to make certain that I'm safe and sound for the dance on Saturday night!]

As Lennon gazed at her and gave her that cute, lop-sided grin of his, Chloe tossed her soft, wavy curls. She had planned for it to be a smooth, movie-star type of move. Unfortunately, several strands landed in her face and stuck to her lip gloss. She quickly swiped them back.

"A word of caution," Lennon said. "Despite the bad press, the pizza has shown no signs of improvement."

Chloe laughed a little. "Thanks for the warning." Her mind raced. Lennon had just made a direct reference to the "Sound Off" column. Not hers, of course, but maybe this was his way of letting her know that he had read it. Chloe glanced away and then back again, waiting for him to say something else.

"Well," he finally murmured. "I'd better get to class." He started to go.

Chloe stood there, stunned. "That's all you have to say?" This question had been meant just for inside her confused head, but somehow it had come sputtering out of her mouth.

Lennon appeared genuinely puzzled. "Oh… um…you look cute today."

Chloe couldn't help but smile her thanks. That was a start, but she had been expecting much more. Finally she decided to simply come out with it. "Did you happen to read my column in the newspaper today?"

"Oh, yeah," Lennon said, his face brightening. "Congratulations on that. It must be cool to see your name in print. I'll see you later." And that was it. He was gone.

Chloe stood there, replaying the scene all over again in her mind. No, this wasn't a nightmare. It had actually happened that way.

Amanda came rushing up to her. "Your column is a runaway hit! E*verybody* is talking about it."

"Whoop-dee-do," Chloe mumbled. "Right now I'd settle for just one person in particular getting the point of it."

chapter
five

Riley and Sierra Pomeroy were in the cafeteria reading Chloe's "Sound Off" column together, stopping to recite their favorite parts out loud. After which, they'd break up into fits of laughter.

Sierra's double life never ceased to amaze Riley. Her real name was Sarah, given to her by strict and old-fashioned parents. They would freak if they ever knew that she went by Sierra, changed into wild clothes before first period, and played bass guitar in The Wave, the same band that Riley's old boyfriend, Alex, was a member of. Small world. Especially since Sierra was dating Larry Slotnick, Riley's neighbor.

[Riley: I have to confess. Watching Larry get over me and enter the dating world hasn't been the easiest thing to deal with. I mean, Larry's had a crush on me since the first grade. As far as stalkers go, he wasn't so bad. I used to wish

147

he would leave me alone, but at times like these I actually miss the way he used to ask me out every five minutes. At least somebody was interested in me!]

"Lennon has to ask Chloe to Save the Seals now," Sierra said. "Because if he doesn't, I would *not* want to be the one who lives with Chloe Carlson this week."

"He will," Riley said. She was sure of it, in fact. But what she wasn't sure of was her own date. "Okay, Chloe is covered, we've got a plan for Mom, the situation for Dad is in the works, and here I am, stuck." Her light mood turned sullen on a dime. "Watch me be the only one without a date."

"Think positive," Sierra said. "Let's work this out like a math problem." She reached into her messenger bag, pulled out a tablet of graph paper, and began scratching out what looked to be a flowchart.

Riley was totally confused. "Exactly what are you doing?" she asked.

"Making sure that you cover all the bases," Sierra said, continuing to mark up the paper. "Let's factor out all possible guy types. For instance, we have the jocks." She scribbled the word on the paper.

Riley shook her head. "Draw a line through that one. There are no possibilities. Except T-Rex. And I won't consider that option until Sunday morning."

Sierra glanced up. "But the dance is Saturday night."

"My point exactly," Riley said.

Sierra laughed. "What about the cool kids?"

"Most of them are holding tickets to the Tribal Council concert. Besides, Save the Seals is not exactly known for its wild mosh pit. And parents will be there, too. The cool crowd would have big problems with that."

Sierra scratched through category number two. "All's not lost. We've got the brainiacs."

"Not this weekend," Riley said. "They leave Friday for the Olympics of the Mind regional finals in San Francisco. Won't be back until Monday."

Sierra inspected her nails. "Okay, I wouldn't normally suggest this, but every girl gets a crush on at least one, so why not get it out of your system?"

Riley leaned in toward the table, intrigued now. "What are you talking about?"

Sierra grinned. "Bad boys."

Riley laughed. "I can't go out with a bad boy! It would never work. You're looking at a girl who feels like a criminal when she doesn't rewind movies before returning them to Blockbuster."

"You have a point." Sierra sighed, eliminating category number four. "We're down to fashion extremists."

"That includes the Goths, right?"

Sierra nodded. "And guys with multiple piercings."

"I'll pass. Not interested in boys who wear more makeup than I do." Riley paused a beat. "Or more jewelry."

Sierra groaned and glanced helplessly at her chart. "Riles, you've got to work with me here. The only category left is, well, *Larry*."

Riley giggled. "Yeah. Larry definitely belongs in his own category."

"But he's taking me to the movies on Saturday," Sierra pointed out. "As *friends*."

Riley gave Sierra a strange look. "Why did you say it like that?"

"Because we broke up last week," Sierra said.

Riley's mouth dropped open in shock. "What? When were you going to tell me?"

Sierra shrugged. "I just did."

"Why did you guys break up?" Riley asked. "I thought you liked each other."

"Don't get me wrong," Sierra said. "Larry's a great guy, but he's just not for me. Besides, all he does is talk about *you*."

"Oh," Riley muttered, feeling a little guilty. But then this got her thinking. She and Alex had broken up recently as well. Maybe they could go as friends, too. Why not? "I'll ask Alex," she announced all of a sudden. "He's still trying to pay off his new guitar, so I'm sure he didn't splurge on Tribal Council tickets. I'll bet he's free. He'd probably love to go to a big dance party."

Sierra directed her gaze behind Riley. "Well, here he comes. Why don't you ask him?"

Riley twisted around to see Alex's lanky, future-rock-star frame walk toward them—and past them—without a word, although he did acknowledge Sierra with a friendly nod.

"Did you see what just happened?" Riley shrieked. "Alex completely ignored me. That could easily go down as the insult heard around the lunchroom."

"Don't take it personally," Sierra said. "It's not Alex's fault."

Riley narrowed her eyes. Alex's behavior was confusing enough. But Sierra saying it wasn't his fault made no sense at all. "Excuse me?"

"It's called cool-guy-disorder. Happens after every breakup. They suddenly have to act like they're so *over it*. You know, basically pretend like you don't exist. In a few weeks it will all be over."

Riley rolled her eyes. "Oh, I can't wait." She paused. "Did *Larry* do this to you?"

Sierra shook her head. "He doesn't have the gene. Not cool enough."

"Lucky you."

Without warning Sierra slapped the table with a jeweled hand.

Everybody jumped.

"Do *you* have a disorder we should know about?" Riley asked.

"Yes, it's called *brilliance*," Sierra said. "I can't believe I forgot this category! It's the perfect one for you."

Riley couldn't stand the suspense. "Tell me! What?"

"Exchange students," Sierra said grandly. "What do you think about Jacques, that dreamy guy from France?"

"Hello?" Riley shouted. "He's only like a walking beautification project for West Malibu High." She scanned the lunchroom. "Where is he?"

Sierra laughed. "Calm down, mademoiselle. He doesn't eat lunch during this period."

"I'll ask him," Riley decided. "I mean, it's important to reach out to our international friends. You know, make them feel at home."

After school at California Dream, Riley sipped on a Vanilla Coke and tried to cheer up Chloe, who was looking pretty depressed slumped in the opposite chair. She had told the story of Lennon not asking her to the dance at least three times already.

"I think we're the only girls at West Malibu who don't have dates for Saturday night," Chloe was saying. "Tara's going out with that cute guy who left West Malibu to be homeschooled, and Amanda's got a date with a trombone player from the Santa Monica High marching band."

Riley slurped her soda all the way to the bottom of the glass. "I told you about Sierra and Larry, right?"

Chloe nodded.

"Well, I was thinking about asking Jacques, the guy from France," Riley said.

Chloe shook her head sullenly. "Too late. Quinn asked him out during study hall and he said yes."

"Ugh!" Riley gave up and put her head down on the table. She glanced around the place, half expecting a magic answer to materialize out of thin air. And one practically did.

Across the room she noticed a new poster plastered on the wall. The supercute surfer boy on it caught her eye. She erupted from her chair and dashed over to get a closer look.

The boy was named C.J. Logan and the poster was for the first annual Waverider International surfing competition. Of course! Riley had known it was coming up soon. Suddenly her heart bolted in her chest. She had a great idea!

Glancing back at the table, Riley made a wild gesture for Chloe to come over in a hurry. When her sister joined her, Riley pointed at the poster as if it explained everything.

Chloe seemed unimpressed. "That is not a cute boy. That is a *poster* of a cute boy."

"Don't you get it?" Riley demanded. "The competition is going on right now. C.J. Logan is actually in Malibu as we speak."

Chloe's expression was blank. "Who is C.J. Logan?"

Riley's focus bounced back to the poster. "He's from Australia. He's fifteen years old. And he's a total hottie. I can't believe I was upset about Quinn asking out Jacques."

"You shouldn't be," Chloe said. "French boys are so five minutes ago. Besides, I have it on good authority that he needs to be introduced to a wonderful invention called the Tic Tac."

Riley giggled, then turned her attention back to the Waverider poster. C.J. Logan was amazing. A surfing whiz *and* an Aussie accent! Now all she had to do was figure out a plan to meet him *and* ask him to go to Save the Seals.

chapter
six

"This is exactly why they invented the phrase, 'Could things get any *more* complicated?'" Chloe whispered to her sister.

It was Wednesday afternoon. Their mom was busy fitting her friend and supermodel, Tedi, for a new dress. Manuelo was front and center in the kitchen, explaining his own dating issues.

"So you see," Manuelo continued, "I couldn't help it. I'm such a good cook that my meals-in-a-minute went for big money at the Dinner at Eight auction. All the proceeds go to the local theater, which is good. But now the chairperson of the fund-raiser believes an invitation to Save the Seals is a great way to thank me, which is bad. Why? Because I don't have a date."

"Neither do I," Chloe said.

"Ditto," Riley added.

Manuelo ignored them. "Look at this," he whined,

holding up the glossy invitation. "It says 'Manuelo Del Valle plus one.'" He frowned. "I have no plus one. It's just me. Manuelo. All alone. So sad. So very, very sad." He looked at Chloe and Riley with pleading puppy-dog eyes.

Chloe sighed. "Don't cry, Manuelo. We'll find you a date. We promise."

Manuelo's mood went into fast turnaround. "Really? This is wonderful, girls. Thank you, thank you, thank you. I'd better get this reply card in the mail right away." He started humming a song and disappeared through the kitchen doorway.

Riley tugged on Chloe's sleeve. "You do realize that we have to find five dates by Saturday. And keep in mind that between the two of us, we can't even seem to find one."

"But what was I supposed to say?" Chloe asked. "He looked liked he was about to cry. Besides, if all of us went to the dance and Manuelo stayed home, it wouldn't be as much fun."

Riley nodded. "I guess you're right. But you have to admit, this is getting ridiculous."

"That's the understatement of the week," Chloe said.

"So what are we going to do about Manuelo?" Riley asked.

Chloe stepped over to the freezer, opened the door, and just let the chill wash over her. Finding Dad a date, finding Manuelo a date, and, how could she forget, finding *herself* a date. Not to mention something cute to wear. This would be one tough order to fill.

"Is the answer behind the Ben and Jerry's?" Riley teased.

"If only it were that simple." Chloe said. She grabbed a pint of Chunky Monkey and shut the door. Maybe all the calories would generate some inspiration.

That same day in the early evening Riley discovered Tedi standing on a small stool in the living room. She was wearing a formfitting animal print number that featured a daring slit up the side. "Wow, Tedi! You look amazing!" she said.

Tedi smiled. "Thank you. It's too conservative for Jennifer Lopez, but for a simple girl like me, it's truly wild." She glanced around and zeroed in on the clock. "Your mother left me stranded to take a phone call, and I have an eyebrow waxing in forty-five minutes." She sighed. "But she's making me look fabulous for the Model of the Year Awards, so I won't complain too much."

"Can I get you anything while you're waiting?" Riley asked.

"Would you please hand me that *People* over there on the coffee table?" Tedi asked. "Since I'm stuck here, I should probably read something educational."

Riley passed her the magazine.

Tedi studied the cover. "Oh, good. The best-and-worst-dressed list."

Riley smiled to herself and settled in on the sofa, tucking her feet underneath her legs. Suddenly it occurred to her that Tedi might have some valuable insight on how to reel in a superhottie like C.J. Logan. "Hey, did Mom mention that we were taking dates to Save the Seals this year?"

Tedi closed the magazine and gave Riley a bright smile. "Yes, she did! So tell me. Who's the lucky guy?"

"That's the trouble. I don't know yet."

Tedi's face registered a moment's pure horror. "You don't know? Isn't the dance this weekend?"

Riley nodded.

"Sweetie, by this point in the week you should be trying to decide on lip color, not who's going to take you!"

"But the boy I want to go with doesn't even know I'm alive."

"If this guy hasn't taken notice of a beautiful girl like you, then he's not worth the trouble."

"No, you don't understand," Riley said. "He *really* doesn't know that I'm alive. We've never met."

"Oh," Tedi said. She thought for a moment then shrugged. "Well, introduce yourself. I'm sure he'll fall madly in love."

Riley shifted in her seat. "It's a little more complicated than that. He's sort of…well, he's sort of famous."

Tedi widened her eyes. "Famous? Sweetie, you're not talking about Prince William, are you?"

Riley shook her head.

"Prince Harry?" Tedi wondered.

Riley laughed. "Nobody in the royal family, Tedi. He's a surfer, one of the youngest competitors ever, and he's taking part in the Waverider International."

"Isn't that going on right now?" Tedi asked.

"Yes," Riley answered. "But how do I get his attention? I mean, this event is huge, and there are probably hundreds of girls who want to meet him."

Tedi glanced around, then stepped off the stool in a huff. "At the very least I hope your mother's on the phone with the President or First Lady." She smoothed out her dress and gingerly settled on the sofa next to Riley. "You came to the right girl for this. Famous men are my specialty. Did I ever tell you the story about Sam Law, the lead singer for Blowtorch?"

Riley shook her head no. She knew the band though. Blowtorch was a regular fixture on MTV, and Sam Law's name always turned up in the celebrity gossip mill. Women fell over themselves just to get close to him.

"Like every other woman in this hemisphere, I had a mad crush on the man. But unlike them, I wasn't going to try my chances at meeting him backstage. Famous guy rule number one: Meet professionally on his turf. I went after a part in the new Blowtorch video and got it, so we were introduced on the set by the director."

"What happened next?" Riley demanded.

"It was a two-day shoot. Our first date was at the wrap party. For the next three weeks we were madly in love—which is pretty much a silver anniversary for rock stars and models—and then it was over." Tedi stared into space for a few seconds. "I can't remember what happened exactly. I just know that we got into a huge argument, and I ended up throwing a banana daiquiri into his lap. Haven't heard from him since. Oh, well." She patted Riley's knee. "So tell me about this guy."

Riley smiled brightly as thoughts of C.J. Logan took flight in her mind. "Well, he's a surfer from Australia—"

"Which is good," Tedi cut in. "That means we know in advance that he's cute with a great tan, perfect body, and a killer accent."

"That's for sure," Riley said.

Tedi tapped a manicured nail to her painted lips. "Can you surf?"

"Sort of. But not well enough to compete."

"Okay," Tedi went on, concentrating hard. "What can you do that would get you to that competition in an official way?"

The perfect solution flashed in Riley's mind. "I can interview him for the sports section of the school paper!"

Tedi clapped her hands. "Sweetie, *you* are thinking like *me*." She paused. "How old are you?"

"Fourteen," Riley replied.

"That's what I thought. Promise me you won't think like me again for several years. Better to quit while you're ahead."

Riley laughed and shot up from the sofa, eager to fill Chloe in on her new plan. "I promise." She started out, then halted, wondering if Tedi might be a strong ally to encourage Mom to go out with Coach Lee. "Tedi, has Mom mentioned anything to you about finding a date for Save the Seals?"

A frustrated breath escaped Tedi. "Don't get me started on your mother. I've offered to set her up with a great guy, but she refuses to let anyone help her find a date. Honestly, I've given up."

"Given up on what?" Macy asked as she bounded back into the room.

Tedi rose from the sofa and took her position on the stool once again. "Finding you a date for Save the Seals."

Macy waved off the subject. "I'm sorry my call took so long. The buyer in Milan just wanted to talk and talk." She surveyed the dress with pinpoint accuracy. "I should take it in about an eighth of an inch at the waist. Other than that, it fits like a glove."

"And feels like a corset," Tedi said. "Remind me not to breathe in this dress. But back to this dating business…"

"No," Macy said, holding up a hand. "I can find my own date, thank you very much."

"By the way, how's that working out?" Tedi asked.

Macy's cheeks blushed a faint pink. "Not so well."

Riley saw an opening and decided to go for it. "You know, Mom, there's a teacher at West Malibu who would love to go to the dance. His name is—"

"I'm not interested, Riley. Besides, aren't you and your sister supposed to find a date for your father?" Macy asked.

"Yes," Riley answered.

"Then concentrate on that," she replied. "I'll figure out something on my own."

"So will I," Riley murmured under her breath. And then she left the living room in search of Chloe. There had to be a way to trick Mom into meeting Coach Lee!

chapter
seven

[<u>Chloe</u>: Last evening I went to bed with finding a
date for Manuelo on my mind. In the middle of
the night I dreamed about Lennon asking me
out. This morning I woke up to see a Post-it note
on my laptop that read, Update Dad's on-line
dating profile. Okay, is it just me, or has all this
dating business completely taken over our lives?
Oh, by the way, in my dream Lennon asked me
out all by himself. No hints. No clues planted in
newspaper columns. Just a boy with a little bit of
romantic nerve. It was an awesome dream.]

Chloe booted up her laptop and went straight to
work on her dad's on-line dating profile. She studied the
original version with a critical eye and ultimately decided
that listing all of his earth-guy qualities just wasn't
enough to get women interested.

Granted, her dad was a truly impressive guy, but on paper he didn't seem that way. One could even argue that he was just an unemployed trailer-park resident. Not exactly bachelor-of-the-year material.

Chloe punched up the answers a bit. After all, a little creativity never hurt. Now Dad was an "entrepreneur in between projects who enjoys coastal living." She smiled at her handiwork and e-mailed the application to the dating service.

All she had to do was wait for Dad's special cyber mailbox to fill up. Hopefully it would. In a hurry!

"Mom," Riley said, staring into her bowl of cereal, "would you mind dropping me off at school and coming into the office for a minute? The secretary needs you to sign a form so I can leave campus to cover the Waverider competition for the newspaper." She didn't dare lift her head now. Her left eye was twitching like crazy, and her mom would know for certain that she was lying.

Luckily her mom was too busy punching buttons on her Palm Pilot to take notice.

"No problem," Macy replied. "But we should probably leave in a few minutes. I'm due at a trunk show in Santa Monica and I don't want to be late."

Riley deposited her bowl in the sink and dashed upstairs to gather her things for school. She stopped in on Chloe, who was still hard at work on the Internet. "How's it going?"

Chloe beamed triumphantly. "I just posted Dad's new profile a few minutes ago and there are already three responses. Imagine how many there will be when we get home from school! What about you?"

Riley brought her voice down to a faint whisper. "Mom doesn't suspect a thing yet," she told her sister. "Wish me luck."

Chloe crossed her fingers on both hands.

"Riley!" Mom called from downstairs. "Are you almost ready?"

"Coming!" Riley waved good-bye to Chloe and dashed to the car. The short ride to school was easy. A fashion reporter had called Mom on her cell phone for an interview about Tedi's Model of the Year Awards dress. While Mom wrapped up the conversation, Riley rushed into the school office to put the finishing touches on her scheme, praying that it would work.

"Good morning, Riley! It's going to be another great day at West Malibu High!" Rebecca Ravitz said as soon as she saw Riley.

The too-eager voice rattled Riley for a moment. Rebecca was the biggest gossip in the ninth-grade class, and, as luck would have it, she was the morning office assistant, too.

"Hi, Rebecca," Riley said, keeping her voice low so that none of the teachers or administrators milling about would hear. "I was hoping you could help me with something."

"Help you with something?" Rebecca asked curiously. "No problem. What is it?"

"Could you please page Coach Lee to come to the office?" Riley's gaze darted to the door. There was still no sign of Mom. Good.

"Why do you need me to page Coach Lee?" Rebecca asked. She narrowed her eyes.

Riley glanced nervously at the adults in the room, then relaxed. Nobody seemed to be paying attention. "I can't explain right now, Rebecca, but it's very, very important."

Rebecca grabbed the intercom system and pressed a red button. "Coach Lee to the office, Coach Lee to the office! This is an emergency! Lives are at stake! Every second that goes by is the tick tock of danger! Coach Lee to the office!" And then she smiled. "There. That should get him here."

Riley buried her face in her hands. What was Rebecca *doing*?

Mom rushed into the office. "Is everything okay?"

Then Coach Lee burst onto the scene, running smack dab into Mom. "Excuse me, ma'am, I'm terribly sorry," he apologized, steadying her shoulders with both hands. And then he did a double take, smiling all of a sudden.

"Oh, I'm fine. Really, I am," Macy said, clearing her throat as she nervously finger-combed her hair.

Coach Lee extended his hand. "I should probably introduce myself since I almost knocked you down. I'm

George Lee. I coach football and teach health here at West Malibu."

Macy shook his hand firmly, and Riley noticed that her hold of it lingered for a moment. "Macy Carlson. I'm—"

"Chloe and Riley's mother," the coach said. "Of course you are. I can see the resemblance. You have lovely girls."

Macy smiled. "Why, thank you…*George*."

"Call me Coach."

"Very well…*Coach*."

Riley watched all of this from just a few feet away. She had counted on some sparks, but this was an electrical storm. A total love connection! Getting Mom a date was going to be easier than she thought!

Riley's celebration came to a crashing halt as soon as Ms. Raffin entered the office.

"Good morning, Mrs. Carlson. How nice to see you. What brings you here this morning?" Ms. Raffin said.

Riley spun around to avoid eye contact and once more came face-to-face with Rebecca.

"This is getting interesting," Rebecca said. "Do you need me to page someone else?"

Yes, Riley wanted to say, a helicopter to get me out of here! But she remained silent instead, listening in on every word of the conversation behind her.

"Riley is so excited about covering the surfing competition for the school paper," Macy was saying. "I just came in to sign the permission forms for her to leave school early."

"I have no idea what you're talking about," Ms. Raffin said.

"Rebecca, who had me paged?" Coach Lee asked.

"Riley," Rebecca said, pointing at her.

Riley could feel the heat of Macy's gaze burning into her back, and she knew that Ms. Raffin and Coach Lee were staring as well. One thing was certain—she would definitely have some explaining to do.

[__Riley__: You probably think I'm in serious trouble, don't you? Well, okay, I am. Things aren't as bad as they seem. Really. The way I figure it, no harm, no foul. Nobody was hurt and nothing was broken. Everybody will probably have a good laugh about this at some point in the future. Hopefully that will be a few minutes from now.]

"Riley, Ms. Raffin and I would appreciate some clarification on a few matters," Macy said.

Bracing herself for the worst, Riley turned around to face them, laughing nervously. "You know, it's the funniest thing. I may have forgotten to talk to Ms. Raffin about this assignment."

"'*May* have'?" Ms. Raffin echoed. "I would definitely remember such a conversation."

Coach Lee had a puzzled expression on his face.

"Will someone please tell me why I was paged to come to the office?"

"To meet me, I'm afraid," Macy said, figuring out the whole thing. "I think my daughter had a little plan up her sleeve this morning."

Coach Lee flashed a charming smile. "Is that so? Well, I'd like to go on the record as saying that I admire your daughter's plan. It introduced me to you."

Macy was genuinely taken aback. "I suppose it was harmless enough."

Ms. Raffin stepped toward Riley. "What's this about a surfing competition?"

Riley quickly explained what the Waverider was, the significance of C.J. Logan being the youngest participant, and how great it would be to do a piece on him for the paper.

Ms. Raffin smiled widely. "This is exactly what I love to see in my reporters—a knack for ideas that are outside the box. Bring back the story. Photos, too."

Riley nodded dutifully, hardly able to contain her excitement.

"Oh, and, Riley," Ms. Raffin added, "please remember that this is for the *sports* page. Your last article about the football team turned out to be more of a dating survey than an athletic feature."

"Yes, Ms. Raffin," Riley said. Then she glanced over to observe Mom and Coach Lee. They were exchanging phone numbers and, from the sound of it, planning a mixed doubles tennis date for later in the afternoon. This last development left Riley completely stunned. Mom didn't know the first thing about tennis!

I guess Mom must really like Coach Lee, Riley thought. She grinned to herself. Cool.

chapter
eight

Chloe ducked into the Newsstand with hopes of running into Lennon before school. Unfortunately there was no sign of him. Disappointed, she waited in line for a hot chocolate.

The girl behind the counter was brand new and very slow. Finally Chloe got her steamy cocoa and started out. Just as she approached the door, she did a double take. Lennon *was* at the Newsstand. He was sitting alone at a corner table, hunched over a book and facing the wall.

Chloe crept up behind him. "Do you want some company, or are you being antisocial?" she asked.

Lennon twisted around and broke into a smile. "Hey, how are you?"

She slipped into the chair opposite him and sighed heavily. "Do you really want to know?"

"That bad?" He gestured to the book he was reading. "Is it worse than trying to learn everything about the Trojan War in twenty minutes?"

Chloe wondered if that was a hint for her to scram so he could study. She hesitated. "Maybe I should—"

"No, stick around." Lennon closed the book and stuffed it into his backpack. "What's up?"

"I'll be so glad when this weekend is over with," Chloe admitted, "and if it doesn't come soon, then Save the Seals just might become Save Chloe."

Lennon cracked a smile. "That's the big dance on Saturday, right?"

"Yes," Chloe said. This was close. She could feel it. He *had* to ask her now! "My parents are separated and refuse to go together, so Riley and I are trying to find dates for them, trying to find dates for ourselves, and, as of last night, trying to find a date for our housekeeper." She let out a heavy sigh. "But so far nobody has a date. And it's Thursday."

Lennon chuckled. "That's pretty funny."

Chloe sat there in expectant silence, waiting for more.

But nothing came. Lennon might as well have been a statue in the park. He made no sound and showed no signs of life.

Finally he gathered up his things to leave. "I guess we'd better start heading out."

"You go ahead without me," Chloe said in a snappy tone. "There's something I've got to do first." Every time she brought up the dance, Lennon either ignored the subject or changed it altogether! Maybe a quick mood swing would get his attention.

But just like he was with everything else that Chloe seemed to say or do, Lennon remained unfazed. "Okay," he murmured with a shrug and took off.

Chloe took a long drink of her cocoa as if she'd find the secret of life at the bottom of the cup. Actually she'd settle for something much more simple. Like the answer to the single question going through her mind: What was Lennon's problem?

Ugh! This playing-dumb act of his was really getting old. They'd already been out on a date, and she *thought* that he liked her. But if he didn't, why couldn't he just make it official—in person, on the phone, by e-mail? "I just want to be friends." That's *all* he had to say.

Chloe sat there, her emotions totally mixed up. One second she was riddled with insecurity, and the next second she was filled with fury. All the back-and-forth had her head spinning!

Why don't boys ever just say what they feel! she wanted to scream. Whoa. She needed to chill. No boy was worth this much drama.

No matter, Chloe couldn't help wondering. Why was Lennon doing this? Did he enjoy watching her make a fool of herself? Or was he really that clueless? Well, Chloe didn't care anymore. As of that moment, her days of playing Little Miss Please-Ask-Me-to-the-Dance were officially over. That's right!

From then on boys were going to fall over themselves to ask her out on dates. Otherwise she just
wouldn't bother. The thought amused her. Wouldn't that
be great? A world where every boy you liked instantly
asked you out for Saturday night? Or if a guy *wasn't* interested, he *told* you straight up—instead of pretending he
liked you for whatever reason.

Really. Guys were so immature sometimes.

Chloe smiled, thinking of all the girls at school who
appreciated her first "Sound Off." They would definitely
love this scenario.

Inspired, she left the table, settled in at one of the
empty cyber stations, and began composing another
"Sound Off." She called this one "Saturday Sounds
Perfect Part II." After all, the first one was a hit, and
everybody loved a sequel.

The column practically wrote itself. Her fingers flit-
ted across the keyboard at a breakneck pace. Within
minutes she was done. On a lark she e-mailed the piece
to Ms. Raffin with a brief note. Maybe there would be
space for a last-minute article in Friday's edition of the
paper.

Chloe was logging off the system when she noticed
a stray flyer screaming the banner headline: IF YOU DON'T
BELIEVE IN LOVE AT FIRST SIGHT, HOW ABOUT LOVE IN FIVE MINUTES?

She picked it up to discover that the Newsstand was
hosting a speed-dating session—that night. She had
seen a story about it once on a morning show. It sounded

kind of cool. Instead of a single blind date that lasted a few hours, you signed up for speed dating, a series of eight mini–blind dates that would last five to ten minutes.

Chloe folded the flyer and slipped it into the front pocket of her backpack. That just might be the perfect plan for Manuelo!

The Waverider thrummed with action and Riley was totally excited to be in the midst of it. Surfers from all over the world were there, not to mention top corporate sponsors, trainers, media pros, and hordes of fans.

Riley fingered the credentials hanging around her neck. Her laminated pass read PRESS—ALL ACCESS, and it was attached to a thick black cord. She looked *very* official. Ms. Raffin had made last-minute arrangements. As it happened, one of her former students was managing the press tent.

Today's waves were no joke. In fact, Riley had never seen them so huge. She watched in awe as each group of surfers skated across the water, instinctively riding the edge of the wave, staying just ahead of the foamy crest. They were like superheroes. It was totally amazing to see.

The wind whipped, the sun beat down, and the tang of the salt water burned in Riley's throat. She had been lucky enough to see C.J. Logan in all three of his heats. Unfortunately he lost to two Americans and another Australian. But for a fifteen-year-old in his first professional competition, he proved himself a force to be reckoned with. The announcers even praised him as a "redhot kid on the rise" and a "young surfer to watch in the years ahead."

After much hand-wringing and nervous pacing, Riley found the nerve to introduce herself to C.J. and request an interview. Now seemed to be the perfect time. All of his heats were over, and he was just hanging out on the beach, scoping out what remained of the competitive action.

"Excuse me," Riley said. But her voice had barely registered above a whisper.

C.J. didn't hear. His gaze remained glued to the two daredevils braving the brutal Pacific waves.

Riley cleared her throat and C.J. glanced over.

"Excuse me," Riley said, much louder this time. "I'm a reporter for West Malibu High. I'd love to interview you for our school paper."

C.J. stepped over in his body-hugging wet suit. "What's your name, mate?"

Riley swallowed hard. The boy was even cuter in person, and she loved the Aussie accent! "Riley Carlson," she managed to say, extending her hand.

"C.J. Logan," he said.

His hand was wet and sandy, but Riley didn't care. "You were amazing out there."

C.J. gave a modest shrug. "Wasn't my best day."

Riley fired off a battery of basic profile questions—

where C.J. had been born, how long he'd been surfing, and what his goals for the future were. His answers were snappy and funny. At the end she pulled out her digital camera and asked permission to take a picture.

C.J. winked at her. "Only if you're in the picture, too."

Before Riley had a chance to answer, C.J. had called over Joey B., another popular surfer from Australia, to snap the photo. Riley gave Joey B. a quick lesson on how to operate the camera. Then she took her place beside C.J., who draped his arm around her for the shot.

Riley was swooning big-time. She didn't want the afternoon to end. C.J. was superfunny, supernice, and supercool! The chemistry between them was natural, as if they'd known each other for a long time.

"I'll be staying in Malibu through Sunday," C.J. said. "Any chance I might see you again?"

Riley's mind raced ahead to Saturday night. She imagined C.J. all dressed up and showing off his moves on the dance floor. "I think that can be arranged."

"How about a surf date tomorrow?" C.J. asked.

Riley stared into the brilliant blue of his eyes. "What's that?"

"I'll show you some long boarding moves, we'll eat a snack on the beach, and then we'll watch the sunset."

Riley hesitated. It sounded like a dream! But part of her thought about Vance and wondered if it was the right thing to do. Whenever she saw him in the halls, she got a funny feeling in her stomach, and she secretly wished that his cousin had never come up with those tickets to the Tribal Council concert.

In the end, though, she reasoned that they weren't exactly a couple yet. Besides, he was busy with his plans. Why should she sit around like crabgrass? A girl was entitled to her own fun, right?

C.J. tilted his head. "Do we have a date?"

"Yes," Riley said. "In fact, I can't think of anything I'd rather do more."

chapter
nine

Chloe had opened the fridge to get a snack when her mother walked…well, *stumbled* into the kitchen.

"I don't know what's hurting me more, the blisters on my hands, the blisters on my feet, or every joint and muscle in my body."

Chloe's dad was sitting at the kitchen table. He took a monster bite out of an apple and laughed at Macy. "Sounds like it was a torture session, not a date," he said.

Macy bristled at the joke. "No. It was a *date*," she insisted. "Coach maintains a very active lifestyle. That's a healthy way to live."

Jake shook his head, grinning. He gestured to Chloe's laptop on the counter. "No thanks. I'd rather relax and let women find me on the Internet." He turned to Chloe. "By the way, how's my favorite dating detective coming along with our project?"

Chloe grabbed a yogurt and shut the refrigerator. "I'm happy to report that your cyber mailbox is full of messages from interested women."

Jake threw a puzzled look over to Macy. "I have no idea what that means, but it sounds good, doesn't it?"

Macy struggled to the table and sat down with a sigh of relief. "Just be careful, Jake. I've heard some pretty crazy on-line dating stories."

"If I didn't know any better, I'd say you were jealous," Jake said, folding his arms.

"Trust me," Macy said, "you don't know any better. Anyway, why would I be jealous? I've got my own date. In fact, Coach is taking me rock climbing tomorrow."

"Rock climbing?" Jake exclaimed. "Macy, you're so scared of heights that you won't even change a lightbulb!"

"I'm not that bad," she protested.

Chloe stared at her mom. Dad was right. Mom was a total chicken when it came to heights.

Macy shrugged. "Well, even if I am that bad, Coach says it's important to face fears of physical challenges."

"Is that so?" Jake said with a smile. "Well, I'll be at the trailer practicing the tango in case anybody needs me." He turned to Chloe. "How does tomorrow night sound for final selection?"

Chloe nodded. "Perfect." She led him over to the laptop. "Look at all these messages in your on-line mailbox. First we have to go through these and decide which ones you want to meet."

Dad was peering over her shoulder, squinting at the screen. "All those are for me?"

"Yes," Chloe said. She clicked the update button. Two more messages popped into the box. "Now there are eighty-six."

"Eighty-six? That's a lot of mail to read. I'm still trying to get through last week's *Buddhist Today* magazine."

Chloe peered up at her father. "Well, I guess Riley and I could weed out the undesirables and set up a meet and greet with the top contenders."

"That sounds great, honey," Jake said. "Well, I'd better run."

As Jake left, Manuelo rushed into the kitchen carrying three sacks of groceries.

"Hello, hello, hello," he sang breathlessly. "Traffic is a nightmare. I should have started dinner over an hour ago. I hope nobody's hungry. We're having paella tonight. An old family recipe. Trust me. It'll be worth the wait. So stop complaining! That means everybody." He bent over to address Pepper. "Including you." Manuelo stood up and noticed Macy's disheveled state. "What happened to you?"

"I had a tennis date."

"Why?" Manuelo asked. "Tennis isn't your game. Can you even play Ping-Pong?"

Macy eased herself onto her feet. "Very funny."

"Thank you," Manuelo said. "I'll be here all week."

"I'm going to soak in a nice hot bath before dinner," Macy said, and shuffled out of the room.

Manuelo began unpacking the groceries. "Where's Riley?"

"She's covering the Waverider for the school paper."

"Ah, the Waverider," Manuelo murmured. "That's part of the reason why I sat in traffic so long. There are cars up and down the beach for miles."

"Oh, I almost forgot," Chloe said. "I've got something for you." She dug deep into her backpack until she found the flyer.

"I hope it's a deed to a French chalet," Manuelo joked.

"It's something better." Chloe unfolded the paper and presented it to him with a flourish. "Ta-da! Your secret dating weapon."

Manuelo scanned the page and frowned. "Speed dating? I don't think so."

Chloe grabbed a spoon from a drawer and opened her yogurt. "Why not? I think it's a great idea."

"Blind dates are risky enough. And you expect me to go on eight of them? No way. I'll take my chances with just one," Manuelo said.

"But what if it's bad?" Chloe said. "It could last for hours. The great thing about speed dating is that the bad ones are over in a matter of minutes."

Manuelo seemed to think this over. "That *is* a better way of looking at it."

"Don't worry. It'll turn out fine," Chloe assured him. "In fact, Riley and I will go along for moral support. Okay?"

"You promise?" Manuelo asked.

"I promise," Chloe said. After all, the odds were against her having a date for the dance. At least she could get one for Manuelo, right?

The next morning Chloe passed through the doors of West Malibu High and received a round of instant applause.

"You must be reading my mind," one girl said.

"Guys are so clueless!" another girl cried.

A trio of truly appreciative sophomores began chanting, "Go, Chloe, go, Chloe, go, Chloe!"

"What's up?" she wondered aloud to herself as much as to anyone.

Tara and Quinn came rushing up to her, waving Friday's edition of the school paper. "Oops…you did it again," they sang.

Chloe grabbed it and immediately turned to the "Sound Off" section. She couldn't believe it. "Saturday Sounds Perfect Part II" took up most of the page. Seeing her own work in print and knowing that so many of the girls liked it made her feel great.

"Hey, Chloe," one girl said. "My boyfriend never takes me to the movies. All he wants to do is sit at my house and play Nintendo. What should I do?"

Chloe thought fast for the perfect answer. "Practice his favorite game. Once you beat him, he'll never want to play again."

Everybody laughed.

Chloe enjoyed being the witty girl with all the right answers. For a moment, at least, it helped her forget about how upset she was with Lennon. "Girls, always remember this: Who needs boys when you've got a supportive sisterhood?" She tried to sound upbeat, but a hint of sadness crept in.

Tara seemed to pick up on it. "Hey, she's right. If a guy is not digging you, it's *his* loss."

chapter
ten

"**N**ot too shabby, wouldn't you say, mate?" C.J. said, proudly displaying the complimentary Waverider surfboard that he received for participating in the surfing competition.

Riley stared at the object in amazement. Definitely the coolest surfboard she had ever seen. The color was a glossy black, as slick as an oil spill, and featured a wild abstract design in splashy purple.

"What do you say we try her out?" C.J. asked.

At first Riley couldn't believe that C.J. actually intended to take this board into the water. It was practically a work of art! "You mean *us*?"

C.J. chuckled. "Who else?" And then he dashed toward the ocean, the board under his arm, his feet kicking up sand.

It was the day after meeting C.J. at the Waverider, and they were already on their first surf date! Riley giggled, zipped up her wet suit, and took off after him, halting at the water's edge.

C.J. was in waist-deep, calling her out. "Come on! Nothing to be afraid of!"

Riley took in a deep breath and charged ahead, reaching him in no time flat despite some rocky waves.

C.J. shielded his eyes to study the water from a distance. "There are some monster waves coming down the pike. Ready for a wild ride?"

Riley felt a mixture of fear and excitement. "Are you sure about this?" she asked him. "Remember, I'm just a beginning surfer."

[<u>Riley</u>: Maybe it's because I just watched a surfing competition. Maybe it's the Wheaties I had for breakfast this morning. Or maybe it's because this guy's smile is so fantastic. But suddenly, I am 100 percent ready to tackle these waves!]

C.J. gave her a cute cocky grin. "You're with me. You'll be fine."

Riley decided to go for it!

C.J. guided her onto the board and swam beside her as she paddled out to sea. For a while it was rough going, waves breaking, the spray of salt water in her eyes, but with C.J.'s encouragement, she kept after it. Soon she was gliding through the water at a fast clip. In fact, C.J. struggled to keep up with *her*!

"Let's stop here," C.J. said. Though treading now and having just put in a major swim, the Aussie boy was barely breathing hard.

What a hottie! Riley could hardly get over it. With his long blond hair, piercing blue eyes, and dark tan, C.J. Logan was movie-star cute.

Suddenly a wild and crazy feeling came over Riley. She had never been out this far in the ocean before. It was scary in a dangerous, fun sort of way. C.J. had started surfing when he was only three years old, so she felt totally safe with him.

"Now it's time for the real fun," C.J. said. He helped Riley straddle the Waverider board, then did the same himself. Together they rode the water, up and down, gathering speed, surfing toward the shore, their legs kicking up a splash.

Riley's stomach did a flip as a major wave lifted them up and swooshed them back down. She screamed in delight. "Wow! That was fun!"

C.J. laughed as they bobbed in the water. "You're good at this. A real natural."

Riley turned back to make eye contact with him. They shared a secret smile. "I want to stand up!" she announced boldly. "I want to surf like you!"

"You asked for it," C.J. said. Within seconds he was standing on the board, the balancing act effortless to him. Then he reached down to take Riley's hands and help her up as well.

After a few stops and starts, she stood steady. Just as she established her footing, a serious wave picked them up and they went gliding across the water, zigging and zagging, twisting and turning, until they crashed into the surf.

Riley went under but stayed calm, allowed the rough wave to pass, and surfaced a few moments later. She filled her lungs with oxygen and scanned the area for C.J. She giggled and spun around to see him directly behind her and back on the board. "That was so much fun!"

C.J. extended his hand and helped her up. "Glad you liked it, but we should probably head to shore. The sun will be setting soon, and we shouldn't be in the water at dusk."

They paddled into the shallow end, and Riley felt an alternating sense of exhaustion and elation as her feet hit the wet sand.

"You're great out there," C.J. said.

Riley was proud to get the compliment. "Really?"

"Oh, yeah. A lot of girls won't do anything but lie flat on the board. You're a daredevil."

She couldn't stop smiling. "Well, what can I say? I had a very good teacher."

"I should probably resign though," C.J. said.

Riley didn't understand. "Why?"

"Conflict of interest," C.J. explained. And then he leaned in and kissed her on the cheek.

For a fleeting moment Riley closed her eyes. C.J.'s lips were soft, and even many seconds after they left her cheek, she could still feel their imprint.

[Riley: Don't worry, I'm not going to say something cheesy like, "I'll never wash this cheek again!" Although, I must admit, the thought did cross my mind!]

The rest of the date passed as if part of a dream. They ate candy on a blanket, watched the sun begin to set, and swapped stories about parents and school and siblings.

Riley didn't know if she had walked home or floated home. But home she was, holding court in Chloe's room, filling her in on *everything*.

"I can't believe he kissed you!" Chloe squealed.

"It was so sweet and so sudden," Riley gushed. "I was completely shocked." She twirled around the room. "That has to be the best date I'll ever go on in my entire life."

Chloe laughed at her. "Oh, please! How can you say that? You're only fourteen."

"Sometimes a girl just knows," Riley said, a stubborn edge to her voice.

"Listen," Chloe began, "best date of your life or not, I'm happy for you."

Riley smiled. "Thanks."

"At least one of us has a date for Save the Seals," Chloe added.

Riley's smile crashed. "Oh, no!"

"What's wrong?" Chloe asked.

Riley flung herself onto the bed. "I was having so much fun on our date that I forgot to ask him to the dance!"

chapter
eleven

"**I** need Tylenol, several packs of ice, and chocolate-chocolate-chip ice cream with rainbow sprinkles."

Chloe and Riley traded worried looks with each other.

"Oh, and the new issues of *Vogue*, *Vanity Fair*, and *Women's Wear Daily*." Mom's requests were croaking out of her mouth, each syllable weaker than the last. "Thank you, girls."

Chloe reached for another pillow to elevate Mom's feet. "Even New York's Fashion Week doesn't leave you in this kind of shape."

Mom managed a hint of a smile. "Don't worry, honey. I'll be fine. I have to be. Coach is teaching me how to scuba dive first thing in the morning." There was a yawn, then a groan, and finally the fluttering of eyelids.

[<u>Chloe</u>: Just between us, I think I'll count to ten before I run around like a crazy person to find

everything on Mom's wish list. This baby is going
night-night. One thousand one, one thousand
two...]

By the count of one thousand six, Mom was sacked
out, snoring, and most likely not to be heard from until
the next morning.

Chloe and Riley breathed collective sighs of relief.
Now they could see about Dad's dating possibilities, who
were scheduled to turn up at his trailer anytime now.

They ran upstairs to grab their clipboards. Then
they rushed out to Vista del Mar, a trailer park on a bluff
overlooking the beach. It was within walking distance of
the house.

A line of women already stood outside Dad's trailer,
the smallest one in the whole park.

Chloe approached the group, wondering for a
moment if a misunderstanding had occurred. These
ladies didn't look anything like their pictures on the
Internet.

"Hi, I'm Chloe and this is my sister, Riley. We're
going to ask you a few questions for our dad. Think of it
as a prescreening interview. After we've talked to everyone, we'll let you know who has been selected to attend
the Save the Seals benefit with him, okay?"

Most of the women scowled in response.

A tough-looking lady stepped forward. "Who does
this guy think he is—Brad Pitt?"

Chloe glanced at her clipboard. The photograph in

this woman's profile must have been taken at least ten years ago. "You must be…"

"Lucy," the woman snapped. "Let's move it along, cookie. I'm already late for a meeting with my probation officer."

Chloe and Riley exchanged concerned glances.

"How are your dancing skills?" Chloe asked.

Lucy grimaced. "Fine. I just stand on a man's feet and tell him to lead."

"Okay, moving on," Chloe said, checking off Lucy's name. "Alexis is next."

A young woman dressed in a bridal gown proceeded to the front of the group. "That's me. FYI, my maid of honor canceled at the last minute, so I'll need one of you to fill in."

Chloe felt Riley tug on her shirt.

"Uh…this isn't a wedding. It's just about a date for Saturday night," Riley said to the woman.

Chloe referred back to the clipboard and made a note that indicated *not* a match made in heaven.

Alexis ripped off her veil, threw it onto the ground, and began stomping on it. "Why are men so afraid of commitment?" she screamed.

Riley leaned over to whisper in Chloe's ear. "Alexis seems a little high-strung. Dad's more laid-back."

Chloe raised her eyebrows. "You think?"

The remainder of the interviews seemed to go from bad to worse. The best of the lot: a puppeteer named

Debbie, whose furry friend, a tiger sock puppet she called Chuckles, never left her side. Yes, she was the normal one of the bunch. The whole exercise had become a least-of-the-ten-evils sort of thing.

Debbie and Chuckles were introduced to Dad, and with great relief Chloe and Riley checked finding him a date off their list of tasks.

Mom was covered, too, provided she woke up from her comalike sleep in time to get ready for Save the Seals! But the girls had one more person to take care of this Friday night.

They marched back to the house and found Manuelo in the kitchen, fretting over which tie to wear with his best suit.

Chloe and Riley consulted and selected a skinny tie that completed Manuelo's hip look.

"You know, we're getting pretty good at this," Riley said as they headed out the door for the Newsstand and an evening of speed dating. "We're finding people dates. We're helping them make important fashion choices."

[Chloe: Don't mind my sister. She's still over the moon about C.J. Logan, so her judgment is a little off. I suppose it seems like we're good at it, but at what cost? We're behind on our schoolwork (I've been reading more on-line romance profiles than Shakespeare this week) and behind on our sleep. (You try getting up before the sun rises to work on Manuelo's love questionnaire!)]

The Newsstand was standing room only with singles hoping to make that special connection. Chloe and Riley practically pushed a nervous Manuelo up to the registration table to sign in. The woman in the FALL IN LOVE FAST—TRY SPEED DATING T-shirt instructed him to have a seat at table number seven.

Chloe and Riley were in luck! They were able to secure a table just off to the side of Manuelo's. From there the girls could see and hear everything that was going on.

"You know, I'm not sure if I'd want to try speed dating," Riley said. "Eight minutes isn't very long to get to know somebody."

Chloe mulled this over. "But what about C.J.? You realized that you liked him in eight *seconds*."

Riley giggled. "This is true."

"Hey, I think it's about to start," Chloe whispered.

Manuelo twisted around and gave them a weak smile.

Chloe gave him the thumbs-up sign. "Just be yourself," she said.

"Yeah," Riley seconded. "You're going to be fine."

But the hour got off to a rough start with Sharon, an efficiency expert who wore her hair in a severe bun that pulled at her face. She never cracked a smile, not even at Manuelo's funniest jokes!

Chloe and Riley had worked out a secret signal with him in advance. If they tugged on their earlobes, it meant DANGER! STAY AWAY. MOVE ON TO THE NEXT ONE.

Greta came next, a female wrestler who towered over Manuelo and probably had a good fifty pounds on him. She was followed by Barbie, an aspiring actress whose energy level dropped off the charts when she found out that Manuelo did not have any Hollywood connections.

"If I pull my ear one more time, it's going to fall off!" Riley said.

Chloe was definitely getting worried now. Manuelo was halfway through and there wasn't even a remote possibility yet.

The second wave of potential dates proved no better. Perhaps the worst of all was Louise, an anger management counselor who spent her entire eight minutes screaming about a motorist who had cut her off on the freeway.

Each and every time, Chloe and Riley tugged at their earlobes in almost perfect unison. What were they going to do? There was only one more woman left for Manuelo to meet.

But with Melina their luck took a dramatic turn. She was a chef, too. Not only that, her signature dish was beef Stroganoff! When Manuelo realized that Melina used a hint of fresh nutmeg in her recipe as well, Chloe knew that this was love at first cooking secret!

For the first time all evening, Chloe and Riley winked at Manuelo. That meant "She's a keeper!"

[Chloe: Okay, you're probably thinking, Wow, this has been one successful night. For about five seconds, I thought so, too. I mean, let's review the facts. Mom is resting. Well, technically she's passed out. Dad is all set up to go out with Debbie. Unfortunately, Chuckles will be tagging along, too, but at this point it was a compromise that just had to be made. And Manuelo has found the perfect match. So I should feel amazing, right? Wrong!]

"Houston, we have a problem," Chloe announced.
Riley turned to her in alarm. "What now?"
"Reality check," Chloe said gravely. "Everybody has a date for Save the Seals. Everybody but *us*!"

chapter
twelve

Chloe woke up with a start on Saturday morning. An unsettled feeling washed over her. This whole situation with Lennon was truly getting under her skin.

The urge to jump out of bed and write another "Sound Off" burned deep. Only this time *nothing* would be left to interpretation. That's right! Mr. Duh-I-Don't-Get-It would have no trouble understanding her latest article.

As the morning dragged on though, Chloe thought better of it. Enough games already. Why use the school newspaper to tell Lennon what she should be telling him herself? After all, if there was any hope of their dating exclusively, then they were going to have to learn how to talk to each other.

[Chloe: Okay, before you say to yourself, Wow, Chloe is very mature for her age to think about relationships on such a sophisticated level, I should probably come clean on something. I have no intention of listening to anything he has to say. I mean, really. I've been listening to him all week, and he's offered nothing worthwhile. As if he'll suddenly be as verbal as those kids on *Dawson's Creek*. Basically when Lennon answers my phone call later today, he'd better pull up a chair and get comfortable, because I have a lot to say! And after that, I might as well just ask him to the dance. Forget about romance. I need a date!]

The final heat of the Waverider had just begun, and the beach crackled with energy and excitement. Riley felt like a true surfing insider. C.J. had invited her to watch his teammate, Joey B., go for the top title that morning.

As Riley and C.J. watched from the shore with a group of Australian surfers surrounding them, Riley felt a strange sense of conflicting loyalty. A surfer from Malibu was in the running to win, too. In fact, his scores were neck and neck with Joey B.'s.

C.J. nudged Riley. "It's okay if you want your guy to win, mate."

Riley grinned. "Do you call *everybody* 'mate'?"

C.J. grinned back and winked. "Only people I like," he replied.

Suddenly the crowd went crazy.

C.J. whooped and hollered.

The Australian was riding a killer wave, skating the top of the water like an incredible aqua wonder, leaning in, swaying out. Judging from what Riley could see for

199

herself and the reaction from everyone on the beach, Joey B. would be the man to beat.

When the final scores were announced, C.J.'s teammate had won by a slim margin. Even the hometown crowd screamed their approval and appreciation. It had been a tough competition, and in the end two surfers had given it their all.

C.J. watched as Joey B. engaged in rowdy victory high-fives. "Do you think that'll be me one day?" he asked quietly.

"I have no doubt," Riley said. "Hey, I'd like to treat you to a victory soda at California Dream."

C.J. pretended to be shocked. "This is a total surprise. I was warned that Americans were sore losers," he joked.

Riley playfully shoved the surfer boy who'd had her smiling for the past few days. "Come on. Stop teasing." She laughed.

C.J. got serious all of a sudden. "Maybe I'd like to treat *you* to something."

Riley was intrigued. "Like what?"

C.J. shrugged. "Anything you want. I leave tomorrow, but I'm free tonight."

"Do you like to dance?" Riley asked.

C.J. rocked his body back and forth. "I've got moves you've never seen before."

Riley laughed again. This boy was nothing but fun! "Then be my date for Save the Seals!" She practically shouted the invitation. "It's a big charity dance. We'll have a great time."

C.J. nodded. "I have no doubt about that," he said. "It's a date."

"Logan, get over here!" a fellow Aussie screamed from down the beach.

Riley and C.J. turned to see the entire Australian surfing team cheering and carrying the big winner on their shoulders.

Almost instantly C.J. broke into a sprint to join them. "You go ahead. I'll catch up in a few minutes," he yelled to Riley.

"See you there!" she called out. Giggling, she watched him join the celebration, then turned and headed for California Dream. To her surprise, she discovered Vance sitting at one of the outdoor tables, looking very bummed out.

"Hey," Riley said. "I never expected to see you here today."

Vance glanced up but didn't offer much. Finally he spoke. "I guess you haven't heard."

"Heard what?" Riley asked.

Vance let out a troubled sigh. "The Tribal Council concert got canceled."

Riley couldn't believe it. Right away she felt pulled in two directions. She was thrilled about her date with C.J., but now she had a chance to go with Vance, too. "What happened?"

"The lead singer has nodules on his vocal cords. A doctor here ordered him to take two weeks off." He ran his fingers up and down his soda glass. "I guess I could have gone with you to the Save the Seals benefit dance after all."

For a moment Riley said nothing. Deep down she wished that she hadn't asked C.J. He was a great guy, but he lived in Australia! And Vance was here all the time. "Actually, Vance, I just made plans to go to the dance with someone else."

"Don't worry about it," Vance said. "I'll see you there anyway."

Riley gave him a strange look. "What do you mean? Are you going to the dance?"

"I asked Ariel to go with me," Vance said.

Riley tried to keep her tone in check. "Who's Ariel?" she asked.

"She's the girl who gave my cousin the VIP tickets in the first place. She does street marketing for Tribal Council and goes to Beverly Hills High."

"Oh," Riley mumbled. "How great for her." It was snippy, but Vance didn't seem to notice. She stood there, stunned at the turn of events, trying to sort out her feelings. She should be happy right now. C.J. was amazing, and he was her date for Save the Seals. But something was bugging her big time.

Before Vance asked out Ariel, he didn't know Riley had a date, and the fact that he didn't even bother to find out had her really steamed! As soon as he found out that the concert had been canceled, she should have been the first person he called. He knew how much she wanted to go to the dance.

Vance stared into his empty soda glass, saying nothing.

I guess all he cares about is the canceled concert, Riley thought. Not me.

Chloe picked up the phone, dialed Lennon's number, and then put it back down before it started to ring.

Oh, just do it, Chloe. Make the call, she told herself. After a few deep breaths, she did.

Lennon's answering machine clicked on. "Hi, this is Lennon. You're about to hear a beep. I hope you know what to do. If not, you've got serious issues. These things have been around for decades."

Chloe didn't smile at the funny outgoing message. She was too wound up. Finally the signal to begin blasted in her ear. Yikes! She wasn't quite ready. Oh, well. No time like the present.

"Uh, Lennon...hi, this is Chloe. Chloe Carlson. I just wanted to ask you a question. Do you have a problem? Because I think you have a very serious problem. I suggest that you see a doctor about it immediately. By doctor, I mean psychiatrist. Okay. That's all I have to say."

Chloe slammed down the receiver with a bang. Unfortunately, she didn't feel better. Plus she forgot to ask him to the dance. Ugh! She hated talking into these things. It made her feel stupid.

But she dialed back anyway, waited for the machine to do its thing, and started in again. "Uh, Lennon, Chloe again. On second thought, maybe you don't need to see a doctor. Maybe you need to just look in the mirror and really ask yourself this question: Do you actually believe that I'm buying this playing-dumb act of yours? Apparently you didn't get the memo, but I was *not* born yesterday!"

Chloe slammed down the phone again. She felt a little better this time, but, strangely, she had a vague sense of incompleteness. Gosh! She forgot to ask him out *again*. So she dialed Lennon's number once more. This time she would tell him that she had decided to forgive him and then ask him to the Save the Seals benefit dance.

Beep. "It's me again…Chloe. Listen, I'm not quite finished yet. I—"

Chloe heard a click. Someone had picked up the phone. Lennon had been screening her calls and listening to her rants the whole time! She drew in a deep breath. "Lennon?" she asked softly.

"No, this is Shari, Lennon's sister. Please stop stalking my brother."

Chloe gasped. "No, you don't understand. I—"

"You're too young to be so disturbed," the girl said.

"Wait!" Chloe cried. But Lennon's sister had already hung up. Chloe buried her face in her hands. She was mortified. So mortified that there should be a new word for mortified.

chapter
thirteen

Riley managed to get through her soda date with C.J. without appearing upset, then dashed home, determined to vent in her journal about Vance!

When she got there, Tedi was in the living room, standing on a stool, wearing the same animal print dress she was wearing the other day.

"Hi, sweetie," Tedi said with a laugh. "Don't worry. This isn't a time warp. Just my final fitting for the Model of the Year Awards."

Riley smiled. "You look gorgeous."

"Thank you." Tedi beamed. "Believe it or not, models can't hear that enough. Deep down we're all very insecure, you know."

"Where's Mom?" Riley asked.

"She went to apply some more ointment to her wound," Tedi explained.

Riley gasped. "What wound?"

"She snagged a nasty cut on a coral reef while she was scuba diving this morning. It's nothing serious." Tedi gave Riley a big smile. "Hey, how did things go with the boy?"

Riley sighed heavily. "Which one?" she grumbled.

"Sweetie, you're going to have to bring me up to speed," Tedi said.

Riley filled Tedi in on the turn of events with Vance. "I don't know how to feel," she said. "I mean, part of me is mad at him, but another part of me feels kind of silly for being mad."

Tedi mulled over the facts for a moment. "All right, first things first. Never doubt your feelings. They belong to *you*. And if you're having them, then they're valid. End of story."

"Wow," Riley said. "That's really deep, Tedi."

Tedi waved off the praise. "Oh, none of that's mine. I stole it from a self-help book. Don't ask me which one—probably a mixture of several. I love those things. Anyway, this could mean one of two things. One, Vance didn't put you first and you should just forget about him."

Riley's eyes almost welled up in tears. She didn't want to forget about him.

"Or two," Tedi continued, "and this reason is definitely easier to swallow—Vance has too much respect for you to ask at the last minute. I'm sure he probably assumed that you already had a date and didn't want to put himself through that rejection. The ego of a man!" She shook her head. "Sweetie, the stories I could tell you."

That instantly made Riley feel better. Deep down she knew that Tedi's second reason was how Vance was feeling!

Chloe was on a mission to find Lennon. She wanted to apologize for all her crazy messages and explain that she was just disappointed that he didn't get any of her hints to ask her out. The Newsstand was her first stop. It seemed as good a place to start as any, because Lennon loved to hang out there.

She searched the place up and down. No Lennon. Since she was already there, Chloe ordered an iced tea and sat down at a table to decide where to look next. That's when she encountered Nick Wexler, one of Lennon's regular running buddies.

"Hey, Chloe," Nick said. He was parked at a table close to the counter, completely immersed in a hand-held video game. "What's up?"

"Nothing much," she answered, trying to sound very casual. "I thought you'd be hanging out with Lennon today."

"Nah," Nick said, distracted by the video game. "He's out of town for the weekend."

Chloe practically fell out of her chair. "What did you just say?"

Nick shot her an odd glance. "I said he's out of town. Lennon's got this cool uncle who's an adventure vacation guide. They went on a rafting trip. Lucky guy. I wish *my* uncle did that for a living. Mine manages a Hallmark store in the mall."

At first Chloe couldn't believe what she was hearing, but now everything made perfect sense. Lennon never asked her to the dance because he could never go in the first place!

An enormous wave of relief rolled over her. But it was quickly followed by a wave of dread. Her weird messages were still on Lennon's answering machine. She had to leave another message on his machine, to explain everything!

On second thought Chloe decided against it. She wasn't having much luck with answering machines lately. Especially his.

Instead of writing in her journal, Riley doubled back to California Dream, hoping the whole way that Vance was still there. She had no idea what she was going to say. All she knew was that she wanted to let him know how sorry she was that his big concert plans went bust, and that he would have been her first choice as a date for Save the Seals.

Riley found Vance sitting in the same spot, staring at the same empty soda glass. She felt really bad for him, because she had never seen him so disappointed.

Obviously, the Tribal Council concert had meant a great deal to him.

"Hey, Vance," Riley said, slipping into the chair next to him. "What's up?"

His mood brightened a little. "What are you doing back here?" he asked.

"I didn't get a chance to say how sorry I was that the concert got canceled. I know how much you were looking forward to it."

Vance sighed. "I was. But you know, I just need to get over it. There's nothing I can do about it, right? Sulking all day isn't going to change the lead singer's throat problems."

"Did they at least announce a make-up date for the concert?" Riley wondered, hoping to spin his attention on the future.

"Not yet," Vance said. "But when they do, Ariel's promised us tickets."

The pronoun caught Riley off guard. "Us?" she repeated.

"Yeah," Vance said. "She had only one VIP ticket left for this concert, but I told her that next time I definitely needed two. That is, if you want to go with me. Do you?" he asked.

Riley knew that her own eyes were sparkling. "Of course I do!" Maybe Tedi *was* right! Vance liked her so much that he was thinking about her on his worst day. Now she realized that as cute and sweet and fun as C.J. was, Riley really wanted to take Vance to Save the Seals.

Vance reached out for her hand and squeezed tight. "One more thing. I know you've got a date and everything for Save the Seals tonight, but will you save me a dance?"

"Fast or slow?" Riley asked him. In her heart she wanted a slow dance with Vance.

"A slow dance," Vance said. "Definitely."

chapter
fourteen

The ballroom of the Standard Hotel in Los Angeles was off the hook! The band rocked and the dance floor sizzled.

Chloe moved her hips to the throbbing music. Once again the organizers for Save the Seals had done an awesome job! As it happened, the only person in their household to show up with a date had been Manuelo.

"Look at Manuelo and Melina!" Riley squealed.

Chloe sought them out and finally captured them among the sea of bodies. They were really working it! Those two were incredible on the dance floor.

Chloe and Riley giggled with delight.

For a moment Chloe looked at her sister seriously. "You know, I didn't think you'd be in such a great mood tonight, especially after C.J. had to cancel."

Riley shrugged. "His sponsors had set up a surf clinic that he didn't know about. They paid for his trip here, so he couldn't say no. Besides," she said, shooting a secret glance at Vance across the room, "I don't think a long-distance romance with a boy in Australia is for me, no matter how cute he is!"

"You can say that again!" Chloe cried. Then she beamed a look over to the table where Mom and Dad were sitting. "You know," she said, "they seem to be having a good time just watching everybody."

"Mom couldn't dance if she wanted to," Riley added. "Her feet are too sore from tennis and rock climbing."

"And don't forget about her back," Chloe put in. "It hurts from carrying all that scuba equipment."

"Well," Riley said, "she's better off alone than trying to keep up with Coach Lee. He's way too physical for her."

"Exactly," Chloe agreed. "And I'm so glad that Dad told Debbie that their date was off if she didn't leave Chuckles at home." She observed her parents, who were looking stylish and talking animatedly with another couple. "Yeah," Chloe said, grinning. "Things definitely worked out for the best."

For almost everybody, Chloe thought. After all, she was there with no date and her insane messages were trapped on Lennon's machine. Hopefully, he would get a laugh out of it. She was counting on that.

The pumping dance beat rocked to a finish, and then the soothing sounds of a love ballad filled the room. Chloe spotted Vance making his way across the crowded dance floor, his eyes locked onto Riley.

"Hey, you promised to save me a dance," he said the moment he reached her.

Riley turned to Chloe, who smiled and gave her sister a thumbs-up. Then Chloe heard a faint buzzing in her beaded Hello Kitty evening bag. It was her cell phone.

She scooped it out to see a message waiting. From Lennon! He was actually contacting her from his rafting trip. The text read: ARE YOU FREE NEXT WEEKEND?

Chloe smiled as she worked the keypad to craft the perfect response: SATURDAY SOUNDS PERFECT. The girls at school sure did appreciate those words. Hopefully Lennon would as well. Nervously she waited out his response.

IT'S A DATE, he sent back.

Chloe beamed. This game was over. And the best part of all, she and Riley had scored!

Chloe
and Riley's

SCRAPBOOK

mary-kateandashley
so little time
boy crazy

by Megan Stine

Based on the screenplay by Randi Barnes

HarperCollins*Entertainment*
An imprint of HarperCollins*Publishers*

A PARACHUTE PRESS BOOK

chapter
one

"Tell me it isn't true, Lennon," fourteen-year-old Chloe Carlson said into the phone. She was lying on her bed, talking to her boyfriend, Lennon Porter. "Tell me you don't have to work the entire winter break."

"I don't know," Lennon replied, "but I have to work today. In fact, I'm supposed to be there right now. I'll e-mail you later, okay?"

"Okay." Chloe sighed as she hung up the phone. Lennon worked at the Newsstand, a cool coffee bar and Internet café with computer terminals all over the place.

Sure. E-mail me. Like that's going to do any good! Chloe thought. Just a few minutes ago she'd been reading through her old e-mails from Lennon. They were all the same. She'd write, *Want to go to a movie*? and he'd write back, *Can't. Gotta work tonight.*

There were ten just like that. Eleven, if you counted the e-mail he wrote *from* work. It said, *Chloe. Wish I were anywhere but here—with you.* It was signed, *Lennon the Latte-Meister.*

Why am I complaining? she wondered.

After all, Lennon was by far the smartest and most interesting guy she'd ever dated. He was cute and honest and funny, too. But lately he was winning in the "Best Boyfriend Who's Never Around for a Date" category.

If he works all week, this vacation is going to be the worst, she thought. With another sigh, she hopped off the bed, brushed her long blond hair out of her face, and went downstairs to see what her twin sister, Riley, was doing.

Riley was sitting in the living room with their mother, Macy. The two of them were hunched over a magazine.

"What's up?" Chloe asked, joining them.

"Mom's going nuts about some movie star," Riley answered. "Are you sure he's famous, Mom? I've never heard of him."

Macy Carlson's mouth dropped open. "Are you kidding? He's a major star! I can't believe you've never heard of Jacques D'Oisseau! Are you sure you're my daughter?"

Riley glanced at Chloe and faked a gasp. "Oh, no! Maybe we were switched at birth!"

"Very funny," Macy said, smirking.

Chloe reached for the magazine and stared at a photo of a French actor. He had dark eyes, a classic tan, and wavy silver hair. "What's the big deal about this Jacques guy?"

"He rented the house right down the beach from us," Macy replied. "I saw him move in yesterday."

"Oh." Chloe tossed the magazine back to her mom.

"I can't believe you aren't more excited!" Macy said.

Chloe shrugged. "Sorry, Mom, but we don't speak much French yet. We've only been taking it a few months in school."

"Besides," Riley chimed in, "he's almost as old as Manuelo."

"I heard that!" Manuelo announced from the kitchen in his Spanish accent. Manuelo Del Valle was a full-time housekeeper and cook for the Carlsons. He had been with them forever—from even before Chloe and Riley's parents had separated. He carried a tray of bagels and juice into the living room and set it down.

"You hear *everything*," Chloe teased him. "You must have the biggest ears in the house."

"Believe it," Manuelo joked, pretending to be proud of them. "And by the way, my little lemonade, how dare you say that I'm as old as Jacques D'Oisseau? He is at least five years older. Maybe ten!"

Manuelo snatched the magazine from Macy and stared at the photo. "I can only hope I look that good when I am his age," he declared.

[Chloe: Yawn. Sorry, but I can't get worked up about some old French guy. Even if he IS a movie star. I'm just wondering what I'm going to do now that winter break is here. So far it looks

like it's going to be boring, boring, boring. Now if
you told me that some YOUNG, hot actor moved
into the house next to ours, THAT might be
worth getting pumped about.]

"Did you know that he's shooting a commercial here
in Malibu?" Manuelo went on.

[Chloe: A commercial? Okay, maybe THAT'S
worth getting pumped about.]

"Where?" Chloe asked, perking up.

"At your favorite hang-in," Manuelo said.

"Hang*out*," Chloe corrected him. "You mean the
Newsstand?"

"That's the place," Manuelo said.

Chloe was suddenly interested. "What kind of commercial?"

"It's some kind of coffee thing for the Superbowl,"
Manuelo said. "I read about it in the newspaper. Jacques is
getting too old for leading man roles, so he's going to focus
on directing instead. Including this major commercial."

"Cool! Maybe I can watch them filming!" Chloe
announced.

"I wouldn't mind watching them shoot it, either,"
Riley said. "I mean, we don't have anything better to do
this week."

"Sorry, my little lemonades." Manuelo shook his
head. "The set will probably be closed."

"Maybe Lennon can get us in?" Riley suggested.

"It's worth a try," Manuelo said.

"Yeah," Chloe agreed. "Why not? We've got to do *something* to kick off this winter break."

Riley made a quick phone call to her friend Sierra Pomeroy and arranged to meet her at the Newsstand.

Twenty minutes later she and Chloe pushed open the glass doors to the coffee house. A bunch of little tables and chairs filled the center of the room. Along one wall was a rack of international newspapers. Another wall was lined with computers. And at the back was a small stage for performers.

"Sierra!" Riley called, seeing her friend head into the rest room. Riley hurried to catch up with her. "Wow," she said, checking out the plaid skirt and boring white blouse Sierra was wearing. "Your mom makes you dress like that even for *break*?"

Sierra nodded and shrugged. She pulled off her scrunchie, letting her flaming red hair fall around her shoulders. "Whatever. It'll be all gone in a sec," she said, gesturing at her clothes.

Sierra's real name was Sarah, but only her teachers and her parents called her that. Everyone else knew the truth—that she was leading a double life.

At home she wore conservative clothes, played the violin, and went by the name her parents had given her. But the minute she was off her mother's radar, she

227

changed into totally hip outfits and let down her hair. Then she became the person she wanted to be—Sierra, bass guitar player in a rock band called The Wave.

Riley watched as Sierra balled up the skirt and blouse and stuffed them into her backpack. Quickly she slipped into a pair of mango-colored silk cargo pants and a lime green top.

"This is getting to be a major chore," Sierra said, nodding toward the backpack with the extra clothes. "I'm so over living a double life."

"How come?" Riley was surprised. "I thought you sort of liked the whole drama of it."

Sierra shook her head. "For one thing, look at these pants! They're so wrinkled, it looks as if I've been sleeping in a mummy case."

"Wrinkled is in," Riley argued.

"Maybe." Sierra sighed. "But it's more than that. I'm running out of excuses to tell my mom every time I have to go practice with the band."

Plus it must be weird not being able to tell your parents the truth about anything, Riley thought. She would hate having to lie to her parents all the time.

"Hey," Riley said. "What if you told them?"

"Huh?" Sierra blinked as she applied some black eyeliner.

"I don't know. It's just an idea, but what if you told your parents the whole story?" Riley suggested. "About your band, your name, your taste in wrinkled clothing…"

"Ha-ha. Very funny," Sierra said.

"No, I'm serious," Riley insisted. "Why not? I mean, what have you got to lose?"

"What have I got to lose?" Sierra's eyes opened wide. "Are you kidding? They could make me stop playing guitar altogether."

"That would be bad," Riley admitted. "But what are the chances? Your parents aren't the worst humans on the planet or anything. They're just—"

"Strict? Old-fashioned? Demanding? And totally convinced they know what's best for me?" Sierra said, filling in the gap. "Pick any two."

"Okay, true," Riley said. "But that's *most* parents, right? I mean, give your mom some credit. She was listening to an indie-rock station on the car radio the other day."

"The tuner was broken. It was *stuck* on that station," Sierra explained.

Oh. Too bad, Riley thought. "Well, anyway, your mom's not so awful," she added. "I remember once she actually complimented my hair, and it was totally messy that day. It was back in my 'How many rubber bands can I use in one hairstyle?' phase. What I'm trying to say is, I'll bet you could make her understand why guitar is so important to you—if you'd try."

Sierra looked doubtful. "I'll think about it," she said as they headed back into the café and ordered two mochas. At the last minute Sierra ordered hers to go.

229

"You're not staying?" Riley was surprised.

"I've got band practice," she explained. "I didn't realize how late it was."

Oh. Too bad again, Riley thought. She checked out the Newsstand. The place was packed with people from West Malibu High, which was cool. But was this really how she wanted to spend her break? Just hanging around with the same people she saw every day of the school year?

"Make mine to go, too," she told Lennon, who was scrambling around behind the coffee bar.

"How come?" Sierra asked. "You're coming to band practice? I thought you and Alex were sort of over."

Alex Zimmer was the lead guitar player in The Wave. He and Riley had dated earlier in the year, but that had cooled down.

"No, I'm going to take a walk through town," Riley said. "It's such a beautiful day. I'm thinking, if I do something different, then maybe something different will happen to me."

"Okay. Call me later," Sierra said as the two of them parted at the door.

Riley sipped her mocha and walked through the crowded streets of Malibu. The weather was perfect, and everyone seemed to be in a good mood. Cars cruised through town and every single convertible top was down.

Now *there's* a cool car, Riley thought, spotting a vintage

red Mercedes sports car with white leather seats. Then she realized that the man behind the wheel looked familiar.

Wait a minute, Riley thought. That's him! That's Jacques D'Oisseau!

No wonder Mom and Manuelo were so psyched about him, she realized. In person, the man radiated glamour. He had a white scarf thrown around his neck, which made his wavy silver hair look cool, somehow, instead of just ancient.

How come he's driving so slowly? she wondered.

Jacques had the top down on the Mercedes, and an adorable little fuzzy white poodle hung over the edge of the passenger-side door. The car was going so slowly Riley could walk faster than he drove. He kept craning his neck, looking around as if he were lost or something.

He spotted Riley staring at him. "Hello! Pardon me," he said in his totally charming French accent. He pulled the car to the curb. "Do you know where Dr. Mandleson's office is?"

"The vet?" Riley nodded. "Sure."

Of course she knew where Dr. Mandleson's office was. She and Chloe had been there a bunch of times right after they got their new cocker spaniel, Pepper.

"It's sort of hard to find," Riley explained. "But it's just two blocks away. Go down that street, turn right behind the muffin shop, and you're there." She pointed. "You can park around back."

Jacques tossed up his hands and looked at her pleadingly. "I've been around the block three times!" he said. "And I didn't see it. Could you possibly show me?"

"Sure," Riley said as Jacques hopped out of the car with his puppy. They started walking. "You're Jacques D'Oisseau, aren't you?"

Jacques smiled. "I'm surprised someone your age recognized me," he said, bowing slightly in her direction.

"Oh, I didn't," Riley blurted out. "I mean, I probably wouldn't have recognized you, but my mom showed me your picture. She said you rented a house near us. I'm Riley Carlson."

Jacques laughed, and Riley instantly blushed.

"I am charmed to make your acquaintance, Miss Carlson," Jacques said, smiling and shaking her hand awkwardly across the armful of puppy he was carrying. "Which house is yours?"

"The boxy white one with a lot of glass and a deck facing the water," Riley said.

"That sounds like half the houses on the beach," Jacques replied with a laugh.

Yeah, I guess it does, Riley thought, blushing more. What is it about movie stars that makes you go all tongue-tied?

"Well, I'm sure I will see you on the beach," Jacques said. "And then you can point out your house to me."

"Okay," Riley said as they reached the end of the street. "Here we are." Riley turned into the alley by the muffin shop. "Dr. Mandleson's office is up those stairs."

"Ah!" Jacques said, as if he never would have found it without her. "Merci. You have saved my life."

"No problem," Riley said as Jacques headed toward the office.

"See you back home on the beach!" Jacques called before he climbed the stairs. "Au revoir!"

"Au revoir," Riley called back, grinning to herself. How cool, she thought. I just said good-bye in French! Then she turned to head back up the street—and smacked right into a guy standing behind her. "Oh! Excuse me!" Riley gasped. Then she gasped again when she saw who it was.

Not just any guy. He was tall, almost six feet, and blond and buff. His pale blue T-shirt fit snugly over his muscular chest. It matched his intense, ocean-blue eyes, which were rimmed with dark lashes. And he had dimples so deep, they made him look as if he was always smiling.

Riley's heart raced. Not just because he was cute, but because she recognized *him*, too.

I don't believe it, she thought. That's Marc Hudson! The son of the famous actor Richard Hudson. What is this? Two-for-the-price-of-one celebrity day?

"Hi," Marc said, giving her a totally flirty smile. He stood there staring, as if he knew her or something. As if he thought they should talk.

"Uh, hi," Riley said. Please don't say something stupid! she warned herself.

"You're the third person I've actually *bumped into* today. I always heard Malibu was a small town, but this is ridiculous," he joked.

"Oh, it's a small town," Riley said, "but there's room for one more."

[Riley: Hey. A little cheese never hurt anyone, right?]

Marc smiled. "Wow, I never thought I'd run into someone like you on my first day here."

Someone like me? Riley's heart did a double thud. "This is your first day in Malibu?" she asked, trying to sound calm even though she wanted to scream, "Hey, everybody! Look! I'm flirting with Marc Hudson!!!"

He nodded. "Winter break. I live in New York, but I'm visiting my dad for the week." He glanced at his watch. "Actually, I've got to go, 'cause he's waiting for me."

"Oh." Riley said. She tried not to let her disappointment show.

"Yeah, he needs to lay a major shopping trip on me," Marc went on. "You know, buying me stuff to make up for the fact that we don't live together twenty-four/seven."

"Yeah, you don't want to miss *that*," Riley said.

"Oh, I don't really care about the stuff," he said. "But you've got to take pity on the guy, you know? It would hurt his feelings if I didn't do the bonding thing with him. Anyway, do you want to have coffee with me on Monday?"

Day after tomorrow? Riley was totally psyched. "Sure," she said. "Where?"

"Starbucks on Pearl Street?" He started walking away. "Meet me at two."

"Okay," Riley called. "But wait! You don't even know my name!"

"Oh, I know who you are," Marc said as he climbed onto a seafoam green motorbike that was parked near the curb. "You're Jacques D'Oisseau's daughter, Danielle. By the way, your English is really good!" He started up the engine and put on his helmet.

Wait! Riley wanted to say. That's wrong. I'm *not* Jacques D'Oisseau's daughter! But it was too late. Marc was pulling away.

Besides, she had always wanted to meet Marc Hudson.

And those eyes! How could she resist those eyes?

"A*u revoir*," she called after him with a guilty wave.

chapter
two

"Lennon, name three things you want to do over winter break," Chloe said as she leaned against the counter in the Newsstand. She was hanging out with her boyfriend while he was at work.

"Huh?" Lennon ladled foam onto a cappuccino without looking up.

"And don't say 'make a mocha, a cappuccino, and a half-caff latte," Chloe joked. "I mean, three *fun* things. Like, we could make a fire on the beach, bring a CD player, and listen to nothing but songs with *fire* in the title," Chloe suggested. "Number Two: we could rent a motorbike, and you could teach me how to ride it. And Number Three…"

Her voice trailed off. He's not listening, Chloe thought, staring at his thick brown hair. He's totally wrapped up in making that coffee, and then the next one, and then the next….

"Sorry," Lennon said, glancing up and shooting her a smile. "I've got to do four more of these and then we can talk, okay?"

"Okay," Chloe agreed. "I have something to ask you." She had been waiting for the right moment to ask if he knew anything about the commercial Jacques D'Oisseau was shooting at the Newsstand. But she knew the right moment was *not* while he was making coffees.

Meanwhile, I'll just stand here for the rest of my life, watching him make lattes, Chloe thought. Not that he didn't look adorable doing it!

"Hi, Chloe," Mr. Horner said, passing her on his way to the back room. "You here *again*? Maybe I should put you on the payroll."

Mr. Horner was the manager of the Newsstand. He was a Type-A bald guy with more energy than a birthday party full of sugared-up three-year-olds. He was getting used to seeing Chloe hanging around all the time.

"Maybe you should!" Chloe joked back. At least that way I'd get to hang out with Lennon once in a while, she thought.

When Lennon finished making the four coffees, he started cleaning the espresso machine.

"Lennon, do you think you'll have any time off this week?" Chloe asked, trying not to sound naggy or anything. "Because I don't know whether you've noticed, but I'm spending as much time with Mr. Horner as I am with you."

"I know, I know. I'm sorry," Lennon said. "You've been here so much, I'll bet you know my job almost as well as I do."

"Better," Chloe replied.

"Hey, don't push it," Lennon teased. "You *know* I'm the Latte-Meister."

"Test me!" Chloe demanded, enjoying the chance to have a conversation with him, even if it *was* about making coffee.

"Okay." Lennon glanced up as he emptied espresso grounds into a trash can. "Tell me, how much is a Tall Mochaccino?"

"Two ninety-five," Chloe said. "Three sixteen with tax."

"Very good." Lennon nodded.

"Test me again," Chloe said, loving the challenge.

"Can't," Lennon said. "I've got to go in the back and get some milk and then make two more lattes for the Randersons, who just walked in the door. They never even order anymore. They just shoot me a look that says, 'Here we are. Serve us.'"

"Want me to make them?" Chloe offered. After all, she thought, it would be better than standing around doing nothing.

"I wish," Lennon said. "Wouldn't it be cool if you could get a job here? Then we could hang out all the time."

Chloe slapped her hand on the counter in excitement. "Why not?" she said. "That would be perfect!"

I could use the money, Chloe thought. And a job working with Lennon would be awesome! Besides, if I'm working here, maybe I'll have a chance to watch Jacques D'Oisseau film his commercial!

"Are you serious?" Lennon's face lit up.

"Definitely," Chloe said. She glanced around for the manager. "Mr. Horner just *said* he should put me on the payroll. Maybe he wasn't joking. I'll go ask him."

Lennon held up a finger. "No, wait. His moods can be tricky. Let me ask him when he's not so busy. We've got to time this right."

Fine with me, Chloe thought. And anyway, two of her best friends, Tara and Quinn, had walked in ten minutes ago, and she wanted to talk to them. Chloe wandered over to their table and sat down.

"Hi," Tara said, sounding as bored as Chloe felt.

"Hi," Chloe said. She reached over and stole a piece of the muffin Quinn was eating. "What's up? Anything good?"

"Nada, zero, zilch," Tara said, shaking her head. "You know what the problem with living in Malibu is? When it's time for break, everyone else in the country heads for the beach to kick back and party like it's 1999. But we already *live* at the beach!"

"I know," Chloe said. "What are we supposed to do? Take a road trip to Canada to go curling or something?"

"What's curling?" Quinn frowned, puzzled.

239

"You don't want to know," Tara answered. "It's like shuffleboard on ice with a broom. Believe me, you've got to be seriously desperate for entertainment to even consider it."

"Actually, I think I've got my winter break plans lined up," Chloe said.

"Can I come?" Quinn asked quickly.

Chloe shook her head. "I'm not going anywhere. I'm staying right here and working with Lennon."

"As a coffee waitress?" Tara looked only mildly impressed. "Hey, whatever floats your boat."

"No, really, it's an excellent plan," Chloe explained. "For one thing, I'll get to hang with him constantly. What could be better? Besides, something cool is going to happen here."

"Tell," Tara said.

Chloe leaned forward and lowered her voice. "Have you ever heard of Jacques D'Oisseau?" she asked.

Tara looked blank, but Quinn nodded.

"French actor," Quinn explained to Tara. "My mom is obsessed with him. He was in some famous classic movie called *Tunnel of Rain*. I think he directed it, too. My mom thinks he's a total hottie."

"Right. Well, he rented a house near us and he's going to direct a coffee commercial for the Super Bowl," Chloe explained in a whisper. "And they're shooting it right here at the Newsstand next Saturday. So I'm hoping I can watch them during the filming."

"Seriously? Now *that* would be way cool," Tara admitted. "In fact, you should totally audition for a part!"

"Oh, no way," Chloe said. "I've heard the set is going to be closed."

"So what?" Tara urged her. "You'll already be *inside*, working here! With your charm, you could talk this Jacques guy into an audition for sure!"

"Have you met him yet?" Quinn asked. "My mom will be so jealous."

Chloe started to shake her head, but just then Lennon hurried over.

"Okay, you've got the job," he said, looking happy and wiping his hands on his apron. "Mr. Horner said you can start Monday."

"Cool!" Chloe jumped up and threw her arms around Lennon's neck. "Thank you, thank you!"

Lennon wrapped his arms around her waist and squeezed. "Hey, don't thank me," he whispered into her ear. "It's going to be awesome seeing you all the time."

Chloe beamed. She couldn't believe she was going to get *paid* to hang with her honey! And with any luck, she might even get a part in a Superbowl commercial! Tara was right. She could probably charm her way into an audition at least.

It looked as if winter break wasn't going to be so boring after all!

chapter three

"**C**hloe, what if he only asked me out because he thought I was famous? Because he thought I was Danielle D'Oisseau?" Riley worried out loud the next morning.

She and Chloe were sitting out on the deck of their house, eating a breakfast of yogurt and fruit.

"No way," Chloe said. "For one thing, I've never heard of her, so you're not *that* famous."

"I'm famous enough!" Riley argued. "My dad's a major French movie star!"

"*Your* dad lives in a trailer down the beach," Chloe reminded her.

[Riley: Oops. Right. Ever since our parents separated, Dad's been living the life of a beach bum. You know, relaxing, doing his own thing. He used to run a fashion business with our mom, but he decided it wasn't for him.]

"But that's only because he's trying to find himself, or something," Riley said. "You know Dad. He's searching for his inner granola. He *could* live in a house like ours if he wanted to."

Chloe nodded. "My point is, Jacques D'Oisseau is *not* your dad, and you've got to tell Marc Hudson the truth."

"Absolutely," Riley said firmly. "Except, what if...I mean, if he..."

"Don't stress," Chloe said. "I'm sure he asked you out because he thought you were cute. Not just because you're Jacques D'Oisseau's daughter."

"Yeah," Riley agreed, glancing at her reflection in the sliding glass doors that led to the deck.

[Riley: Okay, so I have bed-head right now, my eyes are kind of puffy, and my pink pajama top doesn't exactly match my red-and-blue-plaid pajama bottoms. But I'm going to do laundry today—I swear! By the time I see Marc tomorrow, I'll have it together.]

"It is weird, though," Chloe said as she popped a piece of pineapple into her mouth. "I mean, what made him think you were Danielle D'Oisseau?"

"Maybe I look like her," Riley said. "Wouldn't that be cool?"

"Not likely," Chloe said. "Jacques is tall and very European-looking, right?"

"True," Riley admitted. Riley and Chloe both had blond hair, big eyes, perfect teeth, and full lips. They looked as if they should have *Grown in California* stamped on their cheeks.

"So why *did* Marc think you were Jacques's daughter?" Chloe asked.

"I don't know," Riley said. "He probably heard me saying good-bye to Jacques."

"By the way, have you seen Jacques since then?" Chloe asked. "Because I have the most amazing idea. I'm thinking of asking him for an audition for his commercial!"

"Seriously?" Riley's eyes lit up.

Chloe nodded. "It was Tara's idea. She said since I'll be working at the Newsstand already, I should give it a shot. I was hoping maybe you could introduce me to Jacques, though."

"I haven't seen him since we met on the street," Riley said. Then she was quiet for a moment. "I wonder what she looks like."

"Who?" Chloe asked.

"Danielle," Riley said. "I mean, I wonder if I could possibly pass for her."

"You don't *want* to, do you?" Chloe asked.

Riley shrugged. "I don't know. I'm just curious."

"Well, there's one way to find out!" Chloe said, jumping up. "Come on."

A minute later the two of them were huddled over Chloe's computer in their bedroom. Chloe logged on to the Internet and did a search on Danielle D'Oisseau's name. A zillion Websites came up, but they were all about Jacques.

"It says here that Jacques's kids grew up in Europe, but they were kept out of the limelight," Chloe reported. "I can't find a single site with a picture of his kids."

"How old are they now?" Riley wondered aloud.

Chloe clicked down the screen to a biography section. "Danielle is fourteen," she reported. "And she has a half brother who's twenty."

"She's my age!" Riley said brightly.

"Down, girl," Chloe said. She clicked on to another window. "It says here that Danielle was born during a brief marriage between Jacques D'Oisseau and Faye Huntington."

Faye Huntington? Everyone knew who she was: a superfamous American actress who had dark hair and emerald-colored eyes. Her trademark was a beauty mark on her cheek, and she always wore her hair swept up in a French twist.

Riley grabbed her hair and pushed it up behind her head. "What do you think? Do I look like her?"

"No!" Chloe said. "Don't even go there!"

"Yeah. I guess it *is* pretty lame," Riley admitted. She let her hair fall back down. "I'm just nervous about this date. It's going to be so hard to say, 'Hi, Marc. I realize you're the son of a gorgeous, famous movie star, but I'm just plain old Riley Carlson.'"

"Maybe you should throw in *poor little* plain old Riley Carlson. You know, really *sell* yourself," Chloe teased.

Riley would have laughed, but she was busy right then. She picked up an eyebrow pencil and used it to make a small beauty mark on her cheek.

"I told you, don't go there!" Chloe said when she saw what Riley was doing. "Stick to the truth!"

"Right," Riley said, dropping the pencil. After all, that's what she'd been telling Sierra to do.

I guess I'd better take my own advice! Riley decided. She rubbed off the beauty mark, changed into a pair of cute blue Capri pants and a small white camisole, and called Sierra.

"You want to hang out?" Riley asked.

"Definitely," Sierra said. "I'll come over."

Half an hour later Sierra arrived in a pair of preppy khaki slacks and a pink polo shirt. It took her under two minutes to change into low-rise black jeans and a royal blue tank top.

Then Riley grabbed the dog's leash and they took the Carlsons's brown and white cocker spaniel, Pepper, for a walk on the beach.

For the first ten minutes Riley grilled Sierra for ideas about what to wear on her date with Marc tomorrow. Sierra thought black leather pants would make a sophisticated statement, but Riley pointed out that the weather was too warm for leather.

"I'd be sweating like a pig," Riley said. "And then the

leather would stick to my thighs and…forget it. The whole thing is too ugly to discuss."

They finally settled on Riley's cream sweater and brown jeans.

"So did you tell your parents about your band?" Riley asked as they trudged through the sand.

"Are you kidding?" Sierra shot Riley a look.

"No," Riley said. "I thought you were going to consider coming clean with them."

"Well, I did, and I decided against it," Sierra replied. "My parents are hopeless. They wouldn't get it. Listen, guess who just wrote a new song? Marta! Can you believe it?"

Marta was the keyboard player in Sierra's band, but she missed a lot of rehearsals. Riley got the feeling Marta didn't take The Wave as seriously as the rest of its members did.

"Really? Is it any good?" Riley asked.

"It's fabulous!" Sierra said. "It's called 'Random Access Misery.' The lyrics are amazing and the melody is awesome. There's only one problem."

"She wants to sing it?" Riley guessed.

Sierra nodded.

The two of them burst out laughing.

"She really can't hear herself!" Sierra said, jumping to avoid Pepper, who was getting tangled up in the leash. "She thinks she's on key, and no one wants to tell her she's not."

"Well, duh," Riley said. "I wouldn't want to be the one to say, 'Oh, by the way, you sound like a porpoise with laryngitis when you sing.'"

[Riley: Now before you jump all over me for being so heartless about Marta's voice, let me clear up one thing. Those are not my words. I'm just quoting what Mrs. Henry, our third-grade teacher, used to say when Marta sang "The Star-Spangled Banner." Me, personally? I thought Marta sounded more like a Chihuahua choking on a dog biscuit.]

"And it's weird, because she's a great keyboard player," Sierra went on. "It's not as if she isn't musical or anything."

"So what are you going to do?" Riley asked.

Sierra started to answer, but just then Pepper pulled away, making Riley drop the leash.

"Pepper!" Riley called. "Hold on!" She ran to catch up with her dog, but Pepper was already racing toward a fluffy white puppy on the deck of a nearby house. The puppy was on a leash, but the leash was loosely looped over a post.

Hey, Riley thought as she ran to catch Pepper. That's Jacques D'Oisseau's house! The house her mother said he'd rented.

Then she recognized the dog—the same cute little white fuzzball Jacques had taken to the vet.

All at once the puppy got loose and ran down the

248

steps to the beach. It scurried across the sand, romping and playing with Pepper, who began chasing it.

"Pepper! Stay!" Riley called, running and finally catching up with the dogs.

She took Pepper's leash and handed it to Sierra, who was standing nearby. Then she grabbed the poodle's leash and scooped the little dog up into her arms.

"This is Jacques D'Oisseau's dog," Riley explained to Sierra. "Wait here," she said, hurrying to return the poodle. "I'll be right back." She ran up the steps of Jacques's house and knocked on the sliding glass door.

A moment later he appeared and slid it open. "Ooh-la-la, she got away again?" He reached for the poodle. "Chaudette, you bad dog! Thank you for bringing her back," he said, looking up. "Oh! It's you! Hello again, Riley Carlson. You keep rescuing me and my dog!" Jacques reached out to shake Riley's hand.

"No problem," Riley said. "She's so cute. What's her name again?"

"Chaudette," Jacques said, pronouncing it like *show-dett*. "It means little bundle of warmth." He smiled and hugged the dog.

Riley could see why he was a big movie star. His smile lit up his whole face.

"Well, thank you again for bringing her back," Jacques said. "If you see her get loose again, please just open this glass door and put her inside. This door is like your 7-Eleven stores—always open."

249

"Okay," Riley said, laughing. "I will."

Jacques closed the door, and Riley hurried back to Sierra. Wow, she thought. He's so nice! Wouldn't it be cool if I *were* part of his life?

For half a second she thought again about pretending to be Jacques's daughter in front of Marc Hudson. Why not? It would be for one lousy date. Or two. Marc was only in Malibu for the winter break. He'd be going back to New York at the end of the week, right? He'd never have to know the truth.

> [<u>Riley</u>: Okay, so that was a weak moment. What can I say? Besides, you shouldn't judge me until you've walked in my shoes. And by the way, they're size 6½. So if you find a cute pair that goes with these pants, call me, okay?]

Who am I kidding? Riley thought. I just got done lecturing Sierra about leading a double life. So I definitely can't start doing it myself! She had to tell Marc the truth.

And if he doesn't like me anymore and never asks me out again? she thought, trying to prepare for the worst. I'll deal.

But in her heart she was really hoping that wouldn't happen.

chapter
four

"**W**ow," Lennon said, eyeing Chloe the next day at the Newsstand. "You look awesome in that Newsstand T-shirt."

"Really?" Chloe ducked, to try to catch her reflection in the glass of the pastry case.

"But then, you look great in everything you wear," Lennon added. "Except cinnamon. Come here. You got some on your nose." He reached up and brushed it off for her.

Chloe beamed and pulled back her hair, twisting it into a knot on top of her head. This is so awesome! she thought. I can't believe we're allowed to spend the whole day together—and I don't even have to apologize to Mr. Horner!

"I filled the cinnamon container and the milk and creamer things," Chloe said.

"I can see that," Lennon said, staring at a big

251

splotch of milk on her black apron. "Who knew you were such a klutz?"

"I'm *not* a klutz!" Chloe smiled. She loved the way he was making fun of her because she knew he didn't really mean it. "That milk container is heavy, that's all. Anyway, what do I do next, boss?"

"Next I teach you how to make espresso," Lennon said, taking her by the hand and leading her to the machine.

Chloe's heart skipped a beat when he touched her hand. They had been going out for six weeks, but she still got a rush whenever his arm brushed hers.

Cammie, a short girl with curly brown hair who also worked at the Newsstand, was busy making espresso for two customers. Lennon and Chloe stood watching, waiting their turn at the machine.

"Can I ask you something?" Chloe said as they waited.

"What?" Lennon asked.

"You know about the coffee commercial Jacques D'Oisseau is shooting, right?" Chloe asked. "Well, Tara said maybe I should try to audition for a part."

"Yeah, you should ask him," Lennon agreed. "I hear the auditions are on Thursday."

Thursday? Today was Monday, so the auditions were only a few days away.

"He comes in here every morning at around nine," Lennon added.

Chloe shot a glance at the clock. Too bad she was

working the afternoon shift. She'd have to be sure to get to work early tomorrow.

"Lennon?" Mr. Horner called from the back. He gestured toward some messy tables in the café. "Could you tear yourself away long enough to clean up tables three and four?"

"Oh. Sorry," Lennon said, dashing off. "Uh, Cammie can show you how to make espresso," he called to Chloe.

Chloe's heart sank. It would be more fun if *he* could teach me, she thought.

Cammie ran through the instructions quickly, explaining what went into each kind of drink. "The whole thing's pretty easy and obvious," she said when they were done. "So I'll take the orders, and you can make the hot beverages."

Whoa. Just like that? Don't I get to practice for a few days or something?

Nope. Guess not, Chloe realized when Cammie called out the first three orders.

"Regular coffee, tall cappuccino, and a grande mocha, but light on the chocolate," Cammie said.

Chloe made all three drinks and set them on a tray. She carried them out to table seven, where the customers were waiting.

"Hey, Peaches," Lennon said, calling Chloe by a nickname he had started using. "Nice job serving those drinks."

[Chloe: Wait! Before you get the wrong idea, let me explain. I mean, seriously. Peaches? The thing is, Lennon has a cousin called Peaches, and we were talking about it last week—about how we both think it's, like, the corniest nickname in the world. So then he started calling me Peaches, just to be funny. And I laughed every time. So of course he kept it up.]

"Thanks, Sugar-face," Chloe said, joking back.

[Chloe: That's the other part of the routine. He calls me Peaches, and then I come back with some really icky pet name for him. But I use a different one each time.]

"Gag me," Lennon said.

Chloe laughed. "I win!" she announced, happy.

"Excuse me," the man at table seven said, interrupting them. "But you put chocolate in my coffee."

"And there's no chocolate in this mocha," the woman with him added.

Uh-oh. Chloe felt her stomach tighten. How did I mess up that? she wondered.

"What's the problem here?" Mr. Horner asked, appearing from behind the counter.

"Our drinks are all wrong," the man at the table said.

Mr. Horner scowled at Chloe. "This job isn't so hard," he said to her. "You simply have to make coffee, and make it right. That's all I ask."

"Sorry," Chloe apologized, feeling her face turning red.

"Don't worry, Mr. Horner." Lennon scooped up the drinks. "I'll fix it pronto. Don't hold this against Chloe. It's only her first day."

"I won't hold it against her," Mr. Horner said briskly. "I'll hold it against you. You recommended her."

Lennon hurried back to the counter and Chloe followed him.

"Thanks, Lennon," she said softly.

"No problem, Peaches," he whispered, giving her a smile. "Just try not to goof up again. It's the one thing Mr. Horner gets cranky about. You've got to concentrate when you're making the drinks."

Chloe nodded. "Don't worry. I will."

"Did you get those last two?" Cammie called from the register.

"Huh?" Chloe glanced over and realized there was a long line of people waiting to be served. "Uh, no. Can you repeat them?"

Cammie sighed and called out the orders again, and Chloe got to work.

Who knew your hands would get so tired from squeezing this espresso thing over and over? Chloe thought after she'd made about seven of them. She glanced at the clock. It was only one-fifty. She hadn't even been there an hour.

"Chloe! Hi!" a voice called from a few feet in front of the counter. "What are you doing back *there*?"

Chloe glanced up just as she was putting a double latte onto the counter for a customer. "Amanda! Hi!" she called back, seeing her friend Amanda Gray.

Just then the double latte tipped off the counter— toward the customer who was waiting for it. It splattered all over the floor.

"Whoa!" the woman cried out. She was wearing an expensive-looking business suit and heels, but she managed to jump back just in time.

Oh, no! Chloe raced out from behind the counter to clean up the mess. "Did it spill on you?" she asked the woman.

"Almost." The woman brushed at her skirt. "I felt a few drops splash my legs, but I guess I'm all right."

This is a nightmare! Chloe thought. I can't seem to do anything right!

Lennon rushed over and started helping Chloe clean up, mopping the spill with paper towels. "Don't worry. Everyone drops one the first week they work here," he said.

He's being so nice! Chloe thought. She glanced up and saw Amanda watching her with a worried look on her face.

Amanda was another one of Chloe's good friends from school. She had been very quiet and shy when Chloe first met her, but lately she'd begun to come out of her shell.

She waited until Chloe finished cleaning up and

was making a new double latte for the woman. Then she came up to the counter.

"Whoa. Rough day," Amanda said. "I didn't even know you were working here."

"I just started," Chloe explained. Then she lowered her voice. "I thought it was going to be great being near Lennon all day. And it is. But I didn't think working at a coffee house would be so hard."

Amanda nodded. "Tell me about it."

"You want something?" Chloe asked. "I'll be your friend forever if you don't order anything hot."

Amanda laughed. "Okay, give me an iced chai," she said.

"Thank you!" Chloe said, getting to work.

By the time she brought the chai to Amanda, the café had cleared out. So Chloe sat to talk for a minute. "Did you hear about Riley?" she asked, leaning in to share the great news. "She ran into Marc Hudson—you know, Richard Hudson's son—and he asked her out! She's probably with him right now."

"That's cool," Amanda said with a shrug.

That's typical of Amanda, Chloe thought. She wasn't impressed just because someone was a celebrity. That's what Chloe liked about her. Amanda was so real and down to earth.

"And the other really amazing news is that they're shooting a commercial here at the Newsstand on Saturday," Chloe went on. "I'm hoping I can worm my way into it. Lennon says the auditions are on Thursday."

"How about auditioning for the part of coffee waitress right *now*?" came a grouchy voice from behind Chloe.

Chloe whirled around and saw Mr. Horner standing there with his hands on his hips. She jumped up. "Oh, sorry," she said, hurrying back to work. I guess there are *two* things that make him cranky! she thought.

For the next few hours Chloe tried to get the orders right. And she tried not to spill anything on anyone. And she tried not to spend too much time talking to Amanda, Tara, and Quinn, who all came into the Newsstand.

But it was hard—especially the last one. Her friends kept talking to her every time she brought a coffee out to one of the other customers.

By the end of the day Chloe was so tired, she just wanted to lie down in a hot tub and never get up. Maybe this was a mistake, she thought. Maybe working at the Newsstand *wasn't* the best possible way to spend winter break.

"Hey, Peaches," Lennon said as they were closing up that night. "You want to catch a movie?"

Chloe looked at him as if he were nuts. "I'm wiped. I'm going straight home to bed."

"Wow," Lennon said. "You *are* tired. You didn't even call me a sickening nickname."

Chloe didn't answer. She was too tired to think of a snappy comeback, too tired to even speak!

"Okay, well, I'll see you tomorrow morning," Lennon said. "Mr. Horner wants you on the early shift this time, so we'll open up together. Be here at six."

Six in the morning? Chloe's eyes popped open. Was he kidding? She stared at Lennon, waiting for him to laugh.

But he was serious.

chapter
five

Riley checked her reflection in the glass door before she entered Starbucks.

I've got to look good, she thought nervously. Majorly good. Good enough to make up for the fact that I'm not French, not famous, and not the daughter of Jacques D'Oisseau.

In her low-rise brown jeans and cream sweater, Riley thought she'd probably pulled it off. The outfit was totally cute and her hair had been in a good mood that morning. It fell perfectly around her face.

"Hi there," Marc said, standing up the moment he saw her.

Good manners! Riley loved that.

Marc was wearing a white T-shirt under an unbuttoned black cotton shirt. And black jeans. Plus he wore a small woven leather necklace with a turquoise bead on it—just like the one Riley was wearing.

"Hi," Riley said, tilting her head so that her hair swung back and forth a little.

"Great necklace," Marc said, shooting her a smile the instant he noticed it.

"Thanks," Riley said with a grin. "It's my fave because no one else has one like it."

Marc laughed and picked up the cup of coffee on the table. "I got here early," he explained. "Needed a double espresso big-time. What can I get you?"

"Just a regular coffee," Riley said.

Marc went to the counter and got her coffee. Then he sat down, leaned forward, and said, "Okay, tell me everything about you."

[**Riley: Everything about me? You mean, like starting with the fact that my name is really Riley Carlson, not Danielle D'Oisseau? And that I'm totally lying about who I am?**]

Riley tried to think of how to word it, but her throat closed up and her mind went blank. "No, you go first," she said finally.

Marc nodded. "Okay."

Quickly he told her that he was an only child. That he'd grown up in New York City. That he was now a junior at a private school there. And that he loved movies. "Besides that, I love the beach."

"I do, too!" Riley said.

"And hip-hop music, especially Master Crush," Marc

went on. "And I'm a total zombie in the morning. And that's everything you need to know about me."

"That's incredible," Riley said.

"How come?" Marc asked.

"Well, I *adore* the beach," Riley said. "And I'm a complete maniac about Master Crush. And I'm really cranky if I don't get enough sleep."

"Wow. It's as if you're my twin or something," Marc said, grinning.

Riley almost burst out laughing. You have no idea how funny that is! she thought. She had to bite her tongue to keep from saying, "I already have a twin! My sister, Chloe!"

"Okay, here's a question," Riley said. "If you could have gone anywhere for winter break, where would it be?"

"That's easy," Marc said, smiling. "Malibu."

"Really?" Riley felt her face glowing.

Marc nodded. "For one thing, Malibu has some amazing people." He grinned at her even more. "And my dad really wanted me to come out here. He's trying to get me to spend more time with him."

"That's nice," Riley said.

Wow. He's so easy to talk to, she thought. She was having such a great time, she hated to spoil the mood by saying 'Oh, by the way, I'm not who you think I am." But she had to tell him...soon.

"You want to go hang out at the beach?" Marc asked.

"Sure." Riley took one last sip of her coffee.

They headed to the beach, and as they walked past her house, Riley tried not to glance up at the deck. What if Manuelo sees me? she thought. He might call me by my real name. She turned her back to the house and strolled down to the water.

"Want to skip stones?" Marc asked. "I'm a pro."

"Hey, you're talking to a stone-skipping champ," Riley shot back. "You don't want to mess with me."

"Bring it on!" Marc bent down to pick up a pebble.

Riley found a thin flat rock. She turned sideways to the water and flicked her stone. It skipped across the waves in three perfect arcs.

Marc stared for a minute. "Okay. That was good," he admitted. He cleared his throat and walked a few steps. Then he bent his knees and flicked his wrist, sending the rock skipping. It went farther than Riley's, but it only skipped twice.

"I'd give that an eight," Riley teased him.

"No way!" Marc complained. "That thing landed in Japan!"

They both laughed and continued walking down the beach.

"So anyway, Danielle, what's the deal with the commercial your dad is shooting?" Marc asked. "Are you totally pumped about it?"

"Well, uh…" Riley sputtered. Tell him now, she thought. Just say it. He's *not* my dad. He's just the guy who rented a house down the beach from us.

But she was having so much fun, she didn't want to spoil the mood. Besides, Marc didn't wait for an answer. He kept rambling on about how much he loved Jacques's movie, *Tunnel of Rain*. How he had seen it shown as a classic re-release at the Cannes Film Festival in Nice last year. And how he was hoping to hang out at the commercial shoot later this week.

Riley glanced up. They were approaching Jacques's beach house.

"I am so into your dad's career," Marc said. "I mean, I've heard that this commercial he's directing is going to be really cool. People say it's going to be shot in black-and-white, right? Sort of like an old detective movie from the 1940s."

Riley swallowed hard and took a deep breath. "To tell you the truth, he's not my dad," she said.

Marc tilted his head. "Huh?"

"You made a mistake," Riley said. "My name is Riley Carlson, not Danielle D'Oisseau. I'm not Jacques's daughter."

"Are you serious?" Marc looked shocked. And maybe disappointed. Riley couldn't tell.

"Yeah," Riley said. "It was a mistake. I…" She was about to explain the whole thing to him. But as they neared the house, Jacques's little white poodle ran down the steps and onto the sand.

"Chaudette!" Riley called, running to catch the puppy. "Chaudette! Come back!"

The puppy stopped when she heard Riley shouting her name. Then she turned and raced to Riley.

"Sorry," Riley said to Marc. "Hang on a minute. I've got to put her inside."

Riley hurried up the steps of Jacques's house. Marc followed her as she opened the sliding glass door a few inches and put the puppy inside.

"Now you stay where you belong, understand?" Riley said. She closed the door and turned to see Marc standing beside her.

He gazed in through the glass door toward the fireplace mantel. Sitting right there, on top, was a Golden Globe award.

Marc smiled. "Don't tell me you're not Danielle D'Oisseau," he said. "That Golden Globe was for *Tunnel of Rain*, the film your parents starred in and your dad directed."

"They're not my parents!" Riley said. "Honestly! I'm just a girl from Malibu who lives down the beach."

Marc shook his head slowly, grinning the whole time. "You don't have to lie to me," he said. "I know what it's like being a famous person's kid. Once people find out, they try to use you, and it ruins everything. Believe me, I've been there."

Riley tried to interrupt him, but Marc didn't want to hear it. He was sure she was Danielle D'Oisseau.

"Don't worry, your secret is safe with me," he said. "People like us have to stick together. That's why I only hang out with people connected to show business. Other people just don't understand."

What? Riley froze. He only hangs out with people connected to show business? Does that mean he'd dump me if I made him face the truth?

For half a second Riley was going to blurt it all out anyway. How he had mistaken her for Danielle D'Oisseau when she was leading Jacques to the vet.

But she couldn't do it. Not if it meant Marc would walk away. They were having so much fun together! She didn't want it to end. Maybe if he got to know her, he'd start to like her for herself. She could always tell him the truth later, right?

"Yeah, okay," Riley said with a shrug. "But don't tell anyone who I am. I'm trying to keep a low profile."

"No problem." Marc nodded. "I'm all about keeping a low profile myself. So do you want to go out again?"

Huh? Is this date over? Riley wondered. Then she realized he thought he'd dropped her off at home! He was ready to be on his way.

"Uh, sure!" Riley said.

"How about catching *Les Enfants Verts* at the Pepperdine campus Wednesday night? I saw a sign posted in town. It's open to the public, and it's supposed to be a really funny film," he said. "Unless you've already seen it."

It's obviously a French film, Riley said to herself. And judging from the way Marc said the title—with a perfect French accent—he must speak French really well.

"I haven't seen it yet," Riley said. "It sounds great."

"Excellent," Marc said. "They're showing it without subtitles, which will be awesome. I hate how the subtitles get in the way, don't you?"

No subtitles? Yikes! You mean I've got to sit through an entire French movie without understanding more than three words?

"Yeah, great," Riley said, trying to sound enthusiastic instead of morose.

"So I'll meet you Wednesday night at seven," Marc said as he walked toward the deck steps.

"See you then," Riley called, still standing by Jacques's back door.

When Marc was gone, she headed toward her own house.

What have I gotten myself into? she wondered.

Well, at least she had a plan. She'd tell him the truth when he knew her better. When he liked her for herself.

But for now there was only one choice.

She had to pretend to be French!

chapter
six

"**C**hloe! I told you yesterday, no amaretto syrup in the hot-milk container!" Lennon said.

"Oh. Sorry!" Chloe shot Lennon a cute but guilty smile. "I forgot."

Lennon sighed and shook his head. "Well, it's your third day on the job," he grumbled. "Try to remember next time. I just made three lattes that tasted like almonds."

Uh-oh, Chloe thought. That was bad. Lennon *had* told her on her second day to be careful about the almond syrup because some people were allergic to nuts.

She gulped, feeling even more guilty. Still, she couldn't believe he was being so grumpy.

[Chloe: Honestly, I have never seen Lennon in such a bad mood. Of course, I've never spent three whole days with him, either. Especially three days when I've made so many dumb mistakes in a row. Yesterday was the worst. I accidentally spilled a huge bag of coffee beans all over the floor. Mr. Horner said it was a fifty-dollar loss. And Lennon took the blame, even though it was my fault. He was really nice about it, saying, "Don't worry, you'll learn. Those bags are heavy." But that was yesterday. Today he looks like he's ready to toss me into the coffee grinder!]

"What's the problem here?" Mr. Horner asked, looking over Lennon's shoulder.

"Oh, no problem," Lennon said quickly. "I've got everything under control."

"I hope so," Mr. Horner said. He glanced at Chloe and walked away.

Yikes! Chloe thought. Mr. Horner was breathing down their necks already, and it was only eight-thirty in the morning! She waited for the manager to slip into the back room. Then she whispered to Lennon. "Do you want me to apologize to the customers personally?"

"It might help," Lennon admitted. "Go out there and do damage control. I'll remake their drinks and put them up on the counter. When they're ready, you can serve them."

Good deal, Chloe thought. Damage control was something she could do! She wiped her hands on her apron, tossed her hair over her shoulders, and walked up to the group of three women who were waiting for their coffees. They looked like tourists.

"Listen, I'm really sorry about the coffees," she said. "It was totally my fault. But we're getting it fixed right now, okay? I'm new on the job," she added, hoping that would help.

"Fine," one of the women said briskly, as if she didn't want to be interrupted.

Chloe glanced back at the counter. Lennon still didn't have the new drinks ready. And Tara and Quinn had just walked in. "Hi!" she said, thrilled to see some friendly faces. "What's up?"

"Not much," Tara replied. "Except there's a huge sale at Smirmen's. All the bathing suits are fifty percent off. You want to come?"

"I can't," Chloe moaned. "I'm working another long shift."

"I told you this was a lousy way to spend the break," Tara said.

"So what happened with Riley's date the other day?" Quinn asked. "Did she and Marc Hudson hit it off?"

Hmm, Chloe thought. Maybe she shouldn't tell them that Riley was pretending to be French. Tara and Quinn were good friends, but they weren't so great at keeping secrets.

"They totally hit it off," Chloe said. "They're going out again tonight, I think. You guys want something to drink?"

"No, we just came in to talk," Tara admitted.

"And to find out if you're going to be in that commercial," Quinn said. "My mom was so jealous when I told her."

Chloe shrugged and leaned against one of the tables. "I don't have an audition lined up yet. Jacques came in yesterday morning at nine, but I was too nervous to talk to him. I ran and hid behind the pastry case!"

"No way!" Tara said. "Well, you've *got* to talk to him today. The auditions are tomorrow, right?"

Chloe nodded. "He should be here soon." She checked the clock. "He comes in every day at nine and orders coffee, a croissant, and a copy of *Le Monde*."

"What's *Le Monde*?" Quinn asked.

"A French newspaper," Chloe replied.

Tara started to nod, but then she glanced at something behind Chloe's shoulder. "Oops. Maybe we'd better get going."

"Why?" Chloe whirled around and saw Lennon standing beside her with a scowl.

"Can we talk?" he said sharply. He didn't wait for an answer. He motioned for her to follow him into the back room.

"Uh, see you later," Chloe called to her friends as she followed Lennon.

"Look," Lennon said when they were alone. "You can't spend all morning talking to your friends. Those three coffees I made for the tourists were just sitting there on the counter, getting cold!"

"Oh, gosh, sorry!" Chloe covered her mouth. "I

looked and I didn't think you had them ready yet."

Lennon gave her a seriously worried stare. "Listen, I know you're trying, but Mr. Horner is starting to lose patience. He took me aside a few minutes ago and basically laid it out."

"Laid what out?" Chloe asked.

"He said, 'You recommended her, so it's on your head if she messes up. Teach her how to do the job or fire her.'"

"Are you kidding?" Chloe gasped. "It's only my third day!"

Lennon's shoulders slumped. "I know, I know, but you can't make any more mistakes, okay?"

"I won't," Chloe promised.

But even if I do, you wouldn't really fire me, would you? she wanted to say, but she didn't.

He was her *boyfriend*, Chloe decided. No way would he fire her. Not when he knew how much she wanted to watch the commercial being filmed—and maybe get an audition with Jacques D'Oisseau.

Chloe headed out to the coffee bar and took an order. A few minutes later Jacques walked in. He ordered his usual, then sat down. Now's my chance! Chloe thought, glancing around and wondering where Mr. Horner was. Lennon and Mr. Horner had both disappeared.

Okay, Chloe thought as she made Jacques's coffee. I probably shouldn't leave the counter right now, but there are no other customers waiting. And this will only take a minute....

She slipped out from behind the counter and walked to Jacques's table. "Good morning," she said, setting the coffee down beside his newspaper. "Um, you're Monsieur D'Oisseau, aren't you?"

"*Oui*," he answered, not looking up from his paper.

"Um, well, may I ask you something?" Chloe said.

"Chloe!" Lennon called sharply from across the room. "What are you doing? We need you back here!"

Okay! Chloe thought. But can't it wait a second?

She couldn't believe Lennon was calling her right at that moment. He *knew* how important it was to her to talk to Jacques D'Oisseau.

And if I don't ask him for an audition right now, I'll never get the chance! she thought. The auditions are tomorrow!

She opened her mouth to speak to Jacques again, but Lennon had walked out from behind the counter. He shoved a rag into her hands. "Wipe up table six," he said, scowling. "Okay?"

Oh, all right, Chloe thought, trudging back to work.

What ever made me think working together was a good idea?

Riley sat in the middle seat of Mrs. Pomeroy's minivan, smiling to herself. She could hardly wait to see Marc again tonight. Even the fact that she had to sit through an entire French movie without subtitles didn't make her any less excited.

There was just something about him. He was so nice. And funny. And easy to talk to. She'd loved their first date together.

She hoped that he felt the same way and that he wouldn't change his mind when he found out she wasn't Jacques's daughter.

It's not easy leading a double life! Riley thought. I mean, I could probably do it for a while. It might even be fun to pretend to be French for a few days. But I would never want to fake being someone I'm not for months and months, the way Sierra has been.

"So drop us off on the Smirmen's side of the mall," Sierra told her mom. She was sitting next to her, in the front passenger seat.

"You aren't going to get another bathing suit, are you?" Mrs. Pomeroy asked. "I've already bought you three that you never wear."

"Three solid-colored tank suits, Mom," Sierra complained. "They don't look good on me."

"They're not *all* solids," Mrs. Pomeroy said. "What about the navy blue and cream striped one?"

Sierra sighed and turned to look at Riley.

"Tell her." Riley mouthed the words silently so Mrs. Pomeroy wouldn't hear. She gestured at Sierra's mom, trying to get the point across to Sierra that it would be better to tell her mom the truth about her double life. About her music, and her name, and what she liked to wear. Then Sierra could be herself!

As it was, Sierra was sitting there in a navy blue polo shirt and pleated blue jeans. And she was going to have to be *seen* in that outfit as she walked into the mall! At least until she could get to a rest room to change.

"Just do it!" Riley whispered.

But Sierra shook her head and opened her eyes really wide. She was too scared.

Maybe she needs a little help, Riley thought. She reached into her backpack and pulled out a CD. It was a disk Sierra had just given her—a demo of her band.

On a whim—and before Sierra could stop her—Riley leaned forward in the van and popped the CD into the player.

"What's that?" Mrs. Pomeroy asked nicely as the pulsing rock music came on.

"That's Sierra's band!" Riley blurted out.

Sierra turned to glare at Riley.

Mrs. Pomeroy laughed. "Oh, right. I can hear the violin in the background," she said. "You have such a funny sense of humor, Riley."

Sierra hit the eject button on the CD player.

"Yeah, she's a regular hoot," Sierra said as they pulled up to the mall's front entrance.

"Have fun," Mrs. Pomeroy called as they jumped out of the van.

As soon as they were alone, Sierra grabbed Riley's

wrist. "How could you do that?" she said. But she looked sort of excited—sort of pumped up—by the whole thing.

"Did you see your mom's face?" Riley said. "She didn't seem to hate the music. She was smiling!"

"I know, I know." Sierra was talking really fast. "That was kind of cool, wasn't it? But it was probably because she didn't believe it was me."

"Listen," Riley argued, "you'll never know unless you take a chance and tell her the truth."

"Oh, look who's talking!" Sierra said. "You haven't exactly been honest with Marc."

"You're right," Riley admitted. "But I'm going to change that—eventually."

They were walking through the mall entrance, but Sierra stopped in her tracks. "Okay," she said. "I'll make you a deal. I'll tell my mom the truth by the end of winter break if you'll come clean with Marc Hudson."

Riley thought about it. Yeah, that was fair. Besides, she was planning to tell Marc the truth sooner or later.

"Okay, deal," Riley said. And they slapped five, just like they used to when they were kids, to seal the agreement.

The mall was packed, so they didn't do much window-shopping. Too crowded. It was straight to Smirmen's, try on forty bathing suits, buy two, and then crash in the food court.

"Can you believe we've been here two hours and

haven't run into anyone we know?" Sierra said. "That's got to be a record."

Riley nodded, but she wasn't surprised. A lot of people had left town for the week.

Sierra took the last bite of her hot, salty pretzel and wiped her fingers. "Well, I'm over this," she said. "Do you want to go hang out at my house till your big date?"

"Definitely. Besides, you said I could paw through your closet for something to wear tonight," Riley reminded her.

"Right," Sierra agreed, but she sounded doubtful. "Just remember, all my clothes—the ones you might actually *want* to wear—are wrinkled. They're smashed into a big box in the back of my closet where my mom won't see them."

"That's another reason you have to tell her the truth!" Riley urged. "If wrinkled ever goes out of style, you're in big trouble."

They took the bus home, grabbed some fruit for an afternoon snack, and started to head for Sierra's room. But just then Sierra's mom came in and began making conversation, quizzing them about their shopping trip.

"It was good," Riley answered. "I bought a bathing suit and so did Sierra."

"You did?" Sierra's mom glanced at her daughter, surprised.

Sierra shot Riley a glare that said, "Why did you tell?"

Riley leaned close to her friend and whispered,

"What about our deal? I thought you were going to tell her the truth!"

For half a second Sierra and her mom glanced at each other. Mrs. Pomeroy seemed to be waiting for an explanation, and Sierra seemed to be trying to decide what to do next.

Riley reached into her backpack and pulled out the demo CD again. She handed it to Sierra, gesturing toward the CD player in the kitchen. "Go for it," Riley whispered.

Sierra hesitated, but finally she popped it into the machine. "Mom?" she said as the music came on. "Riley was telling the truth in the car. That's my band, The Wave. I play bass guitar."

Mrs. Pomeroy laughed nervously. As if she kind of thought it was a joke but wasn't sure.

"No, really, Mom," Sierra said. She popped the CD out and showed her the label. All the musicians were listed. It said, SIERRA ON BASS. "See? That's me."

"But your name is Sarah," her mother said, shaking her head.

"I know. That's what you and Dad call me," Sierra said, a little impatiently. "But I go by Sierra in the band."

"Your father and I call you Sarah because it's your name," Mrs. Pomeroy said. "Are you feeling all right, Sarah?"

"No, honestly, it's true!" Riley chimed in, trying to help. "And her band is awesome! You should go hear them sometime. They're playing this Friday night at the

Voodoo Lounge."

"Whoa!" Sierra said, putting a sudden halt to the conversation.

Oops! Riley thought. Did I go too far?

Before Mrs. Pomeroy could say anything else, the phone rang. She went to answer it.

"Why did you tell her about the Voodoo Lounge?" Sierra whispered when her mother was gone.

"Why not?" Riley asked.

"I don't know." Sierra twisted her thick hair around her fingers. "It just sort of freaks me out. What if my parents come and they hate it? And they ground me forever or something?"

"Don't worry. It'll be fine. Trust me," Riley said.

She hoped she was right.

chapter
seven

"**B**onsoir. Tu es très belle ce soir," Marc said, speaking perfect French as he greeted Riley that night outside the auditorium. She had just arrived at the Pepperdine campus to meet him for the movie.

"Thank you," Riley said. But instantly her mind was spinning. What did he just say? I've only had a few months of French! she thought.

Okay, so maybe she did know some of those words. Belle meant beautiful. And bonsoir was good evening. She knew that much. But could she actually have a conversation in French? No way!

"Ça va?" Marc asked.

"Hey, let's not speak French," Riley said quickly. "I'm still working on my English, okay?"

Marc did a double take. "Are you kidding? You're still working on it? Wow, you're heavy-duty. I mean, how much more English do you need, anyway?"

"Oh, uh, I don't know," Riley stammered, trying to make up an excuse. "Maybe I'll try out for a part in a Shakespeare play someday."

"Oh." Marc shrugged. "Whatever. Anyway, we'd better go in. They're starting the film in five minutes."

Fine by me, Riley thought. He took her hand and squeezed it. It was nice walking into the darkened theater with Marc.

But mostly she just wanted to get this part of the date over. After the movie, when they would probably go out for coffee—*that's* what she was looking forward to. Then she could start being herself again and talk about something other than French stuff.

They found two seats about halfway down in the auditorium. The place was only about a third full—mostly college students and professors, plus a few older people who were trying to look French, judging from all the long scarves they were wearing.

Riley sneaked a quick peek at Marc as the movie came on. He looked amazing in his gray knit shirt and black pants.

He held her hand and sat back in his seat with a smile as the credits rolled. Then, almost immediately, he started laughing at the screen.

Uh-oh, Riley thought. This is a comedy, and I'm supposed to think it's funny, too.

From what Riley could tell, the movie was about this great-looking young woman with red hair who rode a motor scooter all over Paris. And some guy was trying to catch up with her. There was a scene with a lobster and another scene where a man from a butcher shop chased them, screaming.

Basically, she couldn't follow it at all.

Marc glanced over at her with a little frown as if he wondered why she wasn't enjoying it.

Oops, Riley thought. Guess it's time to fake it! She forced a laugh, but it was a little late. Everyone else was quiet now.

The next time Marc laughed, Riley tried to laugh, too, but it sounded so bogus, he shot her another weird glance.

"You okay?" he whispered.

"Sure," Riley said, throwing in one of the few French words she was comfortable with. "*Oui.*"

Oh, man, Riley thought. Is this what Sierra goes through every day of her life? Pretending to be something she's not?

The next two hours were a lot of work. Riley tried to laugh when Marc laughed, and gasp when he gasped. Finally the film ended, and she jumped up, happy that her ordeal was over.

"So what did you think?" Marc asked.

"About what?" Riley said. Then it hit her. Duh! He wants to talk about the movie!

"You know what?" she said, thinking fast and talking even faster. "It might have seemed really funny to you, but to me—being French and everything—it was just way too obvious and clichéd."

Marc nodded. "Yeah, I kind of thought so, too," he said. "I mean, I went with it, because everyone else was laughing. But it really wasn't all that hilarious. So, do you want to go out for coffee?" he asked, taking her hand again as they walked.

"You bet," Riley said. At last the date could start for real!

Marc led the way to the spot where his motorbike was parked. He handed her a helmet, and they rode into town.

"Let's check out the Newsstand," Marc said, pulling over to the curb.

The Newsstand? Riley thought. Everyone in there knows me, and they know I'm *not* Danielle! They'll blow my cover for sure!

"Uh, that place gets so crowded," Riley said fast. "How about Starbucks instead?"

"Hey, crowds don't scare *me*," Marc said. "I'm a New Yorker, remember? Besides, I want to see this place where your dad is shooting the mega-commercial."

Oh, boy, Riley thought. This is going to be a disaster. But then she flashed back to that afternoon. She and Sierra hadn't run into anyone they knew at the mall. So maybe she'd get lucky. Maybe…

Marc opened the door to the Newsstand, and they stepped inside. Instantly Larry Slotnick spotted

Riley from across the crowded café and rushed toward her.

Not now, Larry! Riley thought. Larry was her goofy next-door neighbor. He'd had a crush on her since they were little kids.

So much for luck. In about two seconds he was going to be close enough to call out her name. There was only one thing to do. "Larry!" she called, rushing forward to greet him before he could say a word. "You darling!"

Quickly she kissed Larry on both cheeks the way she'd seen everyone in the French movie do. Then she whispered into his ear, "Call me Danielle—not Riley. And pretend I'm French. Please! And I'll be your friend forever. I'll explain later."

"Whoa," Larry said, grinning at the cheek kissing. "What did I do to deserve this?"

"Larry, Marc. Marc, Larry," she said, introducing them to each other.

"Hi," Larry said. "You look great tonight, *Danielle*. Very *chic*." He said the last word with a heavy French accent.

Riley rolled her eyes. Don't lay it on too thick! she silently pleaded. "Thanks, Larry. Anyway, excuse us. We're going to sit alone and talk." She motioned toward a small table in a corner. Then she glanced around the Newsstand. Even though it was crowded, none of her friends were there.

Good, Riley thought. We'll have one quick coffee and then we'll go. Maybe I'll actually get away with this!

"What do you want to drink?" Marc asked, walking toward the counter.

"I'll have a cappuccino," Riley said.

Marc stopped and did a double take. "Seriously?"

"Uh, yeah," Riley said. "Is that a problem?"

"No, I'm just surprised." He shrugged. "I mean, I guess you've been in America so long, you're picking up odd habits."

Odd habits? Drinking cappuccino? Riley frowned. She didn't get it.

"Well, you grew up in France, right?" Marc said. "None of the Europeans I know drink cappuccino for anything other than breakfast."

They don't? Who knew? Riley thought, feeling a little silly. She tried to act as if she'd realized that all along. "You're right, I've picked up some pretty odd habits since I've been here," she mumbled, blushing. Such as lying about who I am! "Anyway, do you mind if I sit here while you get it? My feet are killing me."

Besides, Cammie's working the counter. And I don't want to have to kiss *her* on both cheeks to get her to not call me by my real name! Riley thought.

"No problem," Marc said.

Riley waited at the table while Marc ordered. Then he came back and sat down. "They're going to bring it out when it's ready," he said. He glanced around the café.

looking impressed. "This place will make a great location for your dad's commercial. Have you seen the script?"

"Uh, no." Riley made a face. "I get tired of all that…" Her voice trailed off.

"All that what?" Marc asked.

"All that…you know. Show business," Riley said.

"No way," Marc said. "Not when it's your dad. He's a legend."

Riley shrugged.

"So you don't plan to go into the business?" Marc asked.

Riley shook her head. "Not really. I mean, I don't know what I *am* going to do, but I've got time to decide. What about you?"

"I don't know," Marc said. "My dad's sort of a hard act to follow, you know? But I don't have to tell *you* about that."

Riley tried to think of a way to change the subject. But just then she saw Chloe coming toward them. Carrying their drinks.

Oh, no. This is not happening, Riley thought. She jumped up and almost knocked her sister over. "What are you doing here?" she whispered frantically as Chloe tried to keep from spilling the drinks.

"I was just in the back, hanging out with Lennon," Chloe explained. "And he asked me to bring over these drinks."

"What!" Marc said, standing up and staring at

Chloe. "Hold on. You...you two look like...wait a minute...Danielle? You've got a twin? How come I've never read about this? Like, anywhere!"

Think fast! Riley told herself. And then she let her mouth take over. "Ooh-la-la, it's just that we've tried to keep it quiet, ever since we found out about each other," she said, babbling. "My sister, Chloe, and I were separated at birth, see, because Mom didn't feel she could raise both of us. So I lived with my father growing up, and Chloe lived with our mother."

"With Faye Huntington?" Marc jumped in. His eyes were rounder than the coffee cups.

"*Oui, oui*," Riley said, hoping that if she threw in some French he'd fall for this ridiculous story. "And we never even knew each other existed until a few months ago. So now we're together. Isn't it wonderful?" She grabbed Chloe and kissed her on both cheeks—*twice*—as if she hoped that would prove this whole thing was true.

Chloe rubbed at her face to remove the lip gloss.

"Wow." Marc seemed almost speechless. "I can't believe it." He stared at them, amazed, as if he didn't know whether to run to the phone and call the tabloids or to feel lucky that he knew a major secret. "So I'm one of the first people to find out?" he asked, shaking his head in disbelief.

"Yes," Riley said with a sigh. "But you can't tell anyone. You've got to respect our privacy."

"Right," Marc said, nodding. "Okay. I get that. So that's why you didn't want me to know that you're Danielle D'Oisseau."

"Exactly." Riley grabbed at any explanation he'd buy into.

"Wow," he murmured again.

Yeah, Riley thought. Wow. All these lies were exhausting her! "You know what?" she said. "I hate to say this, but I think I should get home. I mean, I have to get up early tomorrow to, um, walk the dog."

"Okay," Marc said, but he sounded disappointed. "But can't you just open that sliding door and let her out? She seems to go out pretty much on her own anyway."

"No, no, we're trying to break her of that habit," Riley said. She took a huge gulp of her cappuccino without sitting down. "So can we go?"

Riley caught Chloe rolling her eyes.

"No problem," Marc said, leaving his coffee behind.

Riley climbed onto his motorbike and put on the helmet. Marc took off, driving through town, toward the beach.

She started to tell him how to get to her house. But then she remembered he knew. Or at least, he *thought* he knew.

Marc drove up to Jacques's beach house and parked his bike. They removed their helmets, and Marc gently brushed some hair out of Riley's eyes.

Then he pulled her into the sweetest kiss she had ever experienced.

When the kiss was over, Riley's head was spinning. "So, I guess this is good-bye for now," she said, disappointed now that the date was over.

"Well, maybe not," he said softly. "Do you mind if I come in? I'd really like to meet your dad."

My *dad*? Riley thought. Oh, no! Now what?

chapter
eight

"You...you want to come *in*?" Riley said with a lump in her throat.

That's not going to happen, she thought, stalling and trying to think of some excuse to say no.

"Just for a few minutes," Marc said eagerly. "Is it okay?"

What am I going to do? Riley wondered, feeling panicked. She glanced at Jacques's house. Luckily, there weren't too many lights on. "Uh, sorry, but *Dad* goes to bed very early," she said. "Especially when he's working on a project."

Marc's face fell. "Oh. Well, can I meet him tomorrow? I'm a huge fan."

Riley put her hands on her hips and narrowed her eyes at Marc, pretending to be suspicious. "Hey, what is this? Are you interested in *me*, or are you just using me to meet my dad?" she asked him.

[<u>Riley</u>: Hey, I know it was a dirty trick, but I'm desperate!]

"Oh, no way!" Marc protested quickly. "It's definitely you I want to spend time with. It's just that—"

"What?" Riley said.

"I've been such a big fan of his forever," Marc explained. "I'd love to talk to him about *Tunnel of Rain*."

"Oh, right. The movie he won the Golden Globe for," Riley muttered. "Okay. Yeah, sure. I just don't know when."

Marc tilted his head to one side and gave her a weird smile.

"What?" she asked him.

"Oh, nothing," he replied, still smiling.

Riley shrugged. "Anyway, I'll try to set up a time when you can meet him," she went on. "But it might not happen before you have to go back to New York."

"Okay. No problem," Marc said with that grin pasted on his face. He moved a little closer. Then he leaned in, tilted his head, and kissed her again.

Riley closed her eyes and felt a sweet shiver.

"I had fun tonight," he said.

"Me, too," Riley said. "Too bad you have to go back home so soon." She half meant that. She didn't want to see him go, but at least she wouldn't have to pretend to be French after he was gone.

"By the way," Marc said with another smile. "I'm not going back to New York. I've decided to stay out here and spend the rest of the year with my dad. Isn't that great?"

Great? Yes! Riley thought. I mean, no. Oh, I don't know...

She was so confused! It *would* be great to see Marc all the time, if she could just figure out how to tell him the truth about who she was.

But if she did tell him, would he still like her?

"Yeah," Riley mumbled, feeling like a complete wreck inside. "I'm glad you're staying. Anyway, I've got to go in...uh...the back door. See you sometime."

"When?" Marc called as she walked toward the back of the house.

"I'm not sure," Riley said. "I'll call you."

"You don't have my number!" Marc said. Quickly he took a card out of his wallet, wrote on it, and handed it to her.

"Thanks," Riley said. "Good night." Then she slipped around to the back of Jacques's house and hurried down the beach to her own home. What a mess, she thought. I'm going to have to find a way to tell him the truth—and soon.

But how?

Today is going to be my fresh start at the Newsstand, Chloe decided. Last night she had apologized for making so many silly mistakes, and Lennon had said he was sorry for being so grouchy. They had cleared the air, and now Chloe was ready to give it her best shot...again.

"Can you put the muffins into the pastry case, Peaches?" Lennon asked in a sweet tone of voice.

"No problem, Dumpling-cheeks!" Chloe said cheerfully.

Lennon laughed.

I'm really going to try today, Chloe decided. She didn't want to get Lennon into any more trouble. And she *definitely* didn't want to get fired now. Not today. It was Thursday, her last possible chance to ask Jacques D'Oisseau for an audition.

The Newsstand would only be open for five more hours. They were closing at two for the auditions.

She glanced at the clock. It was two minutes till nine. Two minutes till Jacques D'Oisseau came in for his coffee and croissant.

Chloe took the large flat tray out of the pastry case and carried it to the back room. She opened a big cardboard box filled with muffins and started piling them on the tray.

But then she heard a voice at the counter. That unmistakable French accent. "*Un café et un croissant,*" Jacques said to Cammie, who was at the register.

Chloe rushed out. "I'll make his coffee," she offered, flashing her best smile at Jacques.

"Why, hello!" Jacques said as if he knew her. "I didn't realize you worked here."

"I don't," Chloe said, and she heard Cammie snicker. "I mean, I work here, but you're probably thinking of my

293

sister, Riley." Quickly she explained that her twin had shown Jacques the way to the vet.

"Ah," Jacques said, laughing. "Well, it's nice to meet you, Chloe."

"Um, listen." Chloe followed Jacques to his table, carrying his coffee. "May I ask you something?"

"Certainly," Jacques said, gazing at her with mild interest.

Chloe took a deep breath and tried to psych herself up. This seemed like a way-too-bold thing to do. But why not? she told herself. You can't get what you don't ask for!

"I was wondering if I could audition for a small part in the commercial you're shooting," she said finally.

"Well…" Jacques started to shake his head.

"I've done a little acting," Chloe blurted out quickly. "And it won't take much time. Please? I'll make sure we save all the best croissants for your crew," she added as a joke.

Jacques smiled as if he could tell she was trying to charm him. "Oh, why not? You will be here anyway, I suppose, yes?"

"Yes!" Chloe said, happy.

"All right." Jacques nodded. "Be ready at two o'clock when we begin the auditions. I will give you a chance for a screen test, but no promises, okay?"

"Thank you!" Chloe said, reaching out to shake his hand. "Thank you very much!" This is the best! she thought as she hurried back to the counter. "I got it! I got an audition!" she told Cammie, who was ringing up some orders. "And I bet I'll get a part! How hard can it be to play the part of a coffee waitress?"

"Let me answer that for you," a voice from behind her said.

Chloe whirled around and saw Mr. Horner glaring at her, his hands on his hips.

Oops. What did I do now? she wondered.

"For *you*," Mr. Horner said, "playing the part of a coffee waitress seems to be almost impossible!" He glanced at Lennon, who was just coming out of the back room with the tray of muffins in his arms. "I've got an appointment," Mr. Horner said to Lennon. "I expect you to handle this." Then he stomped out of the café.

"Handle what?" Chloe asked Lennon. "What did I do this time?"

"It's what you didn't do," Lennon said. "You left these muffins sitting in the back, so Cammie thought we didn't have any. She told about five customers that we were out of muffins, and they left for Starbucks."

Oh, boy, Chloe thought, covering her face.

"Just get to work," Lennon snapped.

Chloe tried not to make any more mistakes all morning. But it was hard, with Lennon watching her like a hawk. She kept wondering when she was going to spill something, make the wrong drink, or get yelled at for what she called "being friendly with the customers" but Lennon called "gabbing on the job."

I'll hang on until two o'clock, Chloe decided. Then I'll quit, and Lennon can stop worrying about my messing up all the time. And I'll have the chance to audition for the commercial.

Tara came in at one-forty-five and ordered a mocha.

"We're closing in fifteen minutes," Chloe said, excited.

Jacques and the video crew had already started to arrive. Chloe quickly served them the coffees they ordered.

"Did you talk Jacques into an audition?" Tara asked.

"Yes! But I haven't had a minute to get ready for it!" Chloe confided. She stirred syrup into Tara's drink and handed it to her.

"Just act natural," Tara coached her. "Be yourself and don't stare at the camera—unless they tell you to, of course. But act as if the camera loves you." Tara took a sip of her mocha and almost spit it out. "Yuck! You put raspberry syrup in this instead of chocolate!" She shoved the drink back toward Chloe, behind the counter.

Lennon came over, shaking his head. "Okay, that's it," he said. "I'm sorry, Chloe, but you're fired."

"What?" Chloe's eyes popped open wide. Was he kidding? "It's just Tara's drink! You can't fire me for that!"

"Thanks a lot!" Tara snapped.

"It's *not* just Tara's drink," Lennon said. "You're a *terrible* waitress. You messed up the last four coffees for the crew!"

Chloe glanced over at the video crew. Some of them

were watching her. And so were the other actresses who had arrived for the audition. They looked like super-models—tall, thin, and totally gorgeous.

Oh, great! she thought as she took off her apron and tossed it onto the counter. Now I look like an idiot in front of everyone!

"Thanks a lot, Lennon." She brushed past him to run to the rest room. But in her rush she knocked over a half-empty cardboard cup of cold coffee. It spilled down the front of her pants. "Oh, no!" Chloe cried, totally upset and desperate to get out of sight. The whole roomful of film people turned to stare at her. A few of them snickered.

Don't cry, she told herself as she pushed into the rest room to hide. Don't cry. Whatever you do, don't cry.

For a minute she just buried her face in her hands. Then she splashed her cheeks with water.

"Chloe? They're calling for you out front," Cammie said, poking her head into the rest room.

Okay, Chloe decided, still shaking inside. I can do this. She brushed her hair, wiped off her pants, put on some lip gloss, and hurried to do her audition.

By the time she came out of the rest room, Jacques's crew had set up lights. They were getting ready to shoot the first screen tests.

"All right, everyone," Jacques said to the collection of actresses. Chloe hurried to join them. "We are auditioning for speaking and nonspeaking parts today. So please just stand in front of the camera, tell me your name, and give us a little bit about your acting experience. Then please read the lines from this script, okay?"

That should be easy enough, Chloe thought. But she was still shaking inside. And so embarrassed she wanted to hide.

She watched as the first actress did her audition.

"Hi, my name is Inga," the model-actress said. "I'm five-eleven, I weigh a hundred and twenty pounds, and my special talents are mime, ballet dancing, and luge." She went on to list all the commercials she'd been in. Then she read the script. She had a cute Scandinavian accent.

Wow, Chloe thought. She's so tall and beautiful!

"Very nice," Jacques said, but Riley saw the other crew people shaking their heads.

"She doesn't sound very real," someone whispered.

"She doesn't even sound American!" someone else said.

"All right, let's see who's next. Chloe?" Jacques motioned to her.

Already? Chloe swallowed hard. She didn't want to have to go on so soon. Her stomach was still turning somersaults, and the stain on her pants was still wet.

She stepped in front of the camera and smiled. "Hi, my name is Chloe Carlson, but you know that already, right? Because, I mean, I just told you this afternoon."

Someone in the background giggled.

My voice is shaking! Chloe realized. I sound like a porpoise with laryngitis, and I'm not even singing!

"Go on," Jacques said. "Tell us something about yourself."

"Um, yeah." Chloe nodded. "Well, I work here in the Newsstand, or at least I did until recently. So I'm very familiar with coffee. And I've done a lot of acting in, uh…school plays."

"Really?" Jacques smiled and tried to look encouraging. "Like what?"

"Well, I got really good reviews in junior high," Chloe said. "I played Woodstock in *You're a Good Man, Charlie Brown*."

The cameraman out-and-out laughed. Some of the actresses giggled, too.

I'm blowing this! Chloe thought. What did I say? I'm very familiar with coffee? Just shoot me now!

She glanced at Lennon, who was standing in the back watching. He had his arms crossed over his chest and was covering his face with one hand.

"That is good," Jacques said. "Can you read the first page of the script?"

"I think so," Chloe said. She picked it up and read. "'If I don't get a latte, I'm going to do something I'll forget,'" she said. "I mean, '*regret*.' Sorry. I read that wrong. Can I do it again?"

"No need," Jacques said. "That was fine. Please leave your résumé and head shot with Patty."

Résumé? Head shot? "I don't have those," Chloe blurted out, and the crew smiled again.

"Well, I'm sorry, Chloe," Jacques said, "but I think we are looking for someone with a little more experience."

"Okay." Chloe wished she could disappear through the floor. This is mortifying, she thought. And it was all Lennon's fault. If he hadn't fired me mere minutes before I had to go on, I would have done a better job! She ran toward the back room. Anything to get out of there.

Lennon followed her. "Are you okay?" he asked.

"What do you care? You made me look bad!" she said, her voice still shaking.

"Well, you served four lattes without any milk!" he shot back.

"But that's not a reason to fire me right before my audition! You ruined my chance to be in this commercial!" she said, her voice rising.

"Hey, don't blame me," Lennon said. "You ruined *that* all by yourself."

Whoa. Chloe was shocked. Did he really say that to her? "Don't you even care one bit whether I get this acting job?" Chloe asked.

"Sure," Lennon said. "About as much as you care whether I keep *my* job."

Chloe's throat closed up. She thought she might cry. "Don't worry. I won't mess up your life anymore," she said sharply. "I'm leaving!"

"Good!" Lennon cried.

Chloe grabbed her backpack and stomped out the back door of the café. But as soon as she was outside, she felt terrible.

Why did I yell at Lennon? she thought. It's not his fault that I messed up my job. Or my audition.

Then a horrible thought hit her—right in the gut.

Wait a minute. What *really* happened back there?

Did I just lose my job, or did I lose my boyfriend, too?

chapter
nine

"**W**ait, wait, tell me again," Riley said to Chloe late that afternoon. The two of them were sprawled on their beds, eating pieces of melon. "What did he say *exactly*?"

"Who? Jacques or Lennon?" Chloe asked.

"Lennon," Riley answered. "Did he say he never wanted to see you again?"

"No," Chloe admitted. "But he made it pretty clear he never wanted to see me *make coffee* again."

"Yeah, I get that part," Riley said. "Manuelo pretty much feels the same way."

Chloe tried to laugh, but it came out more like a moan.

"And Jacques never wants to see you again, either, I'm guessing?" Riley asked.

"Hey, I thought you were trying to cheer me up!" Chloe protested.

"Okay, okay, sorry." Riley thought for a minute. "So

my advice would be, call Lennon and ask him what he meant."

"Call him and say 'Excuse me, but did we just break up?' No way. Too embarrassing. And anyway, what if he says yes?"

"Yeah, that would hurt," Riley had to admit. She took another bite of melon and shook her head. "I don't know, Chloe. Maybe you should ask someone else for advice. I haven't exactly been acing my own social life these days."

"What's wrong?" Chloe asked.

Riley quickly explained what had happened on her date with Marc. "And he's not leaving town at the end of the week," she said.

"But that's great!" Chloe said. "Isn't it? I mean, I thought he was someone you could really like."

"He is." Riley nodded. "But what's he going to think when he finds out I'm not connected to show business? And not French? And not even a little bit famous? Plus he wants me to introduce him to Jacques. The whole thing's a huge mess."

"Yeah, that's bad," Chloe admitted. "Well, you were in the West Malibu High School talent show last year," she joked. "Do you think that counts as a show business connection?"

Riley didn't even bother to answer that. "This is serious!" she said. "What am I going to do?"

Chloe sat up as if she'd just gotten a brilliant idea. "How about this? Jacques comes into the Newsstand every morning at nine for coffee," she said. "Maybe you could make a date with Marc to meet him there at nine."

"What good will that do?" Riley asked.

"When Marc comes in, you tell him the truth about who you are, because you have to do that anyway, right?" Chloe said. "But then right away you offer to introduce him to Jacques. I mean, Jacques will be sitting right there and you *do* know him, right?"

Hmm. Not a bad plan, Riley thought. Jacques was so nice. He would probably be fine about talking to Marc for a few minutes.

"But what about the fact that Marc's dad is a super-star, and Marc said he'd never hang with someone who's not involved in show business?" Riley worried.

Chloe shrugged. "You've got to tell him sometime," she pointed out.

True, Riley thought. She went to the phone and dialed the number Marc had given her.

"Can you meet me tomorrow morning at nine at the Newsstand?" she said when he answered.

"Sure, what's up?" Marc asked.

Riley hesitated for a moment, then she said, "I have something important to tell you."

Riley dragged herself out of bed early Friday morning, considering that there was no school, and got to the Newsstand by eight forty-five.

"Hi," Lennon said, hurrying past her with two coffees in his hands as she walked in.

"Hi," Riley said and immediately went into super-sensitive mode, trying to figure out exactly what his "Hi" meant.

[Riley: I pride myself on being able to read whole chapters into a single syllable, you know? What girl doesn't? So when Lennon said "Hi," I ran through a whole list of possibilities. Was it, "Hi, I wish you were Chloe instead of Riley so I could make up with you"? Or did he mean, "You look exactly like the girl I'm totally over, so get out of my sight"? Or was it just, "Hi, I hope you're not as down on me as your sister is and, by the way, could you be careful not to spill anything, either"? But none of those sounded right. Finally I had to admit that he might have just been trying to say hello. Call me crazy, but it could be true!]

She ordered a cappuccino and hovered around the counter, waiting for Jacques. At nine on the dot he walked in, ordered his coffee and croissant, and sat down with _Le Monde_.

"Hi," Riley said, approaching him with her cappuccino in hand.

"Oh, hello," Jacques said. "Riley, right?"

Riley nodded. "Um, Monsieur D'Oisseau, there's something I wanted to ask you." She cleared her throat. "Would you mind if I sat down for a minute?"

"Please," Jacques said, gesturing grandly to the chair across from him. He even stood up and held the chair for her. "I am forever in your debt for rescuing my petite Chaudette. How can I return the favor?"

That's a tricky one, Riley thought. She had spent half of last night trying to figure out how to tell Jacques that she'd been pretending to be his daughter. But there just didn't seem to be a good way to say it. Finally she had decided to just start at the beginning and tell him the whole story.

"Do you remember last weekend when I helped you find the vet?" Riley began.

"But of course," Jacques said, smiling warmly at her.

"Well..." Riley took a deep breath. She was just about to plunge into the details when the door opened and Marc walked in. Whoops! Riley thought. I should have told him to come later.

"Hi!" Marc said, beaming when he saw her sitting with Jacques.

"Oh, no," Riley mumbled. In a panic, she tried to think of some way to blurt out the whole truth quickly.

Marc rushed over to their table and stuck out his hand. "Monsieur D'Oisseau! It's so nice to meet you," he said. "You have a delightful daughter."

"Oh!" Jacques looked totally surprised as he shook Marc's hand. "You've met Danielle?"

"But of course!" Marc said. "*La jeune fille qui vous accompagne m'a dit qu'elle est Danielle.*"

Whoa! They're going to speak French, Riley thought. That's not fair!

"*Mais, non!*" Jacques said, answering quickly in French. Then he rattled off about five more sentences that Riley didn't understand, and Marc did the same thing.

What a nightmare! Riley thought. She knew they were talking about her, or rather, Danielle. But she had no idea what they were saying! Riley watched their faces.

[Riley: I know what you're thinking, so don't even say it. Now would be a good time to be able to read whole paragraphs into a few syllables, right? Yeah. I wish!]

The conversation went on in French for another few minutes.

Finally Jacques stood up with his coffee and paper and walked toward the door. "*Au revoir*," he called to Riley.

Marc started to follow him.

"Hey! Where are you going?" Riley said. She was just about to tell them both the whole truth! Now her chance was slipping away.

"Your father offered me a job as a production assistant," Marc replied. "So I've got to go. But I have something important to tell you, too. I'll see you tomorrow at the shoot, okay? You're coming, right?"

Coming to the shoot? Uh, no. She wasn't invited. In fact, she knew that the Newsstand would be closed to the public all day tomorrow.

But if Marc was going to be there, and if he wanted to tell her something, she'd have to find a way to get in.

"Sure. See you tomorrow," Riley called as Marc walked out the door.

chapter
ten

"**H**ave another muffin," Manuelo said, trying to cheer up Chloe. "They're still warm from the oven."

Chloe flopped onto the couch and sighed. "My life is a mess, Manuelo. Another muffin isn't going to help."

"It can't hurt," he said, carrying the plate over and leaving it on the coffee table.

Chloe shook her head and went to the freezer. "I'm going to need something stronger," she joked as she took out a pint of ice cream and fished around for a spoon. Then she flopped back onto the couch and picked up the phone.

There's got to be *someone* I can talk to! she thought. Other than Manuelo. Someone who can tell me what to do about Lennon.

She dialed Tara's number and got her answering machine.

Then she tried Quinn. Same thing.

Amanda was third on her speed dial. Luckily, she picked up on the third ring.

"Hi," Chloe said. "You doing anything?"

"Just sitting by the phone, waiting for your next call," Amanda joked.

"Oh, come on," Chloe said. "I haven't called you *that* many times."

"Every half hour since ten this morning," Amanda said. "Have you heard from Lennon yet?"

"Not yet," Chloe said. "That's what's driving me crazy! I can't stand the suspense."

"So call him!" Amanda advised. "If you'd done it three hours ago the way I told you to, you'd at least know where you stand with him."

Chloe thought about it. Amanda was probably right. She should just call Lennon and ask him whether he'd meant to break up with her or not.

It was totally reasonable. But Chloe couldn't do it. "I guess I have too much pride or something."

"Listen, I hate to say it, but I was just heading out the door," Amanda said. "My mom's taking me to the mall."

"Fine," Chloe caved in. "I'll let you go."

What choice did she have? If there was one rule she and her friends stuck to, it was "Never interfere with a shopping trip."

"I'll talk to you later," Amanda promised.

That's okay, Chloe thought. Besides, I think I just heard him come home.

She could always count on Riley for sympathy.

Chloe hung up and waited for her sister to appear in the living room.

"Do I smell muffins?" Riley asked, looking almost as miserable as Chloe felt.

Uh-oh, Chloe thought. Looks like Riley needs sympathy almost as much as I do! "On the table," she said, pointing. "But I've moved on to the ice cream. You want a spoon?"

"No thanks." Riley took a muffin, stared at it, and put it back down.

"Wow," Chloe said. "You must have had a *really* bad day. What happened?"

Riley told her about her coffee date with Marc and Jacques.

"They spoke French for five whole minutes?" Chloe asked, her eyes wide.

Riley nodded. "And I never got a chance to confess that I'm not Danielle."

"I'm betting Jacques already knows that," Chloe teased.

"You know what I mean." Riley covered her face with her hands. "And then Marc said he had something to tell me, which he'll do tomorrow at the shoot. So I've got to get in there somehow. Do you think Lennon—"

"I haven't talked to him since he fired me," Chloe interrupted, shaking her head.

"Oh." Riley nodded.

"But don't think I'm all alone without Lennon," Chloe said, digging into the ice cream container. "Oh, no. I'll be perfectly fine. I still have my friends, Ben and Jerry."

"They're my friends, too," Riley said, standing up to get herself a spoon.

The phone rang. Chloe grabbed it and checked the Caller ID. Her face lit up. It was Lennon!

"Hello?" she said, answering the phone.

"Um, hi," he said. "It's me. I was wondering…can you meet me somewhere so we can talk?"

"Definitely!" Chloe was happy just to hear his voice. But then she froze. What did he want to talk about? Was he going to break up with her—officially? "Where and when?" she asked.

"You pick the place," he said. "Anywhere but the Newsstand."

Yeah, I'll bet, she thought. You don't want to be seen with me there ever again!

Chloe chose California Dream, the beach café just a few blocks from her house. She promised to meet him in an hour, leaving just enough time to change her clothes three times and fix her hair twice.

When she walked in, Lennon was already there, sitting in the booth he knew was her favorite—the one by the windows.

She tried to read the look on his face, but she couldn't. Was he going to dump her? Yell at her? Or was he just waiting to see if she'd apologize?

"Hi," he said, sounding as if he wasn't sure how to act. "I didn't know what you wanted to eat, so I didn't order yet."

"Just a glass of water for me," she said.

Lennon motioned to the waitress and ordered one water and one iced tea.

Then he reached across the table and took her hands. "Listen, I'm really sorry for what happened yesterday," he said. "I was just under so much pressure. Mr. Horner was hammering me, and I lost it. But I really didn't want to fire you right before your audition and in front of everybody. I'm sorry if I embarrassed you. Or if that made you mess up."

He's so sweet! Chloe thought. She let out a sigh of relief, totally grateful that Lennon was saying all the right things.

"I'm sorry, too," she said, squeezing his hands to show how much she meant it. "I mean, I was a totally awful coffee waitress."

"Yeah, you were," Lennon admitted with a laugh.

"I know." Chloe covered her face. "No milk in the lattes? That *was* bad, wasn't it?"

Lennon smiled.

"Anyway, I'm really sorry for acting like I thought you should cover for me on the job," she went on. "And it's not your fault that I didn't get a part in that commercial, either. I wasn't up to the competition."

"You'd be good in a paper towel commercial," Lennon joked. "You've got a lot of experience. You know, wiping up spilled coffee?"

"Very funny." Chloe yanked her hands away, pretending to be mad. But she liked the way he teased her. It was his way of showing how much he appreciated her in *spite* of her faults. "There's only one thing I really wish," she added.

"What?" Lennon asked.

"It would be so cool to hang out and watch them shoot that commercial tomorrow," she said. "Is there any way you could sneak me and Riley in?"

"Done," Lennon said.

"Really?" Chloe asked. "Are you sure?"

"Yup. I already thought of that, so I asked Mr. Horner," Lennon explained. "He said it was okay as long as you don't touch anything or try to make any coffee."

"You got it," Chloe said. She was so happy that she and Lennon had made up. And there were three whole days of winter break left, too! Maybe she could still salvage this disastrous week after all!

"How do I look?" Sierra asked Riley that night at the Voodoo Lounge.

The two of them stood in the rest room, where Sierra had gotten dressed in her black leather pants and red chiffon top with wild, torn sleeves. She twisted a hunk of her wavy red hair into a knot on the side of her head, letting the rest flow free.

"You look amazing, as usual," Riley said. "Are you psyched about tonight?"

"Totally," Sierra said. "And scared. I mean, I want my parents to find out the truth about my band, and I told them to come. But I'm terrified about it, too."

"I know what you mean," Riley said. "That's how I felt about telling Marc that I'm not Danielle."

"But you *didn't* tell him!" Sierra scolded. "You bailed! What about our pact?"

"We said we'd come clean by the end of the week," Riley argued. "I still have time left."

Sierra opened the rest room door a crack and peeked out. "Wow. The place is jammed!" she said. "You'd better hurry if you want to get a good table."

"Chloe and Lennon and Tara and Quinn are saving me a seat," Riley said. "But yeah, I'd better go before someone steals the chair. Anyway, break a leg."

"Thanks." Sierra pulled on a pair of high, spiky black leather boots. Then she turned to the mirror to add some eyeliner and fuss with her makeup.

Riley pushed out through the crowd of high school and college kids who had packed the Voodoo Lounge. The club was mostly dark, with colored lights aimed at the walls in various places.

Indie rock music was pulsing on the sound system while the crowd waited for The Wave to come on.

"Hi!" Riley said, giving Chloe a hug and squeezing into a chair at the crowded table.

She looks so happy! Riley thought. Then she wondered, Can Marc and I ever be as good together as Chloe and Lennon?

Most of the band members were already onstage, getting ready to start playing. Riley gazed at Alex Zimmer, the guitar player she had gone out with for a while. She hadn't talked to him much in the past few weeks, and now she knew why. He was really sweet, and she liked him a lot. But he wasn't as funny or interesting as Marc Hudson. And she didn't feel as if she could totally be herself with him, the way she did with Marc.

That's funny, Riley thought. I feel like I can be myself with Marc, but he thinks I'm someone else!

Finally Sierra came out of the rest room and jumped up onto the stage.

Alex took the microphone. "Hi, everyone. Thanks for coming out tonight," he said in his quiet, shy way. "We're going to kick this off with a song our bass player wrote, called 'Memory Morning.' Give it up, everybody, for Sierra!"

The crowd cheered and applauded, and the band launched into the first song. It was amazing, a really driving beat with a wonderful melody and excellent lyrics.

The Wave is so incredibly awesome, Riley thought. How could Sierra's parents possibly be disappointed if they saw her now?

Riley looked around the packed club, hoping to spot the Pomeroys in the crowd. But they hadn't shown up.

The next three songs were awesome, too. Saul, the drummer, sang on the last one. A bunch of people, including Tara and Quinn, got up and started dancing, so Riley joined them.

When Saul's song was over, Sierra took the microphone.

"We've got a brand-new song that we're going to try out for you tonight," she said. "It was written by our keyboard player, Marta. She really wanted to sing it for you herself, but for her own safety—and yours—we talked her out of it."

Everyone laughed.

"So anyway, Alex and I are going to try to do your song justice, Marta," Sierra said, shooting a smile toward the keyboard player. "This is 'Random Access Misery.'"

Sierra strummed the first chords, Saul kicked off the drum riff, and they launched into it.

"Wow," Chloe said, leaning over halfway through the song. "What a great song, huh? Sierra sounds awesome!"

"Yeah," Riley said. "I wish Sierra's mom could hear her."

Chloe glanced at the door, which was behind Riley's shoulder. "Looks like you got your wish," she said.

Riley whirled around and saw Sierra's parents. They had just come in and were standing near the entrance watching, their eyes wide. It seemed as if they couldn't believe what they were seeing.

Sierra sang the last lines:

"Want to live, want to be
Someone who looks just like me,
But can't let go of the memories
From my random access misery."

The crowd cheered and hooted when the song was over, and Sierra took a jumping-up-and-down bow.

"Thanks, everyone!" she shouted. "We're going to take a break now, but don't go away. We've still got a long night ahead!" Then she put down her guitar and hopped off the stage.

Riley darted out of her seat and ran over to Sierra. "Your parents came!" she said, shouting to be heard above the music playing over the sound system.

"I see them," Sierra said. "They're right behind you."

Riley stepped back to make room for the Pomeroys. She held her breath. What are they going to do? she wondered.

As soon as they could reach Sierra through the crowd, Mr. And Mrs. Pomeroy rushed forward to hug her.

"Honey, that was wonderful!" her mother said. "I had no idea!"

"I'm amazed!" her father added. "Totally shocked but so proud! Your band is really good!"

Sierra beamed. "Thanks," she said, grinning. "So you don't mind if I'm in a band like this?"

"No, of course not," her mother said. "As long as it doesn't interfere with your violin practice."

"And we can see that it hasn't," her father added. "After all, you won that statewide competition last week."

"Right!" Sierra said, so happy she looked as if she might explode.

"There's only one thing," her mother said, stepping back and frowning a little. She looked Sierra up and down. "What on earth are you wearing? What happened to the button-down shirt and plaid jumper you had on when you left home this afternoon?"

Oops. Riley glanced at Sierra, waiting to see what she'd do. But Sierra didn't miss a beat.

"Oh, this? This is Riley's!" she lied. "I'd *never* own anything as wild as this! Riley made me borrow it for the concert, so I'd look, you know, more like a rock star."

Mrs. Pomeroy glanced at Riley. "Well, I'm sorry, Riley, but I think it's a bit too much," she said.

"Oh, right, I see that," Sierra agreed quickly. "Too much. Definitely "

Oh, well. Riley sighed. At least Sierra told them the truth about her band. That was a good start.

Now it was Riley's turn to tell the truth.

To Marc. Tomorrow. No matter what!

chapter
eleven

"I don't believe this!" Riley gasped the next morning, standing outside the Newsstand. "The place is crawling with people. We can't even get to the front door!"

"Lennon said we should go in the back door," Chloe said, leading the way around the corner to the alley.

Good thing, Riley thought. Because with all the trucks parked out front and the production people guarding the front door, they'd never get in the regular way.

They hurried to the back door and found Lennon waiting for them.

"Hi." He let them in. "Mr. Horner said it's okay for you to be here as long as you stay out of the way."

Inside, Lennon put his arms around Chloe's waist and gave her a hug.

"Am I out of the way back here with you?" Chloe asked with a grin.

"See you guys later," Riley called, leaving them

alone. She was on a mission. Today the truth was going to come out—whether Marc liked it or not!

She headed into the coffee shop and found the place crawling with video crew people. Lights and electrical wires were everywhere. She had to watch her step to keep from tripping over metal equipment cases.

"Hi, Danielle," someone said as she squeezed past a light stand.

Huh? Riley's head whipped around. Who said that? she wondered. These people were all complete strangers!

"Hey, Danielle," another crew member said. "You looking for your dad? He's right over there." She pointed to the far side of the coffee shop. To Jacques.

Whoa! Riley thought. What's going on?

Her heart started pounding, and she scanned the room for Marc. There he is, Riley thought. Over near the windows, talking to Jacques. She edged past the camera and cameraman, trying not to bump into anything.

"Hi, Danielle," the cameraman said to her. "You're looking perky today."

What's going on? Riley wanted to shout.

But then Jacques spotted her, and his face lit up. He rushed toward her. "Danielle!" He took her face in his hands and kissed her on both cheeks. "Good morning, my darling daughter!"

Everyone in the room stopped working for a moment. They were all quiet, watching her.

Riley didn't know what to say. She hesitated for a minute. "Dad?" she finally mumbled in a weak voice.

The whole crew burst out laughing.

And Marc laughed the hardest. "Hi, Riley," he said, taking her by the arm and pulling her aside.

"What?" Riley was totally confused. "You know my real name?"

"Yeah," he said with a grin. "I've been on to you for two days now."

Riley was dumbfounded. She stared at him, hoping he'd explain it because she was so surprised, she couldn't think of the right questions to ask.

"You should see the look on your face!" Marc said. He led her off to a corner away from the crew. Everyone else went back to work.

"But how did you find out?" Riley finally managed to say.

"When I dropped you off at Jacques's house after the movie," Marc explained, "you gave yourself away. You said your dad had won the Golden Globe award for *Tunnel of Rain*."

"Didn't he?" Riley asked.

"Nope." Marc shook his head. "Faye Huntington won for best actress in the picture. But she gave the award to Jacques out of gratitude for all his help and support directing her in the film."

"Oops," Riley said.

"Somehow I thought Jacques and Faye's daughter would know that," Marc kidded her.

Duh! Riley covered her face. No wonder he had given her such a strange smile that night! Then she remembered something. "What about yesterday?" she asked, still trying to figure this all out. "When you came in here and you were talking to Jacques in French…"

"I called you Danielle in front of him," Marc admitted. "But in French I told him the whole story. That you were pretending to be his daughter. He thought it was funny, and he liked the fact that I spoke French. So he offered me a job on the shoot."

Well, I'm glad someone thinks it's funny! Riley thought.

"It was Jacques's idea to pull this stunt on you," Marc said, still smiling. "And I figured you deserved it, since you've been basically living a lie all week."

"But I tried to tell you the truth!" Riley protested. "On the beach, remember?"

"Yeah, I know." Marc looked sort of sorry. "I should have believed you, too." His face was serious now, and Riley's heart sank.

"So I guess I know what you wanted to tell me," she said. "I mean, you made it pretty clear that you don't want to go out with an average girl."

"That's right, I don't," Marc said. He stared at her for a minute. "I want to go out with *you*."

Huh? Riley was stunned silent.

"There's nothing average about you, Riley," Marc said, and those dimples of his kicked into high gear.

Aw, Riley thought. That was so nice!

"How about tonight?" Marc asked. "A movie, maybe?"

"I'd love to," Riley said, thrilled. This was working out better than expected! "But there's just one thing."

"What?" Marc asked.

"Promise me I don't have to speak a word of French!"

chapter
twelve

"**S**he's terrible!" Chloe whispered to Lennon. "She's gorgeous, but she can't act!"

The two of them stood behind the counter, watching the video shoot in the Newsstand. Jacques had been shooting take after take of just one scene from the coffee commercial.

"Look at her!" Chloe whispered to Riley. "She keeps serving that coffee as if it's a diamond ring on a pillow or something."

"It's true," Lennon agreed. "Even *you* would have been better in the part."

"Thanks…I think," Chloe said. She wasn't sure if he was teasing her or not.

"Quiet!" Jacques said, clapping his hands to silence the crew. "This is not working. We are supposed to be at the Newsstand, and there isn't a single newspaper in sight."

Marc grabbed some newspapers from the wall rack

and spread them out on the table. "Does that help?" he asked.

"Yes," Jacques said. "No. I don't know." He threw up his hands. "This whole scene is wrong!"

He took the actress aside and talked to her, gesturing rapidly as if he was unhappy with her performance.

I'd hate to be in her place, Chloe thought.

Jacques looked around the room. He seemed to want something. Then he motioned to Chloe. "Um, excuse me? Could you come here for a moment?"

"Me?" Chloe froze.

Jacques nodded. "You auditioned for me, didn't you?"

"Yes," Chloe replied.

"Well, good. We need you, so here's your big chance," he said.

"Seriously?" Chloe's face lit up. I can't believe it! she thought. I *knew* I could do a better job than that actress! She shot a glance at Lennon and Riley, and they both smiled back.

"Great!" Chloe said. "But what do you want me to wear? Am I dressed okay for the part of the waitress?"

"The waitress?" Jacques said with a small smile. "Oh, no. I have something else for you." He led her over to the table where they were shooting the scene.

"Derek? This is Chloe. Chloe, Derek," Jacques said, introducing her to the actor who was playing a customer.

"So am I going to be another customer?" Chloe wondered out loud.

Jacques picked up the newspapers that were spread on Derek's table.

"Yes. Chloe, I want you to sit at the table right behind Derek," Jacques said. "So I can see you in the shot. But you'll be reading this newspaper."

"Is that it?" she asked. "That's my part?"

Jacques nodded. "I am sure you'll be wonderful in it," he said with a kind smile.

Okay. At least I'm *in* the commercial! Chloe thought, still excited. But the minute she sat down and picked up the newspaper, Jacques clapped his hands.

"No, no," he called to her. "Hold up the paper higher. Higher. Higher, please. There!"

"But you can't even see my face now!" Chloe cried out from behind the paper.

"It's perfect!" Jacques said. "Action!"

Oh, well, Chloe thought. At least I'm in show business!

Five takes later they were finished with that scene. Chloe watched the playback on the video monitor. Just as she thought, her face was totally blocked by the newspaper.

"Well, at least I can tell people, 'Those are my hands!'" she said, and everyone laughed.

When the shoot was over, a production assistant gave Chloe a check for one hundred dollars.

"Wow!" Chloe was amazed. "Pretty good money for just holding up a newspaper!" She turned to Riley and the two guys. "You want to go out to dinner? My treat."

"I've already got dinner covered," Lennon said, leading her outside.

Riley and Marc followed.

When they reached the street, Chloe saw two motor scooters parked at the curb. One was Marc's, she knew. But the other?

"What's up?" she asked, turning to Lennon.

"It's just one of three things I wanted to do during this break," he said. "I rented this bike so I could teach you how to ride it."

"Aw! That's so nice!" Chloe said. "You remembered!" She gave him a hug. "But what are the other two things?"

"Well, I thought we could drive to the beach—all four of us," Lennon said. "And make a fire and roast hot dogs and marshmallows while we listen to nothing but songs with *fire* in the title."

I don't believe it! Chloe thought. He was listening the whole time!

Lennon flipped open the lid on the carrier on the back of his scooter. Inside were hot dogs, marshmallows, drinks, and chips. "See?" he said. "Dinner!"

Chloe wanted to melt. "And what's the third thing?" she asked, feeling all warm and toasty inside.

"This," he said, pulling her toward him and giving her a long kiss. "I'm off for the rest of the weekend. Let's get out of here."

Hey, Chloe thought. That works for me!

Chloe
and Riley's

SCRAPBOOK

so little time

Book 12
best friends forever

How did this happen? Chloe wondered. This morning, we were all best friends, now some of us aren't speaking to the rest of us.

And why? Because we couldn't agree on how to handle our Business Studies team project. You would think coming up with a cool product and selling it would be fun and easy. But it's not.

Not when two people want to be in charge.

After the big fight, Sierra had taken sides with Tara. The two of them had decided to form their own team. And they took their product idea with them. They were going to make and sell the Spiral Bracelet by themselves.

Larry had decided to stick with Team Carlson. "I'm not deserting you at a time like this," Larry had said—

not to Chloe, but to Riley. He's had a crush on Riley since forever. "Don't worry. We're still the best."

The best? The best at what? Chloe wondered. We don't have a product anymore!

And that wasn't even the worst of it.

Next Saturday night was the Master Crush concert. The Master Crush concert that she, Chloe Carlson, wanted to go to more than any other concert on the planet.

Last week Tara had scored two tickets from her father, who had major connections, and offered one to Chloe. But then, after the fight this morning, Tara had taken her offer back. "We are so not going to this concert together. Not after this!" she had announced to Chloe.

Now what? Chloe wondered. She sat down at her computer and logged on to the Web. She typed in: MASTER CRUSH TICKETS, MALIBU.

A bunch of ads popped up. They were ads for tickets to the Master Crush concert! Chloe felt a rush of hope.

And then her hope collapsed like a bad hairstyle on a rainy day. She read the fine print.

SINGLE TIX MASTER CRUSH $500 OR BEST OFFER
PAIR TIX MASTER CRUSH 10TH ROW $1000

Five hundred dollars? A thousand dollars?

Chloe's head was spinning. How was she ever going to score a ticket to the hottest concert of the century?

mary-kateandashley

TWO of a kind ™

mary-kateandashley

Meet Chloe and Riley Carlson.

So much to do...

so little time

HarperCollins_Entertainment_    PARACHUTE PRESS    DUALSTAR PUBLICATIONS

TM & © Dualstar Entertainment Group, LLC.

mary-kateandashley

Sweet 16

1. Never Been Kissed	0060092092	7. Playing Games	0060528133
2. Wishes and Dreams	0060092106	8. Cross Our Hearts	0060528141
3. The Perfect Summer	0060092114	9. All That Glitters	0060556463
4. Getting There	0060515953	10. Keeping Secrets	0060556455
5. Starring You and Me	0060528117	11. Little White Lies	0060556471
6. My Best Friend's Boyfriend	0060528125	12. Dream Holiday	006055648X

▣ HarperCollins*Entertainment*

 PARACHUTE PRESS

 DUALSTAR PUBLICATIONS

$14.95 VIDEO

Available Now on Video and DVD

$29.95 DVD

ALSO AVAILABLE: MARY-KATE AND ASHLEY in *WINNING LONDON, PASSPORT TO PARIS,*
BILLBOARD DAD and *HOLIDAY IN THE SUN*

mary-kateandashley

Fashion Dolls

Super Spa Day™

1 Soak their hands and feet in water

Spend a day at the spa with
Mary-Kate and Ashley! You can give
them manicures and pedicures...

...and change their
makeup for a
fun night out!

Transform their
cool spa chair
into beautiful
vanity mirrors.

2 to reveal their
favorite nail color!

3 Use the applicator to change
their eye makeup and lip colors
for a dramatic new look.

Real Dolls for Real Girls

mary-kateandashley.com

DUALSTAR
CONSUMER PRODUCTS

MATTEL